Carbon Copy

MD Hanley

Copyright

Acknowledgements

To my mother and father
Christine Adams and Bob Butch

To my brother and sister
Edward Hanley and Marcia Firsick

Anyone can have a great story, but
you need to be a good storyteller to
make it real and inspire imagination.

Table of Contents

Prologue - Life and Death

"The snake which cannot cast its skin
has to die."

- Nietzsche

Life abhors death. As such, funerals are an
ugly event. Today, it was no exception. Rain
fell on all who were gathered by the graveside.
It dared anyone to not notice it. The continuous
tap, tap, sound of the raindrops on the makeshift awning made it difficult to hear the priest
delivering the last blessings and prayers. Sadly,
the priest standing at the foot of the grave was
doing very little to comfort or ease the pain and
sadness of those gathered here today. As if on
cue, the rainfall increased, once the priest
started to finish the closing prayers.

Funerals are the marking of an end point.
There is no life. This moment is final and
immutable. Ironically, the ugliness of death
yields an unbounded appreciation of life. Birth
represents the antithesis of death. With death,

the body rots, and decays to dust. Birth is life. It's growth beyond imagination.

Both death and life are mighty, make no mistake. All organic life in this world is intensely fighting to persist and exist. Death is equally as ferocious and as strong, fighting to take life away. This is how it was at the beginning of time and will still continue to the end of time.

Chapter 1 - 7-Eleven

The Blue Meanie Slurpee is only sold in Australia

Håvard pulled the shiny red Taurus into the 7-Eleven gas station, parking on the right side of the gas pump, nearest the door to the 7-Eleven. After he stopped the car, a blue pickup truck pulled into the other side of the gas pump to fill up his truck. The big man, with curly red hair, slid off the driver's seat to the ground. He was wearing a blue shirt, with a navy "Jiffy Lube" patch, which said Chucky in bold white letters. The New Hampshire license plate had large letters and read, "CHUKLS'.

Håvard jumped out and put the gas pump nozzle into the gas tank of the rental car he's driving. He ran into the store, and quickly came out with a key to the backroom. The key, like many gas stations, is a small key attached to a big heavy, metal, circular sign which says in all caps, RESTROOM. This common habit usually assures the person who owns the station, will get the key back when the person is through. It also tells anyone watching him he wasn't going to be able to look after their stuff temporarily. At least for a few minutes.

Håvard is late getting to the Boston airport. He will have just enough time to go the bathroom, and change his appearance and clothes. Håvard wants to leave the USA and go back to Iceland, but he doesn't want to be noticed or tracked. This is important because the kind of work he does can be problematic if he leaves a trail of where he has been and also, the country he's in. This new identity is hopefully going to let him not be noticed. Once in the restroom, he pulled out the short cropped, blond hair piece he wants to wear.

Once the hairpiece was properly in place, he pulled out a brush to brush and smooth his new hair. He hated hiding his darker ice blue tinted hair because he loved this particular blue color. He paid a lot to get his normal hair to this color. It was worth it though, because whenever he looked at it, it reminded him of the fjords and springs from home. He took a scrunchy and refashioned it to make a less bunched up man-knot, a more layered and consistent shape.

Taking off his shirt and pants, out of his knapsack he pulled a set of body pads. He put all these pads on and attached them snugly to his body. He thought these body pads would make him look to be someone who is slightly overweight. Not too overweight, but. just enough to let him be a little more invisible. Then, he pulled out some clothes which were oversized for him normally but a perfect fit for his size now.

Håvard had two reasons, for doing this. Overweight people are generally not noticed too much. Oh people, definitely look at people and silently categorize and profile the person they see, but overweight people generally just blend in with the other people in a crowd. Anything above 30 pounds would very subtly steer someone to make a mental note. Less than this is just generally chaff in a crowd.

Håvard also pulled out several taupe skin colored patches which he applied to cover the tattoos visible on his neck, arms and body. He was always surprised when he would do something like this, because it highlighted just how many tattoos he had on his body. At last count it was 62. He didn't regret getting them he just regretted the time it took to cover them up.

These patches were really just skin colored nicotine patches and if anyone questioned him, this was easily explained. These patches weren't really full of nicotine they were just blanks. He got them from a friend, who liked to wear these nicotine patches. He smiled a little because his friend only had these blank patches for the sole reason of substituting nicotine with fentanyl. He would walk around the town crazy high and incoherent.

Measures like these tasks were just one of the many datapoints Håvard used to make himself inconspicuous. It gave him the anonymity he wanted to achieve. When you're unseen, or unnoticed, then you reap the power of doing something other people wouldn't be able to achieve. In the early days of the internet, many people felt empowered by being anonymous. You could do whatever you wanted, or to say whatever you wanted to another person, without the risk of being traced.

After Håvard checked himself over, he walked back to the entrance of the 7-Eleven to return the key. As he came around the comer, he could see the guy in the pick-up truck was looking in the direction of the restroom. He looked right past Håvard.

Håvard hesitated a second before he opened the door of the store. The big guy was using the same gas pump, Håvard had used to fill up his car. But the LCD register showed almost $60 worth of gas pumped out. Håvard didn't really care about the money the guy was trying to steal to fill his truck, but what he did care about was the way this guy was so blatant in his theft. This guy just thought Håvard was dumb and he wouldn't notice. Jerk!

As he gave the key back to the clerk behind the register, he told her the guy in the pickup would be coming in a minute to pay for both cars being filled. She looked at him a little strangely. The credit card used was already approved.

He sensed the confusion and quickly added, "The credit card I put into the card reader sometimes approves it and other times it doesn't. It's something to do with distance away from home. Can you cancel the transaction? My friend in the pickup, Chucky, will be coming in once he finishes filling both my tank and his pickup truck. He's a little shy, but he told me he thought you looked like a really sweet girl." Then, he absent-mindedly winked at her.

Håvard walked out of the front of the store. Now the guy at the pickup noticed Håvard and looked surprised. Then, he recognized him as the guy who went to the restroom. Hastily replacing the nozzle into the gas pump, he knew his hand was caught in the cookie jar.

Håvard looked at him directly and said, "Thanks for the gas Chucky. I appreciate it." He put more emphasis on the word Chucky to reinforce his friendly nature. Håvard didn't know what a friendly nature was, but he said it anyways.

This baffled Chucky. He wasn't able to make the connection. One of the loudspeakers above the gas pump blared with a metallic voice, "Sir your credit card was denied. Please come inside to pay for the gas. Thank you."

Håvard winked at Chucky and smiled. "I think she wants to talk to you, big guy."

Chucky's face started to turn bright red. "Screw you. I ain't payin' for none of ya's gas."

Getting into his car, Håvard smiled as he started to head out of the gas station. Chucky took a small rock which was laying on the bed of the truck and threw it at the car. Håvard saw the projectile coming so he slammed on the breaks. Having slowed his momentum, the rock missed his car and missed hitting another car on the opposite side of the road.

Håvard stomped on the gas to screech out of the 7-Eleven. Another car, which was coming down the road, slammed on its brakes to avoid hitting the red car. The car lost what little traction it had on a road covered in wet autumn leaves and smashed straight into a telephone pole on the right side of the street. This car had five occupants - Lisa, Stanley, Maureen, and their father Julio Harris and their mother Maria.

Looking in the rear-view mirror, Håvard saw everything happening behind him and knew he had caused it. He pressed on the gas. He better get out of Boston sooner rather than later. Now he really has no time to waste and must make his flight out of this city as soon as possible. Six hours later the wheels of the big Icelandair jet touched down in Reykjavik, Iceland.

Chapter 2 - Mercy for the Child

The best and most beautiful things
in the world cannot be seen or even
touched - they must be felt with the
heart.

- Helen Keller

The driver of a car traveling down a road
was forced to make a critical split-second
decision. The 16-year-old girl, Maureen was in
the driver's seat on this day. She was trying to
get a little more experience driving for her
upcoming driver's test. Even though she was
inexperienced, a seasoned driver would have
crashed the car in the same way. A car had
jumped into the traffic lane so quickly it caused
a domino effect of the cars behind her coming
to a screeching stop in order to avoid a collision.
Maureen braked very hard, but the ground was

wet and there were a lot of slick, wet autumn leaves littered on the road.

It was unavoidable and the car with the five passengers lost traction and started to slide in a ditch on the side of the road. The reaction was to turn the steering wheel in the opposite direction. This action caused the car to turn out of the ditch, but traction was lost. The car spun around 180 degrees and slammed into a stone wall on the other side to the road.

The traffic was light on that day, but many drivers saw this car accident and stopped. The other driver was leaving a 7-Eleven and didn't stop before driving into traffic and this sudden action caused the other car to swerve and spin around to slam into a stone wall on the opposite side of the street. The 3 passengers in the front seat of the car were the most hurt.

Tragically, the 16-year-old driver and the father siting in the middle were killed instantly. The mother, siting in the front passenger seat was seriously injured, and was trapped in the front passenger seat unable to move due to the force of the engine pushing into the interior of the car.

Ironically, on this day, a family was just driving down a road with normally light traffic. The fall foliage was at its peak which was usually a big draw for tourists. Saturdays and Sundays brought an increase of people driving through the suburbs of Boston to head north to New Hampshire or Vermont.

The family was heading toward a restaurant that they went to every Sunday. This became a routine for the family and was rarely changed or postponed. It was a nice way for them to catch up and spend time together as a family. They had followed this routine for many years.

The whole family was in their gold LeSabre sedan. In the front bench seat three people were sitting and 2 children in the back seat. The driver today was a sixteen-year-old year girl with pigtails, named Maureen. She was under careful supervision of her father, Julio, who was sitting in the middle. Maureen was trying to get some extra practice driving before her driving test. Next to Julio was his wife, Maria. In the back seat, two younger children were in their seats, buckled in.

The older of the two children in the back seat was a 13-year-old boy, named Stanley. He was sitting behind his mother's seat and reading one of his favorite books. His 8-year-old sister, Lisa was sitting behind the driver's seat. She was singing a song of her own creation and she was the only one who knew the words.

In the front seat, Maria and Maureen were laughing hysterically at Julio. Maureen made bet with her father. She bet him that he couldn't give her any instruction for 20 seconds. It lasted only 4 seconds.

In one split second, everything in the car changed from jovial laughter and good spirits, to a scene of death and tragedy. The little girl, Lisa, was crying and sobbing. She didn't fully understand what happened. It was just the sheer suddenness of it that filled her with fear. Glass was everywhere from all the breaking windows.

Lisa's brother, Stanley, was on the right side of the car behind their mother, Maria. He was pushed up against the right-hand door. On the surface he looked ok, but later it was found the window handle of the door had irreparably damaged his spine.

It so scared Lisa, his eyes were wide open the second before the crash and now they were closed shut. Stanley wasn't moving. He had a cut across his forehead that was just now starting to ooze blood and make a bloody mess of his shirt. She knew it was just a cut and would heal, but the blood scared her.

She checked herself and knew her body was hurt some but not too bad. Her head had hit the driver's seat. The fact her sister was tall and had the seat pushed back all the way, really saved her from more injuries.

Voices of people were heard coming over to the car. The car was on the opposite side of the road up against stonewall. The car spun around 180 degrees and landed on the opposite side of the road. The car was stopped by the stone wall.

The car was not 100% flush with the wall. The car definitely hit the wall very hard, but it also bounced off the wall so there was a space between the stone wall and the right side of the car.

Lisa was pulled out of the car by a big strong bear of a man. She could feel his full beard on her face when he reached into extract her from the car. Later she found his name was Callum. As he was getting Lisa, others tried to get Julio and Maria.

When they got the driver's door open, a grey-haired man, looked inside and knew this situation was dire. His wife was behind him and he looked apprehensively at her. She knew immediately as she sensed the driver and his daughter, the girl with the pigtails, were very still. It was a stillness, which was being felt more than being heard. Because the girl and the father were sitting very closely together the steering wheel became the instrument of death here.

Another man in a dark suit, went to the passenger side of the car. He saw the mother in the front and asked if she could hear him. He touched her skin to see if she was alive. He wasn't a doctor, but he knew there was still some life, but very faint. She was struggling for her life amidst the chaos.

Other people were now showing up ready to help. Stanley, the boy in the backseat needed attention. Like the mother, his pulse was faint. A young woman looked into the back seat. She could see the boy's chest rising and falling so she knew there was still life in him. His body, which had been thrown violently toward the passenger door when the car hit the wall. It was in an unnatural position. His legs came up from the floor and one came to rest on the seat, and the other went back to the floor.

"Where is the ambulance," she shouted to everyone.

It was on its way someone yelled back. People gathered around to start to disentangle the boy from the car. A woman who was also a nurse, asked people to not move the boy. She was concerned that it would cause more harm if they did. The woman said she was a nurse as she advised everyone his injuries might be to his spine or neck.

At the Massachusetts General Hospital, a short time later, Maria Harris was in the operating room and the surgeons were dispassionately trying to save her life. Her head had hit the dashboard of the car. There was a risk that this trauma would cause her brain to swell.

The most serious of the injuries, were two of her ribs were cleanly broken from her ribcage. One of these separated ribs punctured her liver. Her heart kept pumping blood into the liver and instead of filtering the blood it shunted the blood into the abdomen. The circulation of blood in the body was critical for life. If the blood circulation is broken, the body will start to shut down and fail. It wouldn't take long for the body to completely stop circulating the blood. The surgeons were very aware of this condition and they were quickly trying to buy more time by hanging a pint of blood from the I.V.

The liver was severely damaged. The puncture caused a large tear in the upper right quadrant of the organ. The surgeons tried valiantly to repair the damage, but there was too much damage and blood loss. Maria Harris died this night at 8:33 PM.

The boy was strong, and this helped his chances greatly. Stanley Harris was whisked into a room with a massive MRI machine. As this was being done the surgeon and his staff were prepping for surgery of the 13-year-old boy.

The MRI showed his lower spine was damaged. It looked like one of the boy's lower disks was moved out of position. The surgeon had a good idea of where the damage was done. His hope would be that the MRI was accurate. He would know more once he opened this area of his back open. The surgeon who would be performing the operation today was one of the top surgeons in the country for this type of spinal cord injury. He was known for being extremely meticulous, almost maniacal about his steadfast drive for perfection. His staff around the operating room, knew this and were prepared for a long operation.

The 13-year-old boy survived, but he was in intensive care. His spine had received severe trauma. The surgeon was unable to repair the damage to his spinal cord. His lower lumbar disk, L2, was damaged and physically moved out of alignment with the other lumbar disks in his spine. He was able to move his disk back in line, but the damage to his spinal cord wouldn't recover. He knew once he got into the surgery, the young boy would be bound to a wheelchair the rest of his life.

His training as a surgeon did not make him immune to empathy. He knew, sadly, he couldn't do anymore to help the boy. It's times like this, he felt the weight of the responsibility of his work as a surgeon. He could go no farther to help.

Chapter 3 - Bumble Bees

Cricket is basically baseball on valium.

- Robin Williams

2020 - 25 Years Later

Today is warm. Nicely warm. No humidity, no chill, just comfortable. It's a cloudless sky of just pure blue. The sun is making its usual journey in the heavens. A slight breeze coming off the ocean a few miles away. A nice reprise of the last several days of rain. It's a few days past September 1st so by all reckoning, summer has ticked past and it's officially autumn. Stanley Harris is sitting on his porch in the early quietness of the day. He's enjoying his morning coffee, just relaxing, still a little sleepy but sleepiness is slowly wearing away.

Stanley, a 38-year-old man, is sitting on a comfortable chair on his porch. His black hair was cut short. His hands holding the coffee cup were large. Attached to those hands were very large fore arms and biceps. His body was very lean, but not lean in a scrawny way, lean by a healthy diet and physical activity. His physique just accentuated his large chest and upper body.

His attention is commanded by nothing. It's still early in the morning. He's just sitting in the warmth of the sun and acknowledging the life nurturing gift it freely gives.

Stanley is unaware his presence is being considered by something nearby. This thing was aware of his presence and adjusting its dancing routine to factor in the alterations it would need to make. Since the dance was being done on the side of the house, Stanley's presence didn't interrupt, or alter, the course of a few very large and very busy bumblebees.

Bumblebees are large, fuzzy insects with short, stubby wings. They are larger than honeybees, but they don't produce as much honey. However, they are one of the world's most important pollinators and they are a critical piece of the eco-system. Without them, food wouldn't grow. Two-thirds of the world's crops depend on animals to transfer pollen between male and female flower parts. Bumble bees are the most important of all the pollinators in our many different ecosystems. While other animals pollinate, bumblebees are particularly good at it.

The bumblebee continues its own little unique dance to carry out its mission. To someone who isn't well versed in bumblebee dances, they would probably think this was a unique dance and flight pattern. It isn't. This dance has been repeated continuously for eons.

Stanley is one of the chief medical researchers for the Plymouth Massachusetts Thorndike Medical Center or PMT-Med as it's sometimes called. It is located in south eastern Massachusetts. The team he manages are researching a variety of medical advancements which have the potential of enhancing the body's response to new medicines and new medical procedures. The progress they've made is astounding.

Research is a dance of sorts. In essence, it's replicating the dance of the bumble bees. Everyday around the world, researchers are finding new medicines and new medical applications to fix problem areas in the body. Most of the progression in our society has followed an immutable dance of the *scientific method*. Around the 17th century, scientists turned to a process of researching and gathering empirical data which ultimately has helped prove or disprove a hypothesis. Stanley and his team have advanced their projects significantly because of this structured process.

Stanley was enjoying this calm and relaxing feeling to start his day. Today was Friday. One more day to get through, before the weekend. He enjoyed his work. His team constantly kept him on his toes. Not in a bad sense, but completely the opposite. They were all so incredibly smart. If he laid out the parameters of a problem to anyone on his team or researchers, he was constantly surprised when they presented their solution. Stanley was very sharp himself and no slouch in this area of medical research, but many of the solutions delivered by his team were very creative and nailed the goal every time. Sometimes, the parameters got skewed and a problem would have to be revisited to try to come up with a better solution. Very common in most organizations similar to his.

Today is Friday, and he's been sitting here enjoying the morning long enough. He expertly maneuvered his body into the padded seat of his wheelchair. Unfortunately, when Stanley did this, he didn't see a bumblebee who had veered away from the main bumblebee crew who were still dancing on the side of the house. Too late for the bumblebee to move out of the way when Stanley fully sat down in the chair. Out of pure instinct, and also accompanied by the threat of being cornered with no way to escape, the bumblebee stung Stanley several times before dying.

After Stanley came to a rest, he let out a loud yelp of pain. Stanley's reflexes nearly sent him toppling over to the ground, but Stanley was strong and very adept at getting into or out of his wheelchair. He was able to quickly move back to the porch seat he was previously occupying.

Stanley's brain was still trying to catch up with what just happened. He saw the corpse of the bumblebee and cringed. The pain in his butt was great but he didn't want the bumble bee to be killed by his ignorance. Bumble bees are typically peaceful and will only sting if threatened.

He removed the bumble bee from his chair and gently put himself back into his wheelchair. He rolled over to the kitchen to put his coffee cup in the sink.

Behind him someone was putting their arms around his neck to give him a "Good Morning" kiss on his cheek. He turned around to face his fiancé, Ingrid.

"Good morning, my love. I just got stung by a bee right in the 'tuchus.' That little sucker hurt."

Ingrid playfully teased, "If you're expecting a kiss on your boo-boo to make it better, you will be waiting for a very long time."

"Aww. Your hurting me more than the bumble bee," Stanley paused for a second.

"I will be ready in about 10 minutes ok?" he said to her as he turned to give his fiancé a proper good morning kiss.

She smiled as he wheeled into their bedroom to finish getting ready for work. They were still early in their normal morning routine, but it was nice to not feel rushed. They were both fortunate to work in the same building and to live close to their office building and labs.

Usually, on Mondays and Fridays, they blocked out time for them to have lunch together. It helped with the monotony of work, eat, sleep, and repeat. Today was different. Stanley had a very important meeting with the VP of Research and several of the board members of this facility.

This meeting was the culmination of several years of hard work and research. Today would be an update to the board and his boss in a more formal manner. In the past, he has done similar presentations to the board and his boss, Ed Bruinter. Those projects were different than the project update he was going to do today. Several of those other early projects he managed were going concurrently with this one. It was those other projects which kept the company profitable and helped to keep the lights on. Today was the first time he was going to present a comprehensive picture of the state of research they were at. The project was code named Carbon Copy, and this would be a fundamental new solution to medicine, if everything goes ok.

Each of the attendees had a semi-vague idea of what Stanley has been researching. The data he'd been collecting has been astounding. He was pretty sure, at least he hoped the board members would understand the value of this. The company could realistically have a potential to revolutionize the face of medicine. Yes, the face of medicine could change today.

He smiled a little at his audacity of the last thought.

On the drive to the office, Ingrid said casually, "What time is your sister, Lisa, getting into Boston tonight?"

"Last night she sent me her itinerary. She said she'll be at Logan at 2:30. She'll be taking the train down to Plymouth and will be here about 3:45. She insisted she will be staying in Boston on Saturday and Sunday. I was lucky to get her to stay over with us for the one night. I don't know why she wants to stay in the city, but she totally shut me off when I asked her to stay with us on Saturday and Sunday. You know how stubborn she is."

Ingrid laughed a little. "Wait a minute, you inherited the stubborn gene, not Lisa. Honey, she just doesn't like to be told what to do," Ingrid smiled.

For some unknown reason to Stanley, Ingrid always gave him a differing point of view and as usual it was very logical. He smiled at her and said, "Yes. You are right. But I still think she needs to stay with us, not because I am stubborn or trying to tell her what to do. I just hate her wasting money on a hotel, when we've a perfectly comfortable bed in our house."

"I will pick her up at the train station. She and I can have a little girl time on the way back," Ingrid added.

Stanley smiled at his beautiful fiancé, as they turned into the parking lot for work. He often wondered at how lucky he was to be with Ingrid. Their wedding was coming up soon. The excitement was building everyday as the date approached.

As he rode up in the elevator with Ingrid, it stopped at the 5th floor. Stanley went left, and Ingrid went to the right. Just before she exited the elevator, she squeezed Stan's shoulder and said with 100% certainty in a voice who knew his meeting would be a great success and he must call or text her the results after the meeting.

He looked at her and said, "Fingers crossed," and raise his right hand with his index and middle fingers crossed.

His office was close to the elevator. As he rolled his wheelchair to his office, he thought another coffee if there was time. He rolled past the coffee machine, opting to not get the coffee. He didn't want any bladder issues during the meeting.

He flipped the light switch on for his office and opened the white blinds to bathe the office in sunlight. He booted up his computer and logged in. It was the usual Friday morning emails he typically received. Several of them were just status updates of certain project tasks, a couple of emails of the many mailing lists he needed to be on, nothing requiring his immediate attention. A few with questions he could answer quickly. No fires he needed to put out. There was an email from Ingrid who sent it out last night at about 1:30 AM. He opened this email, and it was an animated gif of a picture of Marvell's Avengers Thor. He would raise his mighty hammer calling on lightning bolts from the heavens. Finally, Thor would smash it into the ground. A huge explosion erupted from the ground. Silently he thanked Ingrid for the support.

For the next hour, he pored over his data and the presentation. He knew the information well and had already gone through the presentation in his head. He felt ready. Nervous, but ready.

It was about 9:30, he gathered up his materials and headed over to the elevator. He got off on the 11th floor. Stanley was met by his senior researcher on his team, Phillip Clarkson. They had talked about 20 minutes ago and the plan was to meet him outside the A/V conference room at 9:45.

Phil was joining him to be a backup for the questions he thought might be asked. At least this is what he told Phil. Stanley wanted Phil to attend this meeting solely to get a little facetime with the board members. The research at some point is going to branch off to other areas. He wanted Phil to be leading one of those teams.

Now a decision will need to be made about the future of his team's work. This is a good point in the research to have this work branch off and start to productize it. They aren't out of the woods yet. There could be some really, big challenges ahead. Finding the best way to productize and deliver this to help people with the most difficult illnesses would be a top priority.

Here goes nothing, too late to change his presentation or modify it.

Later that afternoon

Stanley was in the kitchen tenderizing some steaks to get them ready for the grill on the back porch. His rear end felt swollen where the bumble bee stung him this morning. When he was in the office, this feeling was always there but he really didn't have the facilities at work to take a good look at it. When he arrived home, he was able to get a better look at it. It looked like two circles of white and red surrounding the puncture point of where the bee stung him. It looked almost like a target board with the bullseye right at the puncture point of the bee who stung him. The spot looked really bad, but it didn't feel as bad as it looked.

He wasn't allergic to bee's, which is good. He had only been stung probably about 5 or 6 times in his life. This sting for some reason felt different from all the others. It initially hurt and was annoying. After about an hour or two he knew it was there, but it didn't dominate his thinking. He was also distracted by the earlier meeting he presented, the update of the status of the research, to his boss and several members of the board.

The meeting went very well. The material he discussed generated an excitement from the members of the board. This was the goal today. If the board got excited, they could start to see the possibilities of how much his team's research could change medicine, they would stand behind contributing more money into the project.

Like any project, resources would be prioritized. The goal of the project was to develop very sophisticated nanobots, which could create a nano sized 3D printer. These mini 3D printers would be able to target and correct anomalies in the body. The 3D printer nanobots would essentially print new *stem* cells for a variety of issues they targeted for fixing within the body. No surgery, just pinpoint accuracy to navigate to a system in the body needing to be fixed. Once it reached its destination it would reprint new cells and make them specifically purposed for a particular organ. The project was code named Carbon Copy.

It was a complicated project but very exciting to be part of. The focus of the work was to create and print new fully functioning liver, lung, heart, bone, nerve, skin, or any other specialized cells. Those printed cells would correct and fix years of malfunctioning and disabling functions for a patient. Stanley didn't want to get lost in his wanderlust. For a person who was too young for the original Star Trek series but was captivated by the follow-on TV series like "Star Trek - Next Generation", "Star

Trek - Deep Space Nine", "Star Trek - Voyager", or "Enterprise" his work was capturing one commonality contained in those 30 years of television series, the "Replicator". The replicator concept, in the Star Trek world, was a universal tool which could create almost anything you wanted. Whether it was *tea, hot, and earl grey* or a *Jovian sunrise martini,* this was exactly what this type of research is capable of. The difference here being obvious, they were creating human stem cells and not drinks.

However, there was one area they specifically avoided. Making a change in a person's body carries a lot of risk to it. They were developing a very complex treatment for the body. One area they deliberately decided in the beginning was to not focus their research and testing for areas or correcting the brain. The consequences of doing something incorrect would be devastating. The brain is too complex to really be able to just change bits here or there. There was no doubt removing tumors would be child's play for this type of application. They were successful at changing some of the pain/reward centers of the brain. This was limited, and a decision was made to not go further in this direction until more research was completed.

Life after the car accident

Stanley didn't often go back to this part of his life. It just seemed to be something that was a long time ago in a different life. His past was his past, it didn't define him. It was something Lisa and himself shared. It irrevocably changed both of their lives.

Today, Lisa was sober and sharp. This was the sister he grew up with. After the car accident, both of them became changed people. Lisa went down a road of oblivion after both her sister and father were killed in a car accident. This car accident is what has made Stanley dependent to a wheelchair, nearly 15 years ago. It took Stanley many years to come to grips with his disability. He could have taken a different path because of how the car accident left him. Ironically, it was a high school teacher who help Stanley start the process of healing. Stanley was at a crossroad in his life. This teacher had a very profound effect on the way he thought about being disabled. It changed his thinking in many ways.

Mr. Davidson, his history teacher, who was on the verge of failing him, asked Stanley to stay after class one day after they had a midterm test. He made Stanley wait until he corrected the test Stanley just handed in. Stanley scored a 51 on the test.

Mr. Davidson looked at Stanley and asked, "Stanley, you failed this test. Do you want me to give you a special grade consideration because you are in a wheelchair?"

Two things happened. At first, he was angry by the boldness of the teacher's question. The second thing, he thought, was this is just one more thing to add to a pile of responsibilities which he had to shoulder. This is so unfair. Why do I have to take on this and bear the responsibility of all this crap?

At first Stanley didn't answer him. Then his anger came out. White, molten hot, blinding, and thrown at the teacher which a scream, "**YES! I DO**. I never asked for this and I don't deserve this."

"Good! Good. Now, I know someone is alive in there and you aren't totally dead. Stanley don't you understand, you are so much better than this. No, you didn't ask or deserve to have this happen. But it did, Stanley. Don't you see this? It does **not** matter how much you don't want or don't deserve this. It is only what you do with it. Do you think you deserve to be smart? Answer this question, and then we can talk about this test. If you don't think you are smart and intelligent, then I can't help you. You are the only one who can make this choice. No one else."

Stanley mumbled in a quieter voice, he did think he was smart because he studied hard and wanted to learn.

His teacher smiled and nodded his head. "Yes, Stanley you are a very smart boy and you can accomplish anything you want. All you have to do is believe you can."

This teacher made a difference in Stanley's life on this day. The wheelchair for him was a fact of his life. If he wanted to get out of bed, then he had to use the chair to do this. If he wanted to reach for a goal, he had to work for it. Being disabled and a paraplegic didn't award him any free passes in his life.

Lisa on the other hand, had a really tough time after the car accident. For a little girl who was always ready with a smile and a sunny disposition, she turned into the sister who rarely smiled or laughed. She put out a perfect picture for others, but Stanley knew it was just a ruse.

Stanley tried to talk about the accident, but it was a subject she didn't want to talk about. He tried many times, but her shell was impenetrable. As she got into her teens, she started to have an interest in music and singing. There were times when she sang a song she liked, it felt like walking into a time machine and it was the time before the car accident.

This was a direction she might do well in. He would be her biggest supporter if she wanted to do anything in her life which was positive. One radio station she liked paid her some money to record a song that she had sung at one of the high school pep rallies. Her music wannabe friends, got excited and thought for sure they would be super rich and wealthy. She took a path which took a sharp detour. It took her to a very dark place.

The people she started to hang around friends who were finding music and pot helped let them create great music. It wasn't. Pot turned into a variety of other substances, and finally when she was 17, she found her one and only true friend, Vodka. She moved out and worked at a variety of part time jobs to support her drinking and her aimless life. Stanley couldn't talk to her. She changed the subject always. The times he did see her was when she was in the extremes of her use of alcohol. Totally plastered or totally hungover.

Ironically, a friend of hers, and one of her best drinking buddies, got into a horrific fight.

This friend, Theresa, finally had enough of all the partying. Theresa decided to get off the party bus. She stopped drinking and started to live without any substances. Theresa got involved in A.A. Several times she tried to drag Lisa to A.A. meetings. Lisa fought hard against this, and one night she left her friend's place furious.

On her way home she went to another friend's house. This friend, Susan, was older and always kept her personal bar fully stocked. Susan had 3 different types of Vodka. Lisa was determined to drink as much as she could in as short a period as possible, Susan passed out on the couch and Lisa kept drinking more and more. At one point, Lisa managed to crawl over to the bathroom.

Susan woke up about 2 hours later when she needed to use the bathroom. She found Lisa on the floor of the bathroom with a fresh cut over her right eye, and vomit on the floor. Lisa wasn't moving or breathing. Susan didn't know what to do. She slapped Lisa in the face several times. Lisa was able to move a little when Susan slapped her. Susan wasn't terribly drunk, so she had the awareness of knowing Lisa needed a hospital. Miraculously she was able to get Lisa out to her car.

Living a short distance to a local 7-Eleven, Susan tried to get her friend some coffee to help dilute all the alcohol she drank. When she came back out to her car, Lisa was gone. She spied her on the other side of the parking lot passed out. Susan told the girl behind the register of the 7-Eleven to call 9-1-1.

Susan got in her car and drove off. Little did her friend know this is exactly the same 7-Eleven where Håvard caused the car crash Lisa was in which killed her father, and sister. It also left her brother Stanley, crippled losing the use of his legs.

The ambulance came and they were able to pull Lisa back from the edge of an alcohol poisoning death. The doctor and the hospital wanted to put Lisa into an alcohol treatment center. Stanley ultimately agreed with the doctor and the hospital and he signed the paperwork necessary. He knew this was the best course for Lisa. She was going to be very pissed at him though. Stanley legally had guardianship of Lisa after their grandparents died and left the house to Lisa and Stanley. This was important since Lisa was only 17 at the time. Stanley was able to sign her into a treatment facility.

Lisa did get better. She came out of the treatment facility and went directly into a sober halfway house. She stayed in this house for six months. She made several friend in the A.A. program and was able to get and apartment and try to figure out what she wanted to do in life.

She worked at a couple of companies, law firms, or what she could get to at least get some health or student benefits. These companies also allowed her to pay for classes at night. It didn't happen right away, but in one company she found out what she wanted to do. The company she worked at the longest was a relatively small company, so she had to wear many different hats. She picked up a real knack for fixing computers which weren't working correctly. This company was eventually bought by a larger company and her job as an administrative assistant became redundant.

She got along with her old boss really well. He always sent people to her to fix their pc's. When the company was bought, her boss stepped up for her and insisted Lisa be given a position in the new company. He said Lisa was part of the Intellectual Property of the deal. This wasn't 100% true but if a salesperson or a marketing person had a problem with their PC, Lisa usually got called and she would find a way to fix it. She got a nice big raise, and a 2-year retention bonus, and was given a position in the company's IT department.

It didn't happen overnight, but the new team she was on eventually warmed up to her and treated her as an equal.

From there she kept getting more and more responsibilities. She had a special knack for understanding computers. She always found ways to protect the company from hacking. The hacking might be internal or external.

Most companies can't imagine a hack would come from within, but it does happen, and it happens enough to make sure you put in safeguards for it. Companies pay a lot of money for this expertise. They would hire Lisa to break into their company. She always found a weakness or a flaw in how they were protecting their company data.

Stanley was in tears of happiness and pride when Lisa graduated college. She said mysteriously, "*I'm not done yet*". Stanley didn't know what she implied but he assumed it meant going to post Graduate school. It wasn't until many years later that he found out the meaning this statement.

Chapter 4 - Lisa Harris

"Rinse, lather, rinse. Repeat"

- the shampoo algorithm

Leaves flying in the air. They look pretty, full of color, perfectly sized. As inviting as a warm blanket, with hundreds of patches ranging from piercing bright yellows to the life-giving vibrant greens. A multicolor mosaic. Autumn leaves are piled up in small piles, trying to stay together in spite of the wind. The wind always wins.

A pile of a thousand leaves gives way and starts to swirl in a counterclockwise formation. Higher and higher still, they go up. Heights aren't a problem for the leaves because this is where they are born. It is a brief jubilation of singing their song, but with all things it must come down to the ground. Put another record in the jukebox and wait for the next song.

It smells like fall, hints of wood smoke, dampness. Cold. No matter how much heat is applied there is just coldness. A coldness in feeling. A coldness in living. A coldness in thoughts. A coldness of knowing it is going to get colder still. The misshapen lump is shivering underneath a puffy, teal, down-filled blanket. The blanket must surely help? In this case, it does very little to comfort, and is unable to provide warmth.

Temperature isn't the problem here.

The problem for this person, this poor soul, hiding underneath the blanket is slowly being tortured. Tortured is maybe too harsh of a term. The pain being inflicted on this person is a contradiction of terms. They aren't being tortured to death, they are being tortured to heal and live.

The goal of torture typically is inflicting as much pain as possible and then be merciful and let the person die in a quick fashion. This situation was quite the opposite. This torture was playing out in a primal manner. This torture started when we were first given life. The body doesn't like it when you do something which will damage the body. The torture here was the torture necessary for all life; just don't die.

Underneath the blanket, a woman was shivering uncontrollably. She heard a sound above the wind howling outside. A voice. Loud and commanding. Two words, "**NO MORE!**"

"Who's there?", she whispered.

Silence. She said a little louder, "Who is there?"

Still more silence. Shivering cold and sweating. The bed sheet underneath her was soaking wet from sweat. Lisa Harris has been drifting in and out of conscience for the last couple of hours. Now her thoughts are coherent enough to try and rewind in her mind the events and actions which lead her to lying in these sweat soaked sheets. It wasn't surprising, or even scary, knowing she had no idea of how she ended up here. For many hours, the shivering was all encompassing. The only thought screaming in her head was, when will the shivering stop.

She thought, "Ok, let try to piece this together. Whose bed am I in?"

Did she think this, or did she say it out loud? It doesn't matter. The bed felt familiar and comfortable, but this could be any bed.

Not a totally foreign idea for her to have or even to wonder. Sometimes, it was actually comforting to wake up in a foreign bed, somewhere. Usually in the past, if she did wake up in someone else's bed, then there was usually someone else who could help her to piece together what she had done. A couple of times she woke up in a foreign bed and it was in a hospital bed after a car crash.

She had a great knack for getting into car crashes. They weren't car accidents, they were car crashes, and there is a difference. A car accident is if someone does an "oops." This always ends up with a lot of money which is paid out by insurance companies. A car crash, on the other hand, is when a person deliberately gets into a car, and they don't follow the rules. There is no "oops."

Too many rules for driving to keep track of. Don't go too fast; don't cross the line; stay in your lane; failing to stop at the traffic light; don't be distracted by your cell phone. Argh. It's no surprise she got into so many car crashes.

Sometimes her car crashes ended up in a jail. Again, this isn't the worst of all the probabilities to happen. The police would help her piece back the events of the previous night, or day, or even a week. As horrible as a night or two in a local jail can be, it was a safe place. She couldn't hurt others or hurt herself.

It was a predictable place. There was no mystery. If you woke up in jail, then you wouldn't be allowed to leave for a period of time. A person's freedom is the highest possession they can own, but too much of anything can also be toxic.

Lisa was still trying to figure out if there was someone in the room who she heard or was it her mind playing tricks on her. As these thoughts started to form, she started to feel the pull of sleep and oblivion. Finally, she gave up trying to be conscious and succumbed to sleep. In this in between state, she started to drift off, but she was then abruptly, harshly, brought alert. She felt like she was falling backward. It felt like sitting in a chair leaning back too far. If you have done this before, then you know that moment of being in a place which is between balance and no balance. Of course, she wasn't falling. She was lying in this bed soaked in her own sweat. She wasn't slowly gently drifting off to unconsciousness. She was full stop, alert and tensed to spring.

Rinse, lather, rinse. Repeat.

Once again, her mind started to calm down a little. Lisa became a little more aware of her body. It slowly became untensed. Her body clock slowly started to wind down. She could feel a familiar tug to start to let her mind wander and drift off into sleep. Her last thought was, "the definition of insanity, is to do the same thing over and over, and expect different results."

As soon as this last thought registered in her brain, she was abruptly going into a hyper alert state again. This raw feeling of every nerve awake and angry. All screaming at once. A thousand voices yelling. An amphetamine-like adrenaline high coming to its sharp and jarringly abrupt end. The car running out of gas. The light switch being turned off with no more power. Whatever was happening to her body and whatever the seizures in her brain were doing, it wouldn't let her escape one second of it. Death would happen before sleep came. A somber thought, but addiction is somber.

Lisa threw the blanket off of her. Using her arm to push herself up from a horizontal position was painful, but necessary. Her head was pounding. Phil Colins perfected a signature sound when he played the song, "In the air tonight." His drum solo signature is unmistakable. The irony wasn't lost on Lisa. The name of the song and the literal pounding in her head felt exactly like the song.

Lisa knew from experience, getting up too fast would be a mistake. Her body was doing its normal self-check. Her left shoulder dully ached. Her left foot was also hurting a lot. It screamed louder than her shoulder. Once her head stopped spinning, she was able to look down at her foot. It appeared to be ok. No blood, so this was a good start. At first, she thought it looks ok, then why does it hurt?

The light in the room contained long shadows. The nighttime light was clutching the darkness, but as always, the morning comes. As she looked at her foot a little more closely, she looked at the back of her left leg and saw a large black and blue bruise. Seeing her leg like this, helped to dislodge a neuron or two. She did remember the top of a set of stairs vaguely, from last night. The other memory accompanying this thought, was the feeling of wrapping her body into a tight ball and then rolling down the stairs until she crashed into a wall and came to a stop at the bottom of the stairs. Each step was a memory of pain. Just repeating over and over in a seemingly endless loop.

Just those memories semi-pieced together. Nothing in between. Nothing before the fall down the stairs, and nothing after reaching the end of the stairs. If she thought about it more, she really didn't recognize whose staircase it belonged to. This is a pain worse than physical. This is a pain of not knowing.

Now her bladder is screaming for attention. "OK! OK! I get it. Bathroom!" she silently argued with herself. This urge forced her to look around at her surroundings. A long rectangular window near the ceiling was allowing light to come into the room. This room is familiar. Yes, this is her bedroom. Ok, bathroom is across the room. She stands up slowly.

She looks across the room to see where she will need to walk. Just from experience of falling down so much, she plots out every step she needs to make to get to the bathroom door. She alters her path to put her in proximity to items she can hold onto to steady herself if she needs to. She also wants to plot out any areas she would need to avoid which might make it treacherous for her and cause her to trip. There is a pile of clothes near the door she wants to avoid. Her last resort was to crawl, but she didn't think this would be necessary today.

Her head is spinning fiercely. Lisa wobbles over to the bathroom and sits on the toilet. She purposely avoided the mirror. Looking at the mirror might reinforce how she looked exactly like she feels.

Abandoned long ago, was the fallacy of telling herself she was just dreaming, and everything would be back to normal when she opened her eyes. Those thoughts were just a fantasy world her mind fabricated to avoid dealing with the reality of her life. This was real, and she can't remember when the last time she had a nice dream in her sleep.

Once her bladder was satisfied, she started to feel the familiar and unmistakable feeling of being on the verge of throwing up. This is the typical pattern which she goes through consistently about every third day. Not really quite sure why it's only on the third day, but she sensed it was her body just trying to detoxify all the garbage she drank.

After she was done taking care of her bladder, she knew the inevitability of her body wasn't done yet. Her stomach was gurgling and twisting telling her she was about to vomit.

Vomiting when you are drunk is easy. If you don't make a mess, and you repeatedly make what is inside you, now become a mess on the outside; then it bolsters you more and makes more room to drink. If you are really inebriated, throwing up is very easily forgotten. You brain has stopped recording new memories hours ago, so any retention of vomiting is lost. Just like the memories of last night.

Vomiting when you aren't drunk is a different tale. Dry heaves are the worst. Your body goes through this anatomic action and it's born into our physical DNA. It's coming and you have no control over stopping it. Today was no different for Lisa. What she did vomit was red and watery. Was this red wine or blood?

Who knew? This was the least of her worries today.

Once she is finished, at least for the moment, she knows she now needs to face the mirror and have the final reckoning. Lisa Harris stood in front of the mirror and looked at herself. The picture wasn't pretty, but not a total loss. Her face was very splotchy and red. No black eyes, and no visible bruises. So far not so bad. No major reconstruction of makeup, just a little smoothing of the color. Her piercing grey eyes were reddish, and looked very tired. Huge bags under her eyes. Her blond hair was a mess. She quickly bunched up her hair and did a light touch up brushing and re-synched the scrunchie she was already wearing. She looked at her watch and it was just about 4:30 AM.

Praying to any omniscient power in the universe, she prayed to let today be a hangover day. She really didn't want to have any commitments today. She just wanted to stay in bed, and let her body get better. As she thought this, another neuron shook itself from the stubborn neuron tree in her mind. Today is Sunday.

Damn! I have to go to work in a couple of hours and I also promised my brother, Stanley, I would come over later today for dinner with his girlfriend, Ingrid. The last conversation she had with her brother was now replaying itself in her mind.

"Come over on Sunday around 5:00 PM, or whenever you get finished with work," her brother said to her.

"Yeah, sure. That sounds great. I should be out of there by about 4:30 and will come over after I get done," she lied. She would probably be done by about 2:00, but she wanted to give herself room to not be forced to a schedule even if it was just a polite, "*be here when you can.*"

Lisa didn't really want to have dinner with her brother. It wasn't a question of not getting along with him or having a bad relationship. Actually, they got along very well. They both harbored a decade's long memory of shared pain. Ten years ago, Stanley, her older sister

Maureen, and their father were all tragically hurt in a car accident.

These memories are her biggest weakness. She came out of the car accident, not a car crash she quickly corrected herself, physically unscathed. She hit her head and received a small cut. It was gone after about a week. The sadness of that day still consumes and overwhelms her. Memories with this magnitude, weaken even the strongest of warriors.

She got along well with her brother, but she could always tell he didn't like any of her drinking and bad behavior was easy to spot. It was something which he struggled with. He wanted to fix her, or fix "it." Maybe this wasn't really true. He wanted to understand it. Hell, she wanted to understand it herself, so she could then begin to help herself.

If she was truly honest with herself, she knew what the problem was. The day of the car crash, she was in the backseat of the car, she lost any chance whatsoever to be able to normally process particular high stress types of emotions.

Lisa couldn't handle, and she wasn't able to cope with, sadness. Sadness is something in our society which looks like a foreign entity. It isn't foreign at all. Sadness is a state of mind. It is a conscious state of mind though. This state of mind is something you let come into your emotional being and you let it attach itself to any thought or action.

She has been through this mind jag before. She knows how it ends, but she feels incapable of stopping it and must just let it run through its course to the end. If you think about every physical move your body makes, it does these without any emotion associated with it. It is just your hand moving to your mouth to put food into your body. It is just your eyes opening and closing. None of these actions have an emotional tag associated with it. It is buried somewhere in our psyche. It says your body needs to eat, and your eyes are needed to see what it is you are trying to eat.

Now, if you add emotion into this mixture, then the results can be the same or it can be quite different. Sadness and anger are the worst, but coincidently they are almost identical. Sadness is a blanket and we take it on, and we knowingly accept it. This now overshadows everything we do. Happiness goes away. Optimism goes away. Logic is lost. Personality gets warped and twisted. Hope drowns in a pool of sadness. Sadness takes away virtually everything we have to cling to in order for us to be still human. If you replace sadness with anger, then the result is almost the same. There is one exception to this rule though. Sadness is directed inward to oneself. Anger is directed outward to others.

With effort she slowly starts to force herself to get off this useless train of thinking. Sorrow and self-pity are damaging, if you let it go on too long. It is counterproductive. It serves no purpose. She can't stop it 100%, but she can force her mind to try to focus on something without emotion. Force her mind to think of something different. Stop letting her past take charge, and direct her in a direction she felt powerless to control.

Mercifully, our minds allow us to focus on only one thing at a time. We are inherently single threaded. Concentrating on something else which can shatter the thought process and remove all the little, tiny, threads of emotions.

It's a trick she learned when she was going down this pattern of thinking. Think about something you can do which is different than what you normally do. Sometimes, she would change a routine she did every day without even thinking about it. She could try taking a different way to work today and see if it saves her time. Yes, this would work. So, what would be the best way to get there? And if it isn't the best then what is the most interesting scenery to drive past? Typically, she drives from her apartment to get out to the highway. If it's early like today, and it's Sunday, she would avoid the most time-consuming traffic. But she does this every day. She could avoid the highway altogether and drive on the coast road to get to work. At this time in the morning it wouldn't be very busy.

Lisa looks at her face in the mirror again. Sarcastically, she says to her reflection, "OK, Get ready for work. Please try not to puke on anyone this morning."

She kicked the bathroom door closed with a loud bang and turned on the shower. While she was waiting for the water to reach a scalding hot temperature, Lisa tried earnestly to convince herself she could get through all of her social and monetary chores today. It was going to be difficult, no doubt about it. Hopefully, the day will go by quickly. Without realizing it, this thought was a ruse, she started to agree with herself.

"Yes, I should be back home soon and can just be able to really relax later tonight," she thought.

As soon as she let this thought escape, it became alarmingly and starkly apparent. This was just pure rationalization of her mind saying quick, hurry get it done, because you know for certain you will be drinking again as soon as possible. With one last look at herself in the mirror, she stuck her tongue out to her reflection.

Chapter 5 - Humpty Dumpty

Humpty Dumpty was pushed

3:45 PM Plymouth Commuter Rail Train Station

Later in the afternoon, Ingrid is in her car waiting in the parking lot for the familiar face of Stanley's sister, Lisa, to disembark from the train. Friday afternoon is usually not horribly busy at the Plymouth Commuter Rail. The Plymouth stop ended the route for this commuter rail train, so most passengers had already disembarked on previous stops serviced by this train.

Lisa, getting off of the train, was easy to spot. Ingrid waved and walked over to give her a big hug. Ingrid and Lisa had hit it off right from the beginning. The thing Lisa liked most about Ingrid, was she acted as a good counterbalance for her brother. He was totally head over heels in love with her, and she was the same with him.

Lisa was glad to see her and genuinely happy for the both of them. Fortunately, or unfortunately, Ingrid met Lisa at a time when Lisa was in the early stages of trying to be sober and stay chemically free. As most know who have been through something like this, the process is akin to standing naked in front of a hundred people. Every raw nerve showing every ugly, and unflattering, part of yourself. It's a very difficult process to have everything showing up at once like this. It's really not just showing up, the flaws were always there. It was just your brain was so anesthetized it was impossible to see these parts of yourself. Seeing your **true** self can be shocking. Once you get past the psychological shock of these defects and look at them close up, you then have a choice to make. Do I accept these, or do I want to change this and correct them? Dishonesty and selfishness were the part of Lisa that she really didn't like about her behavior. Every day, she tried to do just a little better than the day before. She knew it wouldn't happen in one fell swoop and once done it wouldn't be fixed forever. No, it was something to keep working on and a goal to reach for. Sometimes these goals kept her going.

Lisa had confided in Ingrid once, about these exact things she wanted to change. Ingrid also confided with her about some of her own flaws. She shared with Lisa. about different times she was on a similar path. Ingrid described it as a process she approached in a "*little by slow*" method. She wasn't successful all the time, but she was always open to trying to improve.

Lisa and Ingrid arrive

Just as Stanley was mulling over the meeting from earlier today, He heard Ingrid's car in the driveway. He put down the saltshaker and pepper mill he was using to season the steaks and wheeled over to the front door.

He saw Ingrid and Lisa coming through the door, and he rushed over to give his little sister a big hug. Casually dressed in only jeans and loose-fitting sweatshirt, she pulled her hair back out of her face. It was about a year and a half since he last saw his sister.

Stanley quipped, "Wow, it's great to see you. You look great and also older than I remember."

"Well yes, brother, I am older. But you are balder!"

"Nice you haven't lost your edge. You look great, though. I'm glad to see you. How is the cyber security gig going? You haven't turned into a purple hat or whatever it is, I hope."

"It's black-hat, thank you," she said indignantly. "Besides, why would I do that? It's a lot more fun catching them than it is being like them. Right, now the flavor of the day is Bitcoin and blockchain. I'll tell you later about one of the latest schemes I was working on. I think I laughed for almost an entire day after they were caught."

Lisa added, "Where did you want me staying tonight?"

Ingrid said she would get Lisa sorted out. Stanley called after Ingrid to ask if they wanted him to wait before he put the steaks on the grill.

Lisa answered, for Ingrid, "Stanley, I forgot to tell you, I converted to become a vegan." Ingrid and Lisa both burst out laughing when she saw the look on Stanley's face. He knew she was pulling his leg.

Stanley knew from experience; it was best to just let it pass. Lisa was a lot better at this than he was. It felt good to have his "only" family with him today. He made a mental note to not let this amount of time being out of touch happen again.

3:30 AM Saturday

Plymouth Massachusetts

A noise of something falling and breaking in another room of Stanley's house echoed in the early morning. Lisa woke up from a loud noise. She got up to go investigate. It most likely wasn't anything to worry about. Her curiosity got the better of her. Silently, she slipped on her khaki's which were on the floor next to the bed. She thought she heard the noise from her brother's kitchen.

As she walked closer, one of the motion sensing night lights came on and helped to dully illuminate her path. When she turned the corner to the kitchen, she saw her brother. Stanley was in the kitchen cleaning up the pieces of a large coffee/soup mug which had fallen off the counter. Stanley didn't notice her. He put the pieces of the broken mug in the trash, and went back to his bedroom.

Lisa was speechless. Stanley was most likely sleep walking. This wasn't the problem. When they were younger, Stanley sometimes did this. She was speechless because he was *walking in his sleep*. Literally, walking. No wheelchair. Lisa replayed the scene again in her head. Maybe she was in a dream thinking this. No! Stanley was standing at the sink, bent over picking up the pieces of the coffee mug. He **WALKED** to the bedroom.

Lisa wasn't sure what to do. Should she go wake up Stanley or Ingrid? They would think she was cuckoo. For the third time, she went over this in her head. No, Stanley was standing and walking. She wasn't imagining this.

She knew sleep wouldn't come to her again this night. She took a coffee mug from the cupboard, filled it with milk and grabbed a couple of Oreo cookies and went out to sit on the porch and think for a little bit.

If she didn't do this, she knew she was going to wake up Stanley and Ingrid. It wouldn't solve anything. She needed to think about this and find out the best solution.

Chapter 6 - Lisa - Death Valley

"I think it pisses God off if you walk by the color purple in a field somewhere and don't notice it."

— Alice Walker, The Color Purple

It was late in the evening. There was a full moon tonight and this moonglow bathed the desert landscape in an earie light. The darkness wasn't really black, but it looked like the sheen of a fresh coat of paint or ink. The rocky and flat sandy terrain started to show long shadows around the highway and the lone car driving at this time of night.

A metallic dark green Chevy Blazer was winding its way westbound to Los Angeles on I-15. All four windows of the Blazer were open and the howling of wind and noise was loud. It was even more so driving through Death Valley. It's 11:30 PM and the temperature was just now coming down to the low 90's.

The air conditioning in the car was fully functionable but the driver, Lisa Harris, was enjoying the howling and shouting of the wind and the sound of her little noisy bubble.

The sound of this occurrence was heard long before it arrived, and for a long time after it left. Many of the night predators took advantage of this. Many of the night prey valiantly trying to endure through the night. Always waiting and always still. Predators and prey conducted this standoff every night to see who would blink first. Still. Patient. Waiting. Their survival depended on something being noticed and vulnerable to attack, or to be hidden and not noticed.

The larger predators would wait and watch. Many smaller animals would panic, and confusion would induce them to find another hidden lair. Most larger predators swooped in and took advantage of this. Each night it was a buffet line waiting their turn to take the next animal who was now exposed. Eat or be eaten.

All the windows of the Lisa's car are rolled down. Wind in the car was making Lisa's long, blondish, hair fly in every direction. This was a nice change from the past four days of freezing cold conference rooms. Wind was howling through the interior of the car. The night sky was filled with the moonlight of a full moon. Lisa was driving through a part of the US where several record-breaking temperatures were recorded. The mellow heat was a nice reprieve.

For the last four days, she was attending two different conferences scheduled back to back and being held in the massive MGM Grand hotel/casino on the Las Vegas strip. The warmth of the desolated area she was driving through with the warm air and wind was very comfortable. One conference was focused on some of the newer technologies and advances in the field of IoT, or Internet of Things. Many of the bigger players were involved like IBM, Microsoft, Google, Amazon, etc.) who were starting to invest heavily into IoT advances. It also contained many of the smaller players who created some fresh and interesting devices which the bigger players ignored.

Lisa was heavily involved in cyber security. It was important for her to attend this conference so she could gain more knowledge of who the different players were in the market. For two days she walked around and found a lot of interesting technology being shown in the sales booths within the mammoth conference center. She saw some interesting technologies being hawked, but she also saw several areas where the security was very weak. Lisa made several notes in a notebook she carried with her. She was purposely looking for the different strengths and weaknesses for the tech being sold.

The second conference was a Computer Security conference. Computer Security was a misnomer for this conference. It was really a conference for hackers. It wasn't promoted or advertised. Even the schedule for the different sessions wasn't listed. Each of the sessions were free to anyone who wanted to attend as long as you wore the conference tag.

It's ironic for a conference to be held for computer security, and at least half of the attendees are crooks and malicious hacker criminals. The other half of the attendees are various government officials, or large corporation employees. The reason for several of these different officials being present was for a little friendly truce to happen.

Some of the government officials were invited for perhaps a breach of a company, or a government database, which made its way into the press. Some of the sessions being provided were case studies of those very hacks. It wasn't uncommon for someone who was involved in the hack to be attending in the back row. It was a little passive aggressive to invite the company's IT director to discuss exactly what they had done wrong and how they could've prevented the damage of being ruthlessly hacked at a great expense.

These government officials were called white hats. Lisa was a white-hat hacker. This meant she worked for different companies or institutions and tried to break their security both from outside and within. If she is successful, or even unsuccessful, it's valuable information to give back to her clients. She also helps those clients to make the weak points stronger and less hackable. Lisa works as an independent contractor. She has acquired an impressive client list and also a positive reputation from her clients. A few of her clients gave her some of the toughest security problems to fix. However, she has been able to have a fair record of success.

Even though our society starts to depend on computers more and more, computer security is still a niche field. Being a white-hat hacker gave Lisa good money, and it was a legitimate source of income.

A black-hat breaks the security of some company or institution and their intent is solely on stealing or tampering with their data. It could be done with a virus which would spread destruction across an industry like the Airline industry. Sometimes it could be ransomware. Sometimes it might be a virus which goes out and spreads it destruction silently, jumping from computer to computer.

The other group of hackers is a grey hat. These are normally not malicious but more of a prankster. They may break into a computer system and change the jumbotron at a sporting event or a scrolling news feed in times square.

She had accidentally found out about this conference when she was "lurking" in a darknet chat room. She decided to come to the conference and see what people had to say about security for IoT devices and how to make them more secure.

Most of the *black-hat* hackers knew a lot of the *white-hat* hackers. The people conducting the sessions would take various case studies and dissect them to show how the security was breached. A few of these sessions were familiar to her since she was called upon to help shore up the security of the company or institution after they had been hacked or breached.

The different sessions were a great help to increase her knowledge, but it wasn't really the reason she was at this conference. She was hoping she would run into a person who Lisa has been tracking for several years. She was looking for someone who goes by the moniker of *"6Ix6S!x"*. Recently she had found out the hacker's real name is Håvard Evans and he lives in Iceland.

Lisa assumed he would almost definitely attend this conference. She didn't see him anywhere at the conference. It wasn't like she was expecting him to stand out in a crowd, because she knew it was a long shot. For all she knew, he might have been wearing a disguise. She knows for certain he has used disguises before.

One of his disguises gave Lisa a great cue. She had to go back to the 7-Eleven and find out who the clerk was on the date of the accident. She was also the one who called 911. She saw the whole accident. Two of the customers were arguing about something. She couldn't hear what they were saying but the guy in the blue pickup truck was someone who she knew. His name was Charles Dawson, or as most people called him Chuckey.

Lisa was able to track both of these people down and start to get closer to this person, Håvard Evans. Chuckey said he remembered this day because of one of the tattoo's he wore. He was wearing a patch, like a nicotine patch, which wasn't fully sticking and adhering to his neck.

The tattoo was a very specific tattoo. It was a Celtic triquetra knot symbol which was inked on the left side of his neck. Chuckey said his brother had a tattoo exactly like his. It was put on by a tattoo artist in Rhode Island who had a reputation for his Celtic knot tattoo work. Chucky was positive it was this man in Rhode Island.

At the conference, she knew who some of the people who were attending, and they also may have more information. She needed to be careful about asking around about the person who changed her life so dramatically. She carefully asked a couple of people she knew or had just met here if they knew anything. People don't necessarily wear a name tag saying they are a black-hat or white-hat. Lisa was very good at noticing and reading people. How people react to a simple question can be very telling.

She learned a lot from an exchange she overheard when she was sitting on one of the couches checking her email. Two girls were listening to a young twentyish guy. He was boasting about a famous hack he was involved in. This was the hack with the Ashley Madison website. He referred to one of the other hackers by his moniker of **6Ix6S!x**. He was boasting about how he and **6Ix6S!x** literally blew up all the servers of Ashley Madison. He even put his hands out like he was shooting a gun at each of the servers.

First **6Ix6S!x**, wasn't there. The kid would never have said anything about his work with **6Ix6S!x**. No one ever admits to doing anything illegal. You put everyone else in danger. It does happen, but it isn't the smartest thing to do. If you're involved in stealing the "Mona Lisa", you made sure you kept your mouth shut.

The second thing she learned was more telling. The people who were listening to this kid, showed a trace of fear. Fear means they want to disassociate themselves with anyone knowing this hacker, **6Ix6S!x**, and also the person who was bragging about his past relationship with **6Ix6S!x**. Plausible deniability.

The person who they talked about was ruthless. If he was treated with disrespect or slighted, he would always make sure anyone foolish enough to do this will receive his disfavor and his punishment.

She left the conference feeling a little defeated. She didn't really learn anything useful here. She will have to shake this off and get up and keep trying.

Chapter 7 - Theophilus Weber

Weber BBQ:

The only sport where a fat, bald man is a GOD

Bellevue, Washington

A dirty, white Ford Ranger pickup truck was winding its way to the Amazon Fulfillment Center in Bellevue, WA. It was about 10:30 PM. His overnight shift started at 11:00. The Fulfillment Center in Bellevue was nicknamed KFC4. Each of the Amazon Fulfillment Centers in Washington were given a name of KFC plus a number from 1 to 11.

He rarely told people what his full first name was and made it a point he was only referred to as Theo. He never let anyone call him Theophilus. The only person who could do this was his mother and his older sister. She was older than him by about 8 years, so she claimed her right of seniority in the sibling chain of command. He had a younger brother who paid in blood and colorful black and blue bruises if he called him Theophilus. It was Theo and only Theo.

It was raining. No surprise there. It was always raining, or cloudy with a chance of rain. Theo had just woken up about 2 hours earlier and was heading in to work the 3rd shift, also referred to as the *graveyard* shift. Whatever it was called, he hated working this shift. Come to think of it, he hated all the different shifts. Traffic was light tonight, so he arrived for the 10-hour shift about 20 minutes early.

At the Bellevue, Washington Amazon Fulfillment center his title was, *Ambassador* of the Amazon Bellevue Fulfillment center. This is "Human Resource" speak for an HR robot who was trying very hard to be original, or clever. Theo didn't understand why they just can't just be honest. It's a warehouse job. You spend all your time sorting, loading, unloading, packing, unpacking, categorizing goods. Additionally, you will spend a lot of time walking your butt off. I don't think anyone is fooled by not calling it a warehouse worker.

These fulfillment centers are large facilities with hundreds of employees, sometimes thousands. Employees are responsible for five basic tasks: unpacking and inspecting incoming goods; placing goods in storage and recording their location; picking goods from the computer recorded locations; sorting and packing orders; and shipping of orders. A computer records the location of goods and maps out routes for pickers. This plays a key role for employees who carry hand-held computers which communicate with the central computer and monitor their rate of progress. A picker may walk 15 or more miles a day.

Theo is tall, very thin, with curly, shiny, black hair. Theo had a gaunt, almost anorexic, look in his face. His face looked like it was stretched almost to the point of splitting or tearing apart from his skull. His complexion was gray which matched his piercing gray eyes camouflaged against his skin. The only give away was when he blinked. Ironically, he had a tattoo of a skull and bones on his right arm.

When he got out of his pickup truck, he walked over to the back entrance of the warehouse. His walk was spastic and erratic. He could never quite achieve the ability of being able to *walk in a straight line*. If you were walking down a hall and he was coming toward you, it was hard to know whether you had to sidestep in one direction or not. Since he was early, he went to the cafeteria and got a bowl of cereal and a banana.

There was one absolute here, and this was usually a very common habit among other workers. Get to the time clock early. Punch in at exactly when your shift starts. He got to the timeclock about 2 minutes early, so he was one of the first ten people to punch in. Behind him were about 60 people who had to punch in before three minutes after your shift was supposed to start. If you clocked in after 3 minutes, then you were docked fifteen minutes. Easily rectified though, punch out 3 minutes after your shift ended. There was NO unauthorized overtime.

He had broken this rule several times and many other employees did this also. The last hour of work was usually the worst for Theo. Every two minutes looking at his watch, waiting for his shift to be over.

When it was time to punch out their timecard, a few people who were like him, would punch out 15 or 30 minutes later after their shift. Sometimes you got paid for this, and sometimes your supervisor would hassle you the next day. There was always a legitimate excuse about some package showing up late or it wasn't properly packed or entered correctly in the system. The supervisors loved it when you gave the reason of being just *customer obsessed*. He wanted to make sure this product, in this Fulfillment Center, maintain only the *highest standards*. They bought it every time.

Theo was a jack of all trades here. You had to be. Sometimes he was operating the forklift to carry pallets off the trucks, sitting on the sorting line, or being a picker going into the endless rows of product racks. The warehouse was about 1,000,000 square feet so there were a lot of racks and each rack had a specific address to tell someone where in the rack to look for an item.

Most people would think it must be a terribly daunting task to memorize where to look for different items. Chaos of inventory was the rule here. It wasn't necessary to memorize where the lawn products were or where to find toys etc. If something fits into a space it was put there and the location was recorded. Surprisingly, this actually improved the efficiency of the items being sent out or shipped.

Several Hours Later...

It was towards the end of Theo's shift, so he wanted to make sure he was on the loading and unloading dock filling or emptying one of the large semi-trailer trucks arriving tonight. He went over to Loading/Unloading dock 9.

The loading and unloading docks were an exquisitely orchestrated dance. It was a very impressive form of efficiency. Much likened to an assembly line, there were 12 different tunnel-like bays which the semi-trucks would line up to go into. In this tunnel, the truck would drive in and make two different stops. One stop was for unloading all the contents of the trailer. The other stop was for loading the trailers.

When a truck came to the AFC, it came over to one of the shipping/receiving bays. The truck pulled into a narrow tunnel to a point halfway through the tunnel. This first stop was for unloading the truck.

Each of the 12 different designated truck bays were all the same. Each truck bay was a long tunnel and has two stopping points. The first stop was to unload the truck. At the push of a button, a thick, blue, dimpled steel shelf was extended to the bay immediately opposite it.

An expandable conveyor belt is then extended across the bridge using the metal shelf which just finished locking into place. Now everything was ready to unload the truck. The back part of the truck, where the trailer door was just opened, contained all the loose packages and boxes.

Two of the dock workers started to furiously toss all the loose packages on the conveyor belt. The conveyor belt, which each package was placed on, had small roller wheels.

The wheels made it easy to slide packages into the docking bay. The end of this conveyor belt was a fixed slide where it took each package into the AFC, this was the start of an elaborate process which took each package and ferreted it out to where it needed to go.

It took about 30 minutes to remove the loose packages and put them on their way to the bowels of the fulfillment center. The expandable conveyor belt was taken off the metal bridge of the bay.

The next step in the process was to unload all the pallets of various bulk items like bottles of water, or pallets of 3000 new cell phones.

Two forklifts drivers waited patiently on each side of the bay. One forklift would go in and scoop up a pallet and bring it back onto the dock. While one forklift was driving and unloading the pallet, the forklift on the other side would barrel in and pick up a pallet and bring it back to the dock.

Forklifts look like they would be relatively simple to use. Most people wouldn't think it needed any special training or licenses. It's exactly the opposite. OSHA requires this and since a forklift is commonly seen on a job site or in the public area, the liability of hurting someone is extremely high. The two forklift drivers in this facility so far, at least tonight, haven't maimed or killed anyone yet.

All the goods brought in were worth a particular value, Amazon cared about this and the end customer experience. However, this wasn't the currency of this and many other AFC's. Efficiency and time are the currency used for bottom line profit. This was true for all of the Fulfillment Centers around the globe. If the process was inefficient and took extra time to perform then this effected the bottom line of Amazon. In this instance, it took almost an hour to unload the entire trailer. This was an average time for performing this task.

The metal bridge was retracted, the semi-truck moved forward to the next stop. The second stop was for loading the trailer. So, when the truck moved forward, another truck came into the tunnel behind the first one to unload their trailer.

Once the semi-trailer stopped at the second stop to load up the trailer with a new set of cargo, the process done on the first stop was just reversed. The forklifts went in and loaded all the heavy pallets of items. The loose items were put into the trailer in a way, so every square inch of available space was used.

As Theo and the other workers were unloading one of the trucks on the receiving dock, two boxes strapped together fell off of the track belt. When the boxes hit the floor, the strapping material holding both of the boxes broke when it fell to the ground. The smaller of the two boxes suffered a tear in the box when it hit a sharp edge on the leg for the assembly track. The larger box's top seam ripped slightly. The seam would need to be repacked. The smaller box would need a new box.

A guy with a short crew-cut was looking at his clipboard and saw the boxes fall off the track. At the moment, he was the guy in charge. His manager was in the next bay to load this truck which they were unloading. He saw the boxes fall and he frowned and silently cursed. Theo was the closest to the boxes. The truck was nearly unpacked, so Theo volunteered to fix and repack these boxes. Mike nodded quickly.

Theo took both of these boxes over to an area which was setup for any last-minute packing or repair needing to be done. The first thing he needed to do was to open up each box and figure out the best way to repack these boxes.

The large and small boxes contained about 100 cell phones. The large box had about 25 phones in it. The smaller box contained 75 phones all jammed in the box so tightly there was no room for any packing material. The person who packed this did a lousy job.

The large box on the other hand, was packed so loosely it made the small box weigh about 20 pounds heavier than the large box. When the boxes were strapped together it made the boxes top-heavy.

He got a new box about the same size as the large box of cell phones. He put 50 of the 100 cell phones into a large new box. He could have put all of 100 cell phones into one box. He was going to put the remainder of the cell phones into a new box, but he hesitated for a minute. These phones were top of the line, brand new to the market, cell phones. He hesitated and thought quickly, "what if he sent one of the boxes to a different address?"

If he was going to do this, he needed to act quickly and make sure he wasn't related to this shipment in any way. He went over to one of the computers and changed the bill of lading to one box of 50 cell phones received. He printed out a new label for the box. He packed the remaining 50 cell phones into a new box. He then created a new label for this box and entered in his stepbrother's address. This would be tricky but with a little luck he might pull this off.

These cell phones were the latest cell phones on the market. Each phone was worth about $1000 retail. He knew of several people he had met on the internet who would pay decent money for these phones. He figured if he could unload these for about $700 a piece, it could be about $35,000 he could walk away with.

You need to be careful when you have a cell phone when you didn't buy from a legitimate vendor. Every phone has several pieces of information which are used to make a cell phone work correctly.

A cell phone has a number which is unique and tied to each cell phone device. This could be tracked. Commerce of cell phones has changed several times. Many years ago, vendors and retailers wanted to be able to track down each and every device. It was a little cellular carrier tug of war. Who is using my cell tower? Who is outside their area and wants to use a particular cell tower? Roaming charges were the bread and butter revenue for the cellular companies.

Today, the economy has changed how cell carriers are able to be profitable. The real value is from the cell company attracting more and more subscribers. Each cell phone has a special tiny chip called a subscriber identification module (SIM) card. This SIM card contains your cellular provider information like your cell number and other personal information. With the right software you could easily clear the information and put in other data. This would remove almost all of the vendor information.

He took the first box back to the assembly line so it would go into the rest of the sorting and storing which happens after boxes are received. He told the lead guy, Mike, the box was incorrectly packed, and he condensed it down to one box. He also told the supervisor the second box was incorrectly labeled and needed to be sent out of the facility.

Mike just grunted and said, "Ok. Go over to the shipping bay and put it back on the same truck. But hurry back. We have 2 more trucks coming through and are running about 15 minutes late. Tell Melissa, we need a couple more forklift drivers."

"You got it Mike, I'll be back a couple of minutes," Theo responded, and his face took on a serious look of being given a high responsibility job. His face muscles tried their best to portray this, but it wasn't convincing to his boss.

He took the box and walked very quickly over to the next bay for loading. Walking fast was something which just multiplied his spastic gait. Thankfully, it was only 200 feet from the unloading dock.

He told Melissa, the supervisor of Dock 9, this package was incorrectly put on the wrong truck. She pointed to an area piled with other loose non-palleted items to be put on the truck after the forklifts were done.

He then asked her about some extra forklift drivers. She pointed to one of the guys just coming off the truck after delivering his payload. "Take Jeremy and tell Mike to stop looking at the clipboard and jump on one of the forklift's himself."

Theo just nodded his head. Jeremy and Theo went over to the unloading truck bay. Theo saw a pile of loose cardboard and other bits of trash needing to go out to the trash compactor/recycling area. He told Mike and said he would be right back."

"I'll be back before you know I'm gone."

Theo was a master at manipulating people at work. Theo didn't give a crap about the loose cardboard or trash. It wasn't really documented, but any area with loose items could be something to cause a person to fall or get cut or whatever. They were very stringent about this. If you fell on a piece of loose cardboard or were cut by some trash, then it might turn into a legal issue. Even though they had almost unlimited money to fend off or pay a lawsuit, it was horrible PR.

He knew if he volunteered to get rid of it properly, then he could pretend if asked, he could say he was on a very important mission. But how long did the mission take? Was it 10 minutes? 20 minutes?

On his way to the huge compactor, he thought about the cell phones he sent to his stepbrother's address. At the time it seemed like a logical solution to a problem of making sure he wouldn't implicate himself. Now he needed to think about a plausible excuse to visit Ike.

His stepbrother, Ike, lived in Tewksbury, Massachusetts. Robyn is his first name, but he prefers to be called Ike. Theo understood this very well since his real name is Theophilus.

The package he sent to Ike was supposed to arrive on Tuesday in the AM. Now he needed an excuse to get to his stepbrother's place. He had a lot of mileage points on one of the airlines he could use to get him to Boston. He hated using the points for this, but it was an affordable option to get him to Boston.

Theo had 150 Amazon Gift cards with different values from $1000 to $2500. Theo knew how to work the system and one day he was left in charge of a machine that was used to imprint the value on gift cards. It was the winter holiday rush, so he worked with another person to create these gift cards. It was easy work to be able to palm a couple of cards into his pocket. The methodology was a simple, one card for you and one card for me. He could have created hundreds of Gift Cards, but he knew this is monitored very closely. Any kind of pattern or cards with huge dollar amounts would alert someone in corporate offices.

Ike was into all the tech stuff so he could say he needed his help to configure or possibly buy a new computer. The gift cards could only be used by Amazon stores, but there was a way to get cash for these. He knew of a website that would let you transfer the card value for cash, and of course they took a small fee for doing this,

He only used computers to do a lot of gaming on his off hours. It took a lot of horsepower to play the new games out there so he could always use a newer and faster PC. He could probably sell those cell phones for big money. First though he needed to get the cell phones. He would send a message to him later today. If things worked out, then he could be there to intercept the package. This would be perfect.

Chapter 8 - Robyn Isaac Scott (Ike)

'Holy Mechanical Armies'

- Batman and Robin

Robyn Isaac Scott, or Ike, as he was called, was sitting on his couch typing away at his laptop. Ike had the TV going on in the background on some silly reality program. It was one of the "House Renovation" episodes. He normally enjoyed this show, but it's August and this program won't start airing new episodes until late September. Right now, it was just repeat episodes. Ike was wearing his favorite baggy sweatpants. The minute he got home from work the first thing he did was to get out of the blue button down shirt, beige Khaki's, and tie, and put on his silky multi-colored, flower patterned jammies, or as he liked to say, his "*happy pants*". The living room in his apartment was like someone went to a Pier One and IKEA store and was given only 30 minutes to buy the furnishings for his living room. He wasn't really trying to get the best type of any of his furniture, he tended to buy only the things he felt were practical.

Now his bedroom on the other hand was furnished by someone who took great care in placing every light fixture, nightstand, with the right color theme through the whole room. His queen-sized bed was covered with a large goose down comforter stuffed into a royal navy-blue duvet with beige trimmings on the side. His bedroom was his sanctuary where he surrounded himself with his own theme and his tasteful complimenting color combinations.

Very few men, would be interested or care about decorations in their bedroom. Usually, it's was just a simple quiet comfortable place to sleep. Ike, however, wasn't like most men. His appearance to an outsider was just a regular person who had brown hair with greyish frosted hair tips, was a little shorter than average in height, and had a penchant for sweets evidenced by the small, but noticeable, Buddha belly he was getting. His body language showed someone who would be open and approachable to those he worked with. This was the appearance he wanted to show to most people.

There was another side of him which was strictly reserved for his closest, *get me out of jail* friends. They were his closest confidants, ones with whom he shared most of his secrets. Most of his closest friends were people whom he met over the years at some of the dance bars, or drag queen shows. Sometimes, going a to bar or celebration which was full of men who were very *out of the closet* was an atmosphere which allowed him to relax and have a fun time. People were able to act like their true selves. There was a silent bond with the other gay patrons of a gay bar. Have fun, be loud, or be dramatic, but don't be a shithead.

Don't fool yourself thinking everyone was your friend and it certainly wasn't like an *after school special*. People, generally speaking, understood there was a certain level of being loud, obnoxious, bitchy, and dramatic, or sometimes hilariously funny, which is tolerated. Go beyond this point, and you were just someone being nasty, biting, or mean.

Behaving like this wasn't tolerated at all. People came to these places to give themselves a temporary reprisal of societal chains of being a gay person.

Ike was a hardware/software engineer who specialized in IoT (Internet of Things) devices. He was currently working on a program model to 3D print a part small enough to be inserted into a human body. Many of these items would assist or help the body function normally. It could also print an organ for the body like a new pancreas or a healthy part of a liver. The direction his company, Carbon Copy, was quickly becoming the only player in this field of medical research.

The field of 3D printing was an area of technology which is exploding. 3D printers are becoming a necessity for large and small companies. The model for fabrication or manufacturing of parts has been to use a subtractive model.

A good example of this is how a sculptor might create a statue. They are removing pieces from a larger item. They start with a big block of stone or wood and gradually chisel away at it. Eventually, they have a statue of a man, woman, child, or animal, etc.

The opposite is an additive manufacturing process. This involves adding layer (or bits) after layer. These layers are made up of a variety of materials. When 3D printing emerged in the late 80's and 90's, it used different plastics and polymers, which were heated and softened to make it possible of extruding these materials to form a layer. More and more layers were *printed* to create an object.

Some of the new materials being used kept getting stronger and more adaptable. Metal dust could be sprayed on an object and cured to make a layer of a metal such as titanium or steel. New polymers were being developed showing they were lighter and stronger. One interesting material that had been gaining a lot of attention is called *graphene*. This polymer was stronger and lighter than carbon fibers and could be produced at a microscopic level.

One of the exciting things about 3D printers is they are able to create incredibly small objects. They can print a part down to the micron level. A micron is equal to 0.001 of a millimeter. It's very small. To put this into perspective, a human hair is approximately 20 microns width.

Conversely, the opposite is true. Very large 3D printers can create much larger items. Walls in a building can be printed, large parts for car manufacturing, aviation, pieces of a bridge or signs. With the new advances in materials to use for the output, they might use any color plastics, biodegradable and reusable plastic filaments, metal filaments, ceramics, and many more.

The smaller you want to 3D print an item, the more fragile it is, so the smaller parts were very error prone. They were just not strong enough or flexible enough to make it worthwhile. The advances of materials and different techniques were changing constantly.

Graphene is a substance which has been studied for its unique properties and applications for decades. On a structural level, graphene is just an atomically thin sheet of carbon —it's, a "two-dimensional" matrix of carbon atoms just one atom thick. This might sound like it's too thin to do anything useful, but a single square-meter sheet of graphene would weigh just 0.0077 grams and could support up to four kilograms. No known material can approach this combination of abilities.

His work tonight was on a project he has been working on for a while. This project was to have an implanted device be able to send a signal to a smart device like your phone. The information can be sent directly to the doctor or hospital. In turn, the doctor or hospital could send over settings to adjust an implanted device slightly.

Many implanted devices are usually stationary and once in, they stay in. There are more and more new advances in medicine allowing doctors more options to treat their patients. If your liver has cirrhosis, an implant can assist your body to filter blood and distribution of nutrients and chemicals needed for other parts of the body.

Being able to *print* an organ for the body is really just the tip of the iceberg. Currently, the only way to implant something in the body was through surgery. Now *what if* you could remove tumors or have an antibiotic which could, with pinpoint accuracy, apply medicine to an infection all without surgery?

The company he worked for, Carbon Copy, created new ways to produce or 3D print different body organs. They also created several different types of microbots which could get into parts of the body where many types of tests or even surgery wouldn't be able to easily get into. The heart for example. One of the new products he was working on was to create microbots which had their own 3D printers. You would have a person swallow a couple of pills; and through the Internet of Things, a doctor or a technician would be able to remotely control these microbots. It has been rumored this technology might be a cure for almost all diseases. If you take it a step further this can essentially slow down the aging process in the human body.

At the moment, he is trying very hard to focus on his work. He was trying to modify one of the 3D models he created. It was essentially complete and in the last stages of design. He always made sure all the details of his model were correct. He wanted his work to be irreproachable.

His focus on this project was a losing battle tonight. Earlier he got into a big tiff with a coworker who had a way of making herself look good and trample anyone else's work. Ike never liked her from the beginning and after today, she was definitely taken off his Christmas card list. She called his work out in a meeting today in front of several members of his team and several other groups. She had a way of making a trivial detail to be the biggest thing wrong.

He has seen this before from her. She pulled this stunt on one his co-workers and just decimated him because one of the parts he designed was the color purple in a blueprint. Robyn understood why he did this. He wanted to highlight this piece of his design, so it was easier to see it on a blueprint. Earlier today, she did a similar thing with his project.

One of his measurements was supposed to be using the symbol for microns, which is μ. The labeling for the measure was incorrectly putting the symbol twice, His measurement was written as 30 $\mu\mu$. This was definitely a mistake on his part, and it didn't affect any of his equations or measurements, the numbers were correct.

So, tonight he was seething about this girl he worked with, Savannah Eulanda Jackson. Savannah would only talk to you if you referenced her by her shortened middle name, *Eulie*. If you called her by her first name, she would ignore you until you said Eulie.

Ike didn't like her from the start. He knew she was doing this childish inferiority of who is the *alpha* dog and who is *beta* dog. Ike certainly wasn't going to participate with this little game. Every chance he got he called her Savannah just to piss her off. He smiled a little when he thought of all the times, he did call her by her middle name, but he would put his own little twist on it. He would call her Yogi as in "*Yogi the bear, where's Boo Boo*" or called her Yoda as in "*Yoda, may the force be with you.*"

Sitting here on his couch wasn't helping him concentrate. A bowl of ice cream might help. Twenty minutes later the ice cream did help. Peevishly he smiled to himself as he thought of a perfect way to get her back. Ike knew he was being as childish as she was, but he couldn't resist. It started as a little funny to him and shortly after he was on fire feverishly writing some code and changing his model. By the time he was done he felt much better.

The next day, he submitted his changes he worked on last night. His day was starting out like any other day. After lunch, he could feel like something was up. It was Friday, and at about 2:00 PM his manager came into his office. Now he knew something was up.

Bracing for the worst, his boss explained to him, Ike's mistake, even though it was minor, it made the team and department look very bad. He told him he needed to leave the office today and take an unpaid leave of 3 weeks to let things settle down in the office. Robyn knew taking an unpaid leave was about a half-step to being terminated.

He was upset but he was a professional. He wouldn't cause a scene or act in a way which would change the respect he had worked very hard to earn from his colleagues. He also wanted to make it clear his mistake was minor.

As an afterthought he told his boss he had discovered several issues and defects in some of Savannah's work that still needed to be worked out. He shoved his laptop into his backpack and left the building. There was only one thing right now to satisfy his anger and bruised ego. He certainly didn't want to sit at home sulking over what happened today. He called a couple of his friends and they agreed, tonight was to forget everything and have some fun.

In a couple of hours, he was laughing with his friends and the office was *a long time ago*. He didn't want to drive home, so he took an UBER. On his way back to his apartment, he thought about his little mischief he had done to Savannah. Now it was just a waiting game.

This thought made him laugh very hard. Twenty minutes later he was still smiling about the 'easer egg' he included in his last changes of his code.

Ike put a change in which would wait in the background for a special combination of keys and emit a sound of someone howling like a banshee. It was childish and more likely than not this would just be removed before it went out to production. Every time he thought about it, he smiled.

Chapter 9 - Polishing Silver

Humanity appreciates truth about as much as a squirrel appreciates silver.

- Vernon Howard

Theo and Ike before parent's wedding

Theo's stepbrother, Ike, has a different last name than Theo. Their parents got married about 10 years ago. At the time, both Theo and Ike were 23 years old. Theo realized that because Ike lives near Boston, it would be very unlikely for Amazon to suspect his involvement.

Ike and Theo aren't close. No ill will, just no reason to interact with each other unless needed. Ike always treated Theo with respect and acceptance. Most people Theo met usually just looked at him as different and not equal. They would think he was just a spastic weird person. It was natural for him to attain a special sense of people's real motives. Did they treat him with pity or treat him with genuine respect?

Many years ago, when his father and Ike's mother were going to get married, different tasks were laid out for them to complete together. The first five minutes of Ike and Theo talking and introducing themselves to each other, set the pace for their relationship.

They were tasked with retrieving all the special and expensive wine glasses and silverware from the garage of his father's house in Tewksbury, Massachusetts. Sitting at a kitchen table with a pile of forks, knives, spoons, serving utensils and many different types of glasses, all needing to be polished and cleaned, they both got to work together on this project.

Polishing silverware is a very tedious chore, but it's necessary for special occasions. Polishing each piece becomes a tight balance between perfection and expediency. If you polish a spoon for example, it can be done quickly and easily and nearly perfect. If you polish a fork, then you have to spend a little more time getting it to be acceptable.

Theo asked Ike, "So what do you really think about your mother and my father getting married?"

He was sure Ike, also wanted to ask this question.

Ike said, "Good question. I know my mother is excited about the wedding. If she's happy, then I guess I'm fine with them getting married."

Theo started laughing and tried to smile but his face was too gaunt to really look like a smile. His skin stretched very tight and pushed his lower jaw inwards and left his front teeth to hang forward almost like the big teeth of a beaver.

Ike looked at him and wasn't amused by Theo's reaction.

Theo saw he was laughing, and Ike wasn't. "Ike, don't BS me. That's not any kind of answer. This is the answer someone would give me if it was exactly the opposite of how they felt. I'm pretty good at it myself so don't try to make me think you haven't already been sussing this out."

Ike smiled, and decided in this situation, being completely *real* would serve him better. Theo and Ike would be called into service for different holidays or events and they would be forced into those events. He should at least start out with honesty and be straight with Theo.

"Your right. I have given this some thought. I've only met your father once. He appears to be a decent guy. My mum really likes him, so it doesn't really matter what I think about her marrying or not marrying your father. If they are happy then this is what is important."

Theo said, "Ok, but it doesn't really sound like the total story but more of a watered-down version."

"Ok, if you want to hear this, then here it is. My mother can handle herself pretty well. First requirement is your father needs to treat my mother with respect and love. She is marrying your father. I'm not, but if your father, shows her any kind of disrespect then he and I are going to have a problem. I'm not expecting them to have the perfect marriage. Yeah, they are bound to have an argument once in a while, That's normal. If they care about each other then they will work to make it better. That's all."

Ike continued, "Lastly, these requirements I'm placing on your father also go both ways. I won't tolerate my mother treating your father bad. So, let's have an understanding on this. Their relationship is theirs to make or break. I don't want to get involved or meddle in their relationship. The only exception to this is what I said before. So, you must also have thoughts on this too."

Theo thought for a second and said, "Yeah, I do. I'm not really close to my father, but he is pretty predictable. He is a standup guy. If he says he will do something you can bet, he will. He also doesn't 'beat around the bush' if you're doing something he doesn't like, he will tell you."

Theo comes to visit

About six months ago, Ike had received an email from his stepbrother, Theo, asking for his help in purchasing a computer for XBOX gaming. Apparently, Ike thought, he was now a gaming enthusiast. He was coming back to the Boston area for a couple of days. So, he asked Theo if he could stay with him. Theo knew Ike worked with computers and he wanted his advice on purchasing a new computer system with the right technical specifications for gaming.

At first, Ike was surprised by this request. Theo and Ike never called each other to catch up. It was always for a reason when they had to interact. Usually, it was a holiday dinner or some other function that they were forced to be a part of. There was no bad blood between them. They just both stayed on their side of the road.

Ike replied he could help him out. Theo was coming to Boston on Sunday and would be heading back to Seattle on Monday mid-morning. Ike offered to pick him up at the airport on Sunday. The date in his email was for this Sunday which was in 4 days. He paused a second before he pressed the send key on his reply.

The short time frame of this made Ike suspicious. Getting an airline ticket so quickly and making the arrangements takes time and a lot of extra cost. What if Ike was unavailable? What if he couldn't find a place to stay at? This didn't make any sense to Ike. He suspected Theo shopping for a computer was probably not the truth. But why?

He sighed and just resigned himself to make the best of it. He could take Theo out to shop at a couple of places he knew. He could also probably help steer him into getting a computer system to meet his *gaming* needs.

Four days later, Ike was waiting in the area near security and saw Theo walking toward him. Theo looked even thinner and gaunter than he had remembered. Wearing a jean jacket,

Theo approached him, and they shook hands. A few minutes later, they were in Ike's car heading south of Boston where Ike's apartment was.

In the car they tried to make meaningful small talk to take up the silence which would have been deafening loud. Ike decided he would be safe and just stick to the topics he knew. Ones that were not controversial. He didn't want a repeat of their initial conversation so long ago, about his father and Ike's mother getting married. It was an unspoken truce they made that day. Talk about anything but think carefully before any comments regarding their parents.

Ike started it off, "I was a little surprised you were getting into gaming. You need to be careful on the equipment you buy. A lot of places will rip you off and they will smile as they take your money. I'm glad you asked me, I think I can help get you setup with a decent system and won't cost you and arm and a leg."

"I was hoping you would say that. This all happened very last minute. I had a lot of vacation time and I needed to use it, or I would lose it. I know I didn't give you a lot of notice, sorry about that."

Ike was glad he mentioned the short notice. It sounded plausible but Ike still didn't believe him. He replied, "No problem. I do have to go into work tomorrow though. What time is your flight out again?"

"I have a flight at 3:30 in the afternoon. Is it ok if I just hang out until I have to head to the airport?"

"Yeah, sure no problem. If you call an UBER, it will probably only be 15 or 20 bucks. I was thinking, if you aren't too burnt out from your flight, we could stop by one of the PC stores and take a look at some of the systems they have there."

"Yeah sure. If you don't mind it would be awesome. Thanks."

"My company allows me to get a discount on PC's and equipment so if you find the right system you can save about 30% off the cost."

"Really? That really help. Some of the equipment for PC's are so expensive. I have a friend who I go online with almost every morning, she works third shift also, and I saw the system she has. I mean her computer is a lot newer than mine, but the one thing I noticed was she is doing all this on a laptop and the screen is pretty small. I like the idea of being able to take a laptop to anywhere I want, but I would think the monitor would constantly bug me. Is there a way to hook a laptop to a big monitor or am I just going to have to buy a massive box which stays in one place?"

Ike chuckled a little at this and quickly added, "Theo it's a great question. The answer is yes. A lot of people use what is called a *docking station* to plug their laptop into. The docking station is a device you can connect to pretty much any type of peripheral device you want. For example, when I bring my laptop home from work it will connect to a docking station at home. My docking station has a connection to multiple monitors, a mouse, a keyboard and also three external hard drives. For you, I think this would probably be the best situation."

"I'm up for that, thanks for the advice I appreciate it," Theo beamed at Ike. For a split second, Ike though it seemed genuine.

For the next couple of hours, they went shopping for a PC. Apparently, Theo, had a brand-new credit card he wanted to give a *test drive*. Well, it was quite the test drive that night. It was a fully loaded system with huge amounts of memory, the best graphics, and fastest computer on the market. A great docking station for his laptop and a huge monitor. Theo wanted a gaming chair with lights embedded in it and speakers in the headrest. Theo said this was a must have for him. Ike would never buy a gaming chair, but it was Theo's money to spend. Ike was glad he was asked to give his advice.

After shopping for computers, Theo said he wanted to take Ike out for dinner. They stopped at a local restaurant called Woody's which Ike had been to many times in the past. Decent food and reasonably priced. Ike was not expecting anything from Theo, he was genuinely happy to help him. For some reason however, he still couldn't shake the feeling there was a hidden agenda to Theo's visit.

During dinner, they talked about the usual things. How their jobs were doing; how they liked where they were living etc. Ike was curious about the online friend he mentioned. Theo said she was a friend from a different Amazon facility. She was the person who introduced him into the world of online gaming. He really liked playing with her on these teams. He said they were very good and worked well together on these teams. They usually dominated these games because they would crush and kill anything or everything in sight. Ike said he used to be an avid gamer, but he couldn't afford the time. He could easily get lost in the time it required.

Ike asked him what he wanted the computer for, other than gaming. He mentioned he wanted a computer for surfing the internet, email, and he said he was interested in doing some video editing. He bought a drone a little while ago and wanted to be able to put different videos he had taken and mix it with music or other video clips.

"Well, you have a decent computer for doing this. Serious software for doing any kind of video editing requires a lot of horsepower. The computer you got tonight has everything you need for this. I have used some different software packages out there and some are better than others. I can help get you get started on some of the software when we get back to my apartment. You must be exhausted after a long day of flying and shopping."

"I'm good. I'm glad I asked for your help. I would have been totally clueless without it."

"I was glad to help you out."

Later after Theo got situated and unpacked what he brought with him. Ike showed him a couple of the programs he had on his laptop for editing video's and audio files. He also showed him a couple of other general-purpose tools, virus software and malware tools. After Theo got all of this downloaded and was in the process of installing them, Ike said he needed to go to bed.

Theo said goodnight and thanked him again.

The Next Day

Theo woke up about 10:00 AM. He went out into Ike's kitchen and got some coffee which was left in the coffee pot from Ike that morning.

There was a note from Ike:

Theo,

I'm glad you came back east from Seattle. I am sure you will be able to get a lot of use out of your new computer. Let me know how the video editing goes. Send me a video if you want.

All the best

Ike

Theo thought to himself, one down and one to go. He checked his phone to see where the package was in the system, the one to be delivered to Ike. Theo came here for one reason only and it was to intercept the package that he had sent to Ike. It looked like it was on schedule and should be here by noon time. Ike's flight back to Seattle was for late tonight but he told Ike he was leaving at 3:30. He wanted to have some cushion if this package of cell phones doesn't get here in time.

If Ike was ever able to untangle anything about Theo's ruse it would be overflowing in lies. The first three lies are all one in the same. The girlfriend, the online-gaming, and the need for a computer. He had none of those. The lies about video editing and drone video, well it was partly true. He did have a drone and he did take video of people who didn't want to be videotaped. It never went any further than that.

The only thing he came back to Boston for was a plausible alibi for getting the cell phones he intercepted. He was hoping to sell these. Maybe he could get some money or eBay. Maybe on craigslist. There were many places he could probably unload these. You didn't have to look that far to find a place to sell these types of commodities.

The FedEx truck was early, and Theo was able to get the package and sign Ike's name. This was what he came all this way for. The only issue right now was he wanted to kill some time before his plane later tonight.

He noticed Ike did not take his laptop with him to work. Hmm that was odd, he thought. Theo turned it on, and it came on in a second. Theo would have thought Ike would have a password or something, but it didn't ask for one. He saw a couple of folders on the screen. He double clicked on to see what was inside. He was just being nosey. One folder caught his attention though. One of the folders was called *CarbonCopy*. Theo knew Ike worked at a company called *CarbonCopy* and they were doing some cutting-edge medical stuff.

In the top-level directory, there were a couple of document files. He opened them up one by one. The first document was just a simple text file which appeared to be a lot of legalese for copyrights and licensing of software. The next document was a changelog text file. This again was not really interesting, and it talked about each change made to the files in the directories below this one. The last document was a large document laying out all the technical specifications of the software below this top directory. It described everything about what the software does and how to run it, what are the limits, what it can do, and on and on. Theo at first couldn't make any sense of it. All of the software below could be used to print out new body parts. At least, that was Theo's understanding of it at a high level. This could be a gold mine for the right person.

In a millisecond, Theo decided to copy all of these files and he would figure out what to do with this later. He hooked up his new laptop to Ike's laptop the way he had shown him last night. He then copied everything in all of those directories. It took a while, but it finished with no problems. Theo started looking in other parts of his computer and found a couple of things which might be interesting and copied them also. The *CarbonCopy* directory and all the source code was a great find.

Now, he looked at his watch and it was nearing 3:00 PM. He jumped into the shower, packed all of his gear into his backpack, called for a taxi and locked the door when he left.

When he got to the airport, he assumed he would have a long wait for his flight later in the evening. He was able to change his flight to a time much earlier and was flying home to the Emerald City of Seattle, Washington. It was good to be home.

Chapter 10 - Kópavogur Iceland

"Show a little faith, there's magic in the night."

— Bruce Springsteen

1 year ago

Kópavogur, Iceland

Håvard Evans

Iceland is an awe-inspiring place where your eyes grow weary from trying not to miss anything. How easily it becomes to be overwhelmed and humbled by nature. Iceland is a sacred place. It's unlike any other on the planet. Everything is out in the open and nothing is hidden. Although, many areas are designated as tourist areas, it feels redundant. The wonder and the splendor of nature is available to all. No introduction, tour guide or fare is needed.

In Kópavogur, Iceland, there is an old fish processing warehouse, with several large loft-like apartments carved out of the building. In one of these apartments, very loud heavy-metal music is pulsating from the main living area of the loft. The heavy, highly amplified distortion, and emphatic beats are making the walls vibrate. The building has two other lofts, but they are both vacant now.

A 39-year-old man, with a tightly trimmed beard and long, dirty blond hair set into a low man-bun is sitting in front of a white L shaped workbench. It is impeccably organized. On the left side two laptops stacked on top of each other are in their own little cubby. Below the work bench, sits a large computer. Above the desk surface of the desk are three monitors stacked on top of each other. The bottom monitor was tilted out a little, the middle monitor was flush to the vertical bench struts. The last monitor at the top was tilted in for better viewing.

Next to these monitors were shelves of small bins which were filled with all kinds of conceivable small electronic pieces. Several breadboards of different sizes were neatly stacked together. A breadboard (a.k.a. plugboard, or a terminal array board) holds connection holes which don't require soldering. It is reusable. This makes it easy to use for creating temporary prototypes and experimenting with circuit design. These boards allow for fast prototyping of electronic devices without soldering into the holes of the board.

Finally, at the base of the bench was a long horizontal strip of powered plugs. Also, affixed above the bench was an additional horizontal metal bar containing another row of powered plugs if needed.

The housing of the computer underneath the desk is a clear plexiglass which allows you to see all of the components stored inside. Inside this casing are several tubes lighted to an orangish color and filled with pure distilled water. These tubes contain the liquid cooling for the processing power of the computer.

In front of Håvard Evans was a breadboard with several wires going in and out. All of these wires were connected to a small Raspberry Pi computer. His Raspberry Pi computer is a small device and contains only the barebones of hardware necessary to run a program which he has uploaded to it. In the world of IoT, or Internet of things, this computer will represent just one of the possible things which someone might want to use. When you use an app on your cell phone to control the thermostat of your house, or when you have someone ring your doorbell and it sends you a video of who is at the door; then it is something similar to the device that is in front of Håvard now.

Cell IoT

Håvard is trying to correct a program he wrote for this small device in front of him which is hooked up to a cell phone. The program is trying to send a signal to the device but every time it attempts to connect, the device turns off and then turns on again. After about 5 minutes, he found exactly where the issue was located. Once he corrected and recompiled the code the connection to the device was working again. He had two green led lights connected to the breadboard. They are now lit up.

He unhooked the cell phone from the device in front of him. He restarted the application on the cell phone and as he was expecting, the two green led lights lit up again. Now, he pressed a sequence of numbers and the numbers started to show up on his monitor.

Håvard sat back and look at all the devices in front of him. He was pleased with the progress. He also went through a mental checklist to be sure all the connections were correct. Yes, all the inputs are correct, and he was now ready to go.

The next step of his work this morning, was to add some new changes which would finish his application. The application was an eclectic mix of many different pieces of software. Some of it was source code which was hacked to bypass license checking or serial number keys.

Parts of the code he was modifying to make the device behave the way he wanted. It involved a lot of cutting, stitching, pasting, and writing large chunks of the source code to make it bend to his will.

Håvard was modifying this code to work on this cell phone and send new signals to another device recently released in the medical field. The devices were supposed to be part of a breakthrough in curing many diseases in the world. It is really a phenomenal discovery. Håvard thought when he heard about this a year ago, if he could get into the guts of this, he could sell this to people who wanted to do more than cure diseases. What if he could repurpose these devices to not just cure cancer or leukemia, but cure aging?

Applications for this technology and also his repurposing of the software, would have almost an unlimited choice of applications. Theoretically, this could also kill someone if the right signals were sent. Foreign entities or different world militaries might want to get this powerful ability to indiscriminately kill a public figure. How much would a government or company pay for this technology?

He needed to be mindful of these thoughts because his imagination would jump in. Thoughts of him becoming uber wealthy could side-track him. He needed to stay focused.

5 Years Earlier - Ashley Madison Website

About five years ago, Håvard made a lot of money stealing user data from the Ashley Madison website. Håvard, who was only known as 6Ix6S!x, was part of a team of other hackers who cracked and breached the security of the parent company, Avid Life Media, which operated the Ashley Madison website and its sister site, Established Men website.

The hack involved a team of hackers who found a way into the company's internal network. Once they had access to all this data, they took down almost 10 TB (Terabyte) of information of approximately 150 million users. Many of the users gave fake email addresses but real street addresses and real phone numbers. All of these profiles were simple to track down to real names and information. Håvard, remembered how charged up he felt after pulling this off. Then the whole thing went south.

After the data was taken, someone on the Impact Team, as they were called, told Ashley Madison they had stolen the information and would release it unless they shut down the site. He didn't see it coming. He didn't understand this. It also could put his involvement in this heist at risk.

They didn't shut down the web site. The leader of this Impact Team two weeks later released 60 GB's of user information to the public. Many high-profile people were included in this 60 GB of data.

Every person who had ever created a profile on Ashley Madison was released. Everything in this 60 GB's of data contained all user data, addresses, work info, phone numbers, and credit cards. All of the chat scripts and pictures of the users were passed around. Some of the pics were really graphic. Pictures of every type of anatomy and sex act. Ironically, it also contained all the emails for the CEO of Avid Life Media, Noel Biderman. For this group of hackers this was the mother lode of all mother lodes of bounty,

More importantly on this particular hack, all of the chatroom chats, company emails and even financial databases were all living on one server. It was literally like taking candy from a baby. All of the data lived on one server and backed up in a different folder on the same server.

It took about 10 hours to copy all the data. Once they finished, they deleted all the data and also deleted all the backup data. Having everything on one server wasn't smart on the company's part. They thought if they backed up regularly, then any data associated with the user was backed up.

Most companies follow a regular backup process which will have local backups and also remote backups. The remote could be in a machine stored in a different office, or physical media like tapes, drives, or disks secured in a safe. They never leave it on the same server machine. This is just plain lazy and stupid.

It also uncovered an even shadier side of the Ashley Madison website. If you were a user, and let's say after a while you decided not to use Ashley Madison website. You could request to have your profile and data deleted. Ashley Madison's user agreement stated you would have to pay a fee to have your profile deleted. If you paid the fee, you would incorrectly assume your information was deleted. It wasn't. This information was also included in the data which was later released.

Even though this was about 5 years ago, he still sees people asking for any data from those databases which could be used for extortion or ransom ware on these users. When it was first released a couple of weeks after the hack, rumors were going around about a few people were committing suicide over this release of information. Once this started happening, Håvard was done and wanted out. He collected

148

his $1.25 million in Bitcoin and removed any data he had which could be linked to him and this hack.

1 year ago

One year ago, he was hanging out in one of the darknet chat rooms where he would occasionally go to. The chat rooms were like a county bazaar. Some people in the chat room were people who he has chatted with or traded warez within the past. Warez are software programs or source code which has been illegally copied or 'cracked' the licensing of the software. This chatroom only allowed entry to someone if another member vouched for you. This helped to reduce many of the white hat or grey hat people sniffing around to gather information to provide to different government intelligence agencies.

Every once in a while, people would be allowed access faking to be black-hat users. Most people in this room could sniff them out pretty easily. There is always a trail somewhere of what networks this person has recently surfed. So, if last week you were communicating with the FBI, CIA, MI-6, etc. many of the nodes in your history would show up. Those nodes were certainly not named FBI-2 or MI6-XX. It would be too obvious and probably a goof of someone in the room who got a kick out of it. Hiding in plain sight so to speak.

The monitor on the top of the other two monitors was endlessly scrolling the back and forth the chatting going on in one of general chat areas on a busy chatroom. If you are new to this public room chatting, tread carefully. When you post anything in the public feed of the room then you are vulnerable to the many trolls and troublemakers who come on to get a kick out of saying the nastiest, outrageous, funny, amusing, demented, and cruel things. You have to have a thick skin. If you do say something which is funny or clever you may garner a few LOL's or if you are very clever then you might be tossed a few ROFL (Rolling On Floor Laughing), or LMFAO (Laughing My Freaking A** Off). These acronyms are very Grated. There are too many to count of these which are in the R-rated section.

Most deal making was done in a private chatroom and not in the main feed of the chatroom. Håvard was just trolling in one of those main chatrooms to see if a friend, he knew, was online. Friend is probably the wrong description. This was a person who like, Håvard, was very adept at finding weak spots in a company's security defenses of their network.

GrillMan299

Someone called GrillMan299 sent him a private message. The message read:

GrillMan299: Hi u online?

(pause)

GrillMan299: u there? Someone told me to contkt u if I got a hot item to sell? U there? This guy said he knew u from impact taem? U there?

Håvard sat there for a second. He didn't like it when people IM'd him when he was just lurking and not active in the chatroom. The only way for this guy to send him a message is to know his screen name exactly. He decided this person was a fool and a noob. He ignored the message.

The next day when he logged on still in invisible mode, he received another message this person.

GrillMan299: HEY MAN U ALIVE OR JUST IGNORING ME - OK, FINE BE A DICK. YOUR BUDDY TOLD ME YOU MIGHT BE INTRESTED IN BYING A BUNCHof new non aktivated cellies I have about 50

I also got some source code I took off someone's pc which has prototype of carboncopy gadgets stuff.

I also have 100 AMAZON GIFT CARDS WITH $2500 BUCCKS ON THEM. I CANT US THEM.

Against his better judgement he replied. He wanted to know who this buddy was he mentioned.

6Ix6S!x: yeh I might be int's in the cells. First who told you to find me? And STOP YELLING with all caps. That's rude

GrillMan299: yeah ok sorry abouthe caps – didnt know. Cells are brand new clear sims – got them from friend totally clean. prob worth $1500 a piece! sell for 750. guy who told me to talk to you was someone calls Z3bra-m9er

Håvard thought if these phones were new and non-activated, he knew several people who would buy these for at least 700 hundred to 1000. The carriers were all trying their best to sell phones and depending on the deals you leased a phone for some dollar amount per month plus you are locked into a particular carrier. The carriers make bank by tying you to their service. Non activated phones are like gold.

The other thing he mentioned was Amazon gift cards. It wasn't hard to figure out GrillMan299 probably worked at Amazon or had some tie-in to the tech giant.

The person who directed GrillMan299 to Håvard, Z3bra-m9er, was someone who Håvard knew. It was about 5 years ago, he worked on a global hack of a company called Avid Life Media. Avid Life Media was the parent company of the Ashley Madison website and also its sister website called, Established Men.

It irked him intensely about who told this fool to look for him. It broke a silent rule in these spaces. Most times, the person who you knew would make the introductions or at the very least send a heads-up message. Damn. Håvard had no idea who this person was. Is he real or fed? Well ok, let's see if he is real.

Håvard knew the cards would be easy to distribute in the network of people he has worked with around the world. For some reason, the Japanese and Indian people were addicted to Amazon. Håvard would make a little bit of money on the Gift Cards but he would sell these very cheap and this would increase his reputation among the network of black hats. This money would be a drop in the bucket to the money he could make getting this code and documentation on CarbonCopy.

This was a wind fall for Håvard, but he haggled a little with this person, GrillMan299. He instantly recognized the person wasn't really experienced in negotiating deals on the net. He looked up the person who vouched for him, it all looked pretty safe to deal with GrillMan299.

The deal was a straight trade and a lot of cash. GrillMan299 had about 100 Amazon gift cards. He wanted to unload these for $1500 apiece. He negotiated a little and got him down to $1000 a card plus $50,000 for all of the source code, architecture and documentation of the device called CarbonCopy. Finally, 50 cell phones for $600 apiece. In total, GrillMan299 wanted $180,000 in Bitcoin (approximately 19.45 BTC @ $9254).

Selling his modifications of CarbonCopy would require a lot finesse and delicacy. He couldn't just put a sign out on Craigslist or eBay, to sell a fountain of youth. His list of contacts contained some very powerful and well-connected people. People such as these would be able to do the proper introductions and also understand the need to be discrete. People who would want this would pay top dollar for this. The understanding being if a person will be willing to pay a large amount of money for something, then you must absolutely deliver what you promise.

If you don't deliver exactly this promise, then their disappointment can have a mortal repercussion on Håvard.

Chapter 11 - If Truth Be Told

My family could only afford to get me the box of eight Crayola crayons, but I craved the one with all 24 colors. I wanted magenta and turquoise and silver and gold.

- Joni Mitchell

For the last half hour, Lisa has been sitting on her brother's porch in the early dawn. She was feeling several emotions all at once. Her brother just walked out of the kitchen. Walked! She was very surprised. Speechless! She was happy, ecstatic, and joyful for her brother. He can walk now, and he had the choice of where and how he went. The wheelchair made those decisions before, but not now. The last feelings, she felt was just raw anger and hurt. Why didn't he say anything about this? It hurt her. She knew it was irrational, but she couldn't really define it any better. Stanley was less than 2 feet from her on the day of the car accident. Stanley wasn't the only victim who suffered from this accident.

Afterwards, Lisa went down a totally different road than the one Stanley took. Her road was a ferocious battle to search for a meaning to the incredulous and the irrational events in her life. Sometimes, she felt like she was a potter, trying to mold the clay of her life to become something useful, as it comes out of the kiln.

Now she can deal with this. She has to.

Lisa came out to the porch to sort through what she had just seen. The dawn was still makings it way into the sky. There was a wind chime on Stanley's porch, lightly tinkling in the early morning. She was thankful for the silence and the gentle wind chimes.

Ingrid must know about this change with Stanley. There's no way she couldn't know. Lisa knew Stanley was doing some type of advanced medical research. They had talked about this at one point. About a year ago.

They happened to be talking about some new research in the area of implanting devices into people. It was becoming more and more common to have the device possess the ability to access the internet. Doctors and hospital could now harness the power of the internet to send and receive data from these devices which also have the ability to be remotely configured or tweaked. Stanley was asking a common question about the possibility of those devices being hacked. She heard these questions from her different clients and colleagues.

Devices definitely have the ability to be hacked. Any manufacturer can create devices to talk to the internet, many manufacturers provide at least common configuration for those devices. Basically, the manufacturer creates the default configuration to satisfy the most common customer.

Home devices, like Alexa and Google Assistant, are becoming very popular. You can connect these devices to control everything from your alarm system, house lights, garage door, or any other appliance or device. Most items such as these, are mostly benign. Self-driving cars or medical devices take on a much higher risk of use. Your self-driving car could make a right hand turn unexpectedly and drive you off a cliff. The insulin pump will give a deadly dose of insulin. Scary to even contemplate such a thing, but it has every potential to act this way in the hands of a malicious force.

At the time, Lisa didn't really think much of it. Just idle conversation. She knew Stanley was working on a way to create and produce new therapies using *stem* cells to help correct various medical anomalies. Lisa didn't really know much more than this. She knew that he was very excited by his work.

Ingrid was working for a different company that created printers. As she thought about this, she had to admit to herself that she really didn't know much at all about her work. Why was this? Ingrid wasn't secretive about her work. It was just something that didn't come up in conversation. This will not do, Lisa thought to herself wryly.

She got up from the porch, grabbed a cup of coffee and brought her laptop outside with her on the porch. She brought up her search engine and started to search for printing in Plymouth, Massachusetts. The initial hits she got back were a laundry list of links about the history and the significance of Plymouth Massachusetts, and the original settlers. Nothing terribly useful.

At the bottom, she saw a company called DoubleDigit. They were a medical device outsource company. They made 3D printers, to create bio-compatible cardio & vascular devices. They were using state of the art materials with remarkable strength and durability. She would have missed it, but one of the product pages caught her eye. One sentence mentioned a little blip about the ability to print *stem* cells. This had to be it.

But wait, Ingrid worked with Stanley at his company called Carbon Copy. Did they have a relationship with DoubleDigit? She went to the Carbon Copy webpage and eventually found a mention of Carbon Copy purchasing the bio printing part of DoubleDigit.

Like turning the light on in a dark room, she connected the dots. Is it possible for Stanley to have his spinal cord fixed using *stem* cells? This seemed to be surreal. She needed more information.

Over the course of the next couple of hours, Lisa kept searching for any information about *stem* cells and 3D printing. What she read was incredible. In different laboratories around the world, scientists have been able to make big leaps in the field of medical devices and bio-engineered *stem* cells. If she was understanding this correctly then it did seem like it could be possible to correct Stanley's spinal cord. *Stem* cells were the key factor here.

Lisa lost track of the time. It was about 9:30 AM. She heard motion in the kitchen. Looking into the kitchen, she heard Stanley's voice. He was talking to Ingrid about making plans for cooking breakfast. The voices in the kitchen were lost in noises of pans being taking out to start cooking pancakes. Lisa picked up her coffee cup and went into the kitchen.

Stanley was in his wheelchair and Ingrid was at one of the cabinets taking out some dishes. Stanley saw her come in from the porch and said, "Good morning. How did you sleep?"

Both Ingrid and Stanley were looking at her to respond. In Lisa's mind a large inaudible battle was happening. She quickly kept her face expression neutral.

She lost the battle and responded, "I slept fine. I'm little jet-lagged, so I woke up early."

Ingrid jumped in and asked, "Are pancakes ok? Or do you want some scrambled eggs or an omelet? Whatever you want."

Stanley piped in, "I have some nice fresh blueberries if you want some blueberry pancakes?"

"Pancakes sound great. And maybe another coffee. Anything I can do to help?"

For the next hour, Lisa did her best to keep conversation light and not go into the dialog she was having with herself about how to broach the subject of Stanley walking. She had made a snap decision that she would ask Stanley and Ingrid this morning about what she had seen, after she could pull her thoughts together.

After Lisa finished her second cup of coffee, she got up and walked over to the sink with her plate. She decided it was now or never. She turned around and asked, "Hey, I was wondering if I could talk to you about something?"

After they both nodded sure, Lisa sat down at the table where they had just finished breakfast. She looked at Stanley and asked, "I saw something early this morning that I don't understand or even believe. I woke up this morning about 3:30 am. I heard something crash and break. I came out to the kitchen to make sure everything was ok. Stanley, one of the coffee mugs, fell and broke. I saw you cleaning it up."

She paused, to inhale a deep breath. She continued, "Stanley you were out here bending over and cleaning up the pieces on the floor. You were bending over to pick up these pieces. You weren't in your chair. You put the pieces in the trash. And you walked back to the bedroom. Stanley, you **walked** to your bedroom. You did not wheel yourself into your room from the kitchen. You walked!"

Again, she paused to breathe, and said, "Stanley, I know I'm not losing my mind here. Is this really true that you can walk now? Please don't say I was just imagining this. I have been thinking about this since 3:30 this morning."

Lisa turned to face Ingrid. "Ingrid, is this something you're working on? It, kind of makes sense. If you're working on new tech with 3D printing and Stanley is working on getting and growing *stem* cells. It makes sense. It is unbelievable, but I can understand how these two areas could combine. This could totally change the world."

Ingrid looked at Stanley, and Stanley nodded slightly. "You're right about combining Stanley's work and mine. It's strange, the way it happened though. Stanley's work was focused on *stem* cells. These cells are like templates for cells. You can make them and transform them to be almost any type of cells. Now, the work I was doing was to make a device that could 3D print those cells. This part of the solution is working and has been for about a year now."

"Ok, I think I get it. So, you printed new spinal cord *stem* cells? Is this how he can walk with these new cells in his body? Is this change going to be temporary or is it permanent?" Lisa asked.

Stanley jumped into the discussion at this point and said, "Well it isn't exactly like that. We knew we could print *stem* cells, but we were running into a problem where the cells we printed weren't going through the full cell cycle. Our theory was to inject the body with approximately 1000 nanobots. Each of those nanobots would act like a 3D printing factory and print out 1000 3D printer nanobots. Each of those nanobots would print 1000 *stem* cells. This was the theory at least."

Stanley continued, "We were hoping to have all these cells go through the normal cell mitosis. The purpose of mitosis is to produce more cells. One cell divides and replicates into two cells. Now the two cells divide and replicate. And this goes on and on. The problem was our little nanobots weren't replicating the way we wanted them to."

Lisa sat there, listening intently, waiting for Stanley, waiting for him to finish the story. Stanley looked like he was finished explaining. Lisa, a little perturbed said, "Ok, I can see this, but what I really want to know is how is it you can walk now?"

"Lisa, this is the funny part. About a year ago when you came here last, Ingrid was in the lab and she was trying to inject an animal to try out the latest revision of the mini 3D printer. This serum also contained the latest revision of the *stem* cells we had created in our lab. I went into the lab and Ingrid was about to inject one of the small animals we use for this research. I came up behind Ingrid and surprised her. I surprised her so much, she fell into my lap and ended up injecting me with the serum."

"Come on, really?"

"I know, I know. It sounds crazy but this is the way it happened. Neither Ingrid nor I were concerned about getting injected with this. The injected solution would run its course and eventually leave my body naturally. At the time, our theory was that the little nano-bots would go to an area which needed to be fixed and then be flushed out normally. On the day this happened and also for the next two weeks, nothing happened. We had almost forgotten about this. After two weeks, we did see a change happen. My legs were moving around when I was sleeping. Poor Ingrid got kicked one night and woke up. She thought she was imagining things."

Ingrid smiled at Lisa, "I thought I was going crazy or I was just dreaming. The next night nothing happened. The night after that, Stanley's legs were moving around under the covers again. It seemed to be something like restless leg syndrome. This cannot happen if you have a spinal cord damage in the way Stanley has. I took a sample of Stanley's blood and ran some tests on it."

"Did you have to take blood from his lower back or just take blood from his arm?"

"I did both. The results of those test showed Stanley's blood full of millions and millions of nanobot 3D printers who were making millions and millions of *stem* cells. Over the next month, we watched it slowly increase in the number of cells. About a month after he received the injection of this serum of nanobots, more changes started to happen."

"Lisa, do you remember when we were kids, I asked you to help me with tying my shoes. You always tied them too loose. You said it would be hurtful if you tied them too tight. To a normal person they feel their shoelaces being tied too tight. For me, I couldn't tell whether they were tied too loose or too tight. Now, I can *feel* it if they are too tight. The changes for me came in incremental pieces. Feeling pain in my feet was the first thing. Then it was feelings in my calf's and then my thighs. What you saw last night was new for me. I have only been able to stand or walk on my own for short periods in the last month. I can't do this full time but getting out of bed to come into the kitchen is now possible for me without overexerting my muscles. I still need the chair because my leg muscles are still not strong enough. I also don't want to attract any attention."

Lisa asked playfully, "So, big brother are you going to be wheelchair free now?"

Her brother smiled and nodded his head.

She didn't understand why, but she started to be overcome by a wave emotion, and she started to cry. A happy cry. A joyful cry. Lisa stood up and gave Stanley the biggest and tightest hug she could. She whispered through her tears, "I'm so happy for you. I love you so much and I'm just so happy for this."

Lisa went over to Ingrid and hugged her as tight as she could and said, "Thank you. Thank you so much."

Teary eyed, Ingrid said she was also so happy. Ingrid interjected playfully, "You realize, the next thing he will want is a candy apple red corvette now he can walk. He won't need me anymore."

Stanley smiled, "I will always need you"

After finishing breakfast, Lisa decided to not go back to Boston as planned but stay with Stanley and Ingrid for a couple of days. They were both thrilled by this.

For the rest of the day, Lisa hung out with them. Several times through the day Lisa asked Stanley to demonstrate that he could walk. For Lisa it was just too surreal to see this. Lisa couldn't help but smile as she watched him. She knew she was being a pest, so she stopped asking. It still made her smile though.

That night, she went to sleep, and she felt a bit of emotional relief knowing that her brother could really walk again. However, she has been on the hunt for the person who caused the car crash so many years ago. Every day, she still missed her father, her mother and sister Maureen. Nothing could replace that ache in her heart. A hurt like this is with you always and really never goes away. Over time it will morph slightly and eventually you just have to accept it. Acceptance doesn't mean forget. It means an acknowledgement of the facts and truth. It also means an acknowledgement of the power it could have if she chose to let it.

The last thing she thought about before falling to sleep was her search for Håvard Evans, or his online name, **6Ix6S!x**.

Chapter 12 – DefCon 2020

Black Holes are where God divided
by zero

- Albert Einstein

Sunday morning the silence was broken by the sound of the Boston Globe newspaper being placed inbetween the front door and the screen door. Stanley and Ingrid had a routine they followed. They both woke up early, briefly showered, and were out the door to go to a local church they liked. It was close to the house and Ingrid and Stanley had made a lot of friends over the years who also attended this church service. The priest was young and very charismatic. His message each Sunday was uplifting and relevant for the time.

Lisa was just waking up when they returned. They didn't have any plans set out for the day. At some point later today, she was going to get on a train and head up to her hotel in Boston. This coming week was a conference she had gone to last year, in Las Vegas. She was happy this year they decided to host it in Boston. As she thought about this, she realized she hasn't told Stanley why she is going to these conferences.

Both Stanley and Ingrid were looking at the Boston Globe, sharing different sections. Lisa sat on the couch with her laptop.

"Hey, Stanley I'm not sure if I ever told you the reasons why I go to these conferences. Of course, there is the obvious reason I go which is to learn about some of the new technology out there and also some networking with different vendors and technology leaders. There is an additional reason why I go to these conferences."

Stanley just smiled and kept reading his section of the paper, not really listening that intently.

"Ok, this is important. It has taken several years to uncover this information, but I am trying to track down a person who might be attending the conference this year. Last year, I went to the one in Las Vegas. I didn't find anything useful though. I am hopeful he might turn up at this year at the '*DefCon*' conference I'm going to."

Lisa was cut short as Stanley jumped in, "Is this your new boyfriend? Did you fall in love with him in a chat room? It's ok, I get it. I just wish you could have told us, and we could have gone up and met him. Are you going to get married or wait – are you pregnant?"

Lisa looked at Ingrid for some help to make Stanley stop talking. She just shrugged her shoulders, as if to say, "once he gets started you can't turn him off."

"Stanley, come on, I am serious here. Please."

Stanley saw from her face his needling wasn't being taken the way he intended. He smiled and mimed zipping his lip and turning an imaginary key.

"Thank you. This is serious. The person I am looking for is very personal for both you and me. The day so long ago, which changed both of our lives irrevocably, was caused by one man who was driving a car and jumped out in front of our car. He is the reason we got into the car accident. This person also took away Dad, Mom, and Maureen. I never told you this because I thought I would be adding more things for you to worry about. I know who the person was who drove the car on that day."

The smile long gone from Stanley's face was now blank and he was speechless. "Wait, uh wait a minute, you're talking about the red car exiting the 7-Eleven that forced our car into the telephone pole? How? This was over twenty years ago, how is it possible you can know it was him on that day and at that time?"

"I am very good at this! I found out the name of the owner of the 7-Eleven. Luckily, the woman I spoke with was very helpful. She remembers the day clearly. They had to shut down the station for a couple hours while the EMT's and police arrived on the scene. She told me the name of the person who was working at the time. I spoke with the woman who worked on that particular day. She remembered the day and told me there were two customers outside pumping gas. One guy came in and gave her his credit card and he wanted the restroom key. When he came back with the key, he looked different. A lot heavier and bigger than she first thought."

"Do you think he was wearing or putting on a disguise?"

"Yes, he was. He told this cashier, the other guy outside pumping gas liked her. He wanted her to tell him his card was declined, and he needed to come in. She announced it over the speakers outside, and apparently, they got into an argument and were yelling at each other. She then remembered the car not stopping to exit the 7-Eleven, and just floored it to exit into traffic. This is what caused our car to crash into the telephone pole. After I got this information, I couldn't find out anything else. I thought I had run into a dead end."

"It doesn't sound," Ingrid affirmed, since Stanley was still speechless, "like this was the end of it for you, was it?"

"Yes, you're correct, grasshopper."

Lisa continued, "It gets even better. I thought what if he was at the gas station to top off his rental car before he dropped it off at Logan. I hit paydirt here. I had to use some *unconventional* ways to get the information from the rental car company. Are you ready for this? The name of the person is Håvard Evans and he lives in Iceland. Well, at least he was living in Iceland at this time."

"Hoovered?" Stanley asked.

"Sounds like Harvard, as in Harvard University, but the 'a' is a long aahh. Like Haahhverd," Lisa said.

"Wow, I can't believe you were able to get this information out from so long ago. When did you start doing this?"

"I don't know exactly when it happened, but I made a decision, I didn't have to die drunk and I had a choice about it. The car accident changed everything for the both of us. Something happened to you a little while after the accident. You were really tortured by not being able to use your legs. Something happened and you changed. I remember it because I knew something was different for you. I kept waiting for the same thing to happen to me. It never did. I just kept getting farther and farther away from you and everyone else."

"It was my high school teacher, Mr. Davidson, who made a difference for me. Lisa you have changed so much since then. You're a hundred times so much better and wiser of a person than I could ever attempt to be."

"Well, thanks big brother, love ya too. So, I think this guy might be here this week. This is the closest I have ever gotten to him. I'm not sure exactly what I will do once I find him. I can't call the cops or anything. I honestly, want to just get him face to face and tell him exactly what he did and how much he affected us so many years ago. I haven't really thought any more than that."

Lisa understood exactly what Stanley was going to say to her, so she beat him to it, "I know I need to be careful with this guy and I know how he will react if I do something or I cause a huge scene and the police get involved. Don't worry. I have thought about this long and hard. I'm not going to go berserk on him. He isn't worth it. I think I've been working on this for so long, I think I just need to meet him face to face and tell him what he did to both of us. After I do this, I think I can officially end this chapter and move on."

Stanley understood and knew she was the director, and this was her show. He also knew from past experience to get out of the way and let her run this. Just to re-enforce his support he added, "I understand this. If you want me to do anything just let me know."

Off to Stanley's side, Ingrid explain, "Oh boy. Lisa do you know what this guy, *Haaverd*, looks like? I am reading an article in the Globe about a guy from Iceland who is going to be traveling to Boston this week, to present a talk about a new medical miracle. It says he is going to be at one of the convention center's in Boston. What place is your *DefCon* conference being held at?"

"The Hynes Convention Center. It's a huge facility and sometimes they host a couple of conferences at the same time."

"They don't have a picture of him in the article, but the way they are propping his image up is, it sounds like this person is going to unveil a huge breakthrough in medicine," Ingrid finished.

This got Stanley's attention, and he said to Ingrid, "This is new to me, have you heard anything about this, honey?"

"No. Nothing, but this isn't unusual. You would probably hear it sooner than I would."

Lisa was trying to readjust her picture of the person she knew as Håvard Evans. Some of the scraps of information she had about Håvard, she knew some people might say he was a hacktivist and his medical breakthrough was his benign way to shake up the machinery of healthcare. Lisa couldn't classify Håvard as a person who was benign or trivial. Håvard was a cyberterrorist and he didn't think twice about loss of life. Håvard was cold, calculating, and from what she knew of him from her research, he never forgot the slightest offense or insult to him.

After the Ashley Madison hack, she tried to find some of the other hackers who were part of it. Over the years, she was only able to find one other person on the *impact team,* as they were called back then. With little to go on, she was only able to find 3 references to another hacker called *Z3bra-m9er*. A corny username meant to be a clever way of saying *zebra-miner*.

Lisa changed the subject and asked both of them, "It's about noon, how about I take you guys out for lunch and then I can catch a train back to Boston, yeah?"

They both nodded affirmative. Lisa got up, dropped her coffee cup in the sink and went in the bathroom to clean up and pack-up her things. For the next couple of hours, they had a nice lunch at one of their favorite seafood places which was only known by the locals. This is the way the restaurant wanted it.

Over lunch they laughed and got caught up on all the news of their lives. It was so nice to be around people you knew you so well, it just became effortless to have nice conversations, a little joking or ribbing, and all in a good-natured way. Lisa has always admired Ingrid. She has been a very positive force in Stanley's life. She knew about Lisa's rough past and has never showed her anything but kindness and honesty. If you have gone through the hell like the one, she went through, then having this subtle affordance is a big deal and much more comfortable to be around.

Monday Morning – Sheraton Boston Hotel

Hynes Convention Center

DefCon 2020 Conference

Lisa woke up early the next morning. She was staying in the Sheraton Boston Hotel which was right across from the Hynes Convention Center. Last night she checked into the hotel but also checked in for the conference. They gave her a green and blue card with her name (or user pseudonym – if she wanted to) on the front of the badge. It also contained a little pocket in the badge itself which contained a small map of the convention center.

She walked over to a small breakfast area to get some coffee and a large granola and strawberry yogurt concoction that she took out from a small freezer. There was a small area with some comfortable couches and chairs. She had an idea of what sessions she thought she wanted to attend.

There was no mention of anything about medical devices, new research, or medical protocols being used. She thought this might pop up here in this conference after what she learned from Ingrid and Stanley. This didn't seem to be the case.

This conference served a couple of different areas. The training part of this conference started about 2 days ago on Saturday. These training sessions were very intense and crammed a lot of information in a very short time. After those training sessions were completed, the next couple of days of the conference offered a number of sessions on topics of all sorts involving computers. It's just a place for similar like people to gather amongst other hackers, either underground hacking or above ground hacking, security vendors, and some 3 letter organizations.

There was time for people to stroll through the enormous showroom to meet and greet several vendors, or thought leaders, in attendance. It was also a way to grab a lot of tchotchke's like little wireless mouse or what have you.

For Lisa, this conference served two purposes. Her main goal was hopefully finding Håvard. She couldn't explain why, but this time she had a feeling she might get lucky and find him. The second reason why she was here, was to network and maybe find a new client who she could work with.

The next talk she thought would be interesting was a discussion of safety protocol for IoT devices. This starts in an hour, so Lisa had some time to check email or work on the program she had been working on for the last month. It was a simple program, but it could be a life saver for someone having their network hacked.

It was getting close to the time of the first session she was thinking of attending. Lisa picked up her backpack, her coffee, and headed over to the room conducting the session. She kept her eyes open for anyone she knew in her area of security, or even some hackers she might have worked with in the past. Some of them were people she worked with and some were people she was working against.

She hoped going to this conference wasn't a waste of time. Strangely, for the first time, she thought what will I do after I find him? Is she *Ahab* and Håvard is *Moby Dick*?

Chapter 13 - Renegade Six

"I wonder if other dogs think poodles are members of a weird religious cult."

- Rita Rudner

While Lisa was attending one of the talks about the new layers of security for Internet of Things devices, Håvard was conducting his own little meeting. Håvard arrived last night to the Sheraton Boston hotel. Additionally, six other people checked into the hotel also. This group of six expected to meet Håvard in one of the session rooms he rented for the purpose of this meeting.

He told the event planners, he wanted to rent one of the session rooms for an invite only session. He also provided them with the networking and presentation materials he would be needing. For Håvard this was a subtext he needed. The invite-only part was important to coordinate the execution of the master plan he was proposing. Everyone he dealt with was very helpful and tried their very best to make his event experience excellent.

Håvard didn't think along the line of the in-betweens. If something was sort of good, not too bad, or it was an excellent job. His thought pattern was just the opposite. His view of people was through a binary lens. People did what they were supposed to do, or they didn't. To most people, he would be considered as cold and calculating. This was also very true.

The other six people involved in this caper, thought in a similar way Håvard thought. This wasn't a playground, not an exercise. It was necessary to work together and if it was accomplished, the payoff would be great.

Each person in this group, all had their own moniker, for the purpose of this job, Håvard assigned each one a name. There were 4 men and 2 women. The first hacker had obsidian black hair with a perfect goatee with a razor-

sharp groom of a 'V' to shape his face. He was
assigned the name of *Hydro*. He was also from
Iceland, he was the inside man for a critical part
of this operation. He worked at one of the main
factories for bottled water called Gullfoss.
Håvard and Hydro had some inner whispered
mumblings in Icelandic. The next guy was a
slightly hefty guy, with blonde dyed hair. He
was given the moniker of *Homer*. His real first
name was Bartholomew. His job was to take
care of the logistics of interfacing with the
Hynes Convention Center.

The next person was in their mid-forties
with brown hair. The only thing which was kind
of out of place was he wore a denim leather
motorcycle jacket. This is the type of jacket you
would see from a heavy biker getting off their
Harley-Davidson motorcycle. He was given the
name of *Batman*. There was no reason for his
name except that he requested to be called by
this. His responsibility was to work with
another person in the group, Homer, on the
logistics of the loading docks.

The next three members of this group were also given a unique name or nickname. A woman with totally dyed grey hair and bright blue tips was in her fifties to early sixties. She was given the name of *Bleu*. Her part in this caper was to work with Hydro on the water bottle dispersal inside all the common areas. She was also from Iceland and spoke in Icelandic sometimes directly to Håvard.

A kid in her early twenties, with a losing battle of acne, was given the name, *Edie*. She was responsible for controlling the power grid of the Convention Building. This was critically important for any of the alarms or doors she could control with the flick of a switch. Håvard only called her Edie in front of other people. If they were alone, he called her by her given name of Ruth.

Finally, a hacker who was very polite and tried to not ruffle any feathers was a late twenties man now called, *Carbon*. Håvard didn't change his user id, he still went by his handle **Six6S! x.**

The plan Håvard envisioned was to spread his nanobots on a regional scale. Boston was the test run for his plan. The planning for this event started a couple of months ago. *Hydro* and *Bleu* both had access to a natural water bottling company in Iceland. *Hydro* and *Bleu* were given a specific recipe of how and what was needed to create specialized nanobots. These nanobots each contained 1000's of nano sized 3D Printer Factories. Each of these factories in turn created millions of 3D printers. Each of these 3D printers could then print thousands of *stem* cells for the body to use. The bottling company was filling each of its water bottles with hundreds of thousands of nanobots which were in a dormant state just waiting for a signal to be activated. These water bottles were sold in America under the name of *GullFoss Natural Water.*

Once those special *stem* cells were created, Håvard would then start the next procedure in the plan. The cell phones he got from **GrillMan299**, would have the modified code he put on them. His code would essentially turn on those 3D printers that lay dormant until it received a signal from one of the phones Håvard supplied. It would also allow someone with those phones to be able to scan a person to see if they had ingested a sufficient amount of nanobots. What those 3D printers would print was only known by himself and each of these six people.

What they didn't know was, Håvard held back a little part of the plan. He gave each one of the six, a secret module they could turn on to make themselves immune to these nanobots. What Håvard didn't mention was he also created an override to the override switch. His phone was the only one which could do this.

For the next six hours they all worked together to execute the plan. Each member was also responsible for an area of penetration.

Hydro and *Bleu* were responsible for the Icelandic water, Gullfoss, which was being exclusively provided by this team.

Homer was responsible for all the HVAC systems and the necessary overrides.

Batman was handling the interface with the Hynes Convention Center and any logistics like the loading docks. He also implanted several hidden bugs in the control center for the building.

Carbon was responsible for killing the cell towers, and also to reject all calls except from the phones or devices entered into the hack to work normally.

At approximately 4 PM, all of them exited the rented space and headed back to their hotel rooms. Everything was set to go off at 1:00 PM tomorrow afternoon.

One person of those six, or as he went by online, was *Z3bra-m9er*, and now was being called *Carbon*, was walking out of the session room, and walking to an escalator to go to the first floor. This escalator took people down to the first floor to exit the building. The Boston Sheraton Hotel was across the street. *Carbon* was walking toward the front part of this long wide hall. He spotted someone he knew from a long time ago.

He spotted Lisa Harris sitting on one of the couches near a coffee stand provided by the event conference. He recognized her, from a long time ago. God, it seems like years ago, but he definitely recognized her. It was extremely important, right now at this moment, to not be recognized. He fell a step back from the group. He was still walking with them to the escalator, but he was about a pace behind. Lisa looked up in his direction. As quickly as he could, he did a quick shake of his head as if to say *no not at this time*. Thankfully, she understood. It was very dangerous for him, and also for her sake, to not be talking in front of Håvard.

10 years ago

Z3bra-m9er, or his real name being Austin Mark Alexander, knew Lisa from his past. Just remembering his past life was jarring. He was sent to the same treatment center Lisa went to. She came in about a day or two before him. Memories of those initial days are bits and pieces strung together by the thinnest of lines.

The memories from ten years ago, were sparse and spotty. Memories which are sketchy like this, increase your anxiety. Always dredging up a question, "Is this real, or did I imagine it." Austin and Lisa had created a bond in those initial *drying out* days. As he thought again about this period, the memories were fleeting and scattered. A couple of things he did remember, was one day, Lisa was angry. Very angry in fact. On the other hand, he was probably as angry as she was.

One morning, they were both in one of the common areas where they were getting coffee and breakfast. Lisa was in line with Austin waiting to get a cup of the decaf swill they called coffee. He thought the line was moving forward and he moved a little forward. Lisa was filling her mug with very hot black coffee. She had just filled her mug and he accidentally bumped into her causing some of the hot coffee to spill over onto her hand.

"OW!!," Lisa exclaimed. Medusa wouldn't have nearly the amount of venom as to how Lisa looked at him right now. "You asshole!"

"Shithead!"

"Jack ass!"

"Jerk."

"Fat ass!"

"Bitch!"

This last insult pushed it too far. Lisa turned to him and threw the entire contents of her hot coffee at him. In return, he was holding a glass of orange juice which he threw at her. She picked up the pitcher of milk on the table and threw it at Austin, snarling, "Would you like a little cream with your coffee!"

From somewhere off to their side, someone with authority shouted very loudly, "**Enough!**"

For Austin, unfortunately, Lisa had grabbed a cream filled doughnut and was in mid throw at Austin's face. The creamy inside of the doughnut exploded on his face and hair.

The woman who shouted for them to stop, quickly walked inbetween them. "Enough you too. Enough! If you want to continue to act like kids, then we've a place for you outside those main doors to this facility. Do you understand?"

Lisa looked like she wanted to throw coffee at this counselor. She glared at Austin. The counselor told them to clean all of this up and to go back to their rooms after this was done. Both Lisa and Austin went over to a closet containing cleaning supplies. He grabbed a mop and she grabbed a bucket for the mop. She went into the kitchen to fill it with hot water and a cleaning solution.

When she came back, she took a bigger view of the mess they made. Lisa looked at him and started laughing uncontrollably. He didn't know what Lisa was laughing about. After about a minute, between uncontrollable waves of laughter, she told Austin he had a big dollop of cream on the top of his nose. He reached up and took it away.

He had to stop and take a look at the incredible mess they had both made. Lisa's clothes were covered in orange juice. His brow was still leaking little bits of milk and coffee. He started to laugh uncontrollably as well.

For the next 20 minutes, they both cleaned up the mess they had made. While they were cleaning, they kept saying little snide comments to each other and every time they did, it started the fit of laughing again.

Lisa probably didn't know it at the time, but he was ready to break out of the treatment facility right after breakfast. The withdrawals were just too much and too severe. He kept lying to himself, saying he could do this on his own.

He didn't leave that morning for just one simple reason. The breakfast was free. His plan was that once he finished breakfast, he would find a way to walk out without causing any drama. Laughing and to laugh uncontrollably, was something he hadn't done in very long time. He credited Lisa for that day. He went back to his room, showered, and put on a fresh set of clothes. He remembered saying to himself, let's leave after lunch. Lunch came and went, and dinner came and went. He never did leave the facility earlier than he was scheduled to leave.

During this time, he struck up a friendship with Lisa. He was about 8 years older than Lisa, and it was strictly a friendship. Neither of them wanted any type of relationship entanglement.

In the first couple of years, they kept in touch pretty regularly. In many ways this was the helpful support they both needed at the time. Going to a place where Austin and Lisa went to, was a start of a process many people hope to have.

At some point, Austin came to a profound realization. He learned that just completing a stay at a facility like the one he and Lisa went to, doesn't necessarily mean everything in life is great now, and it's all fixed. It's a long line of very difficult knots to untangle and set right.

At the time he went to this treatment facility, he was working as a software programmer for a company which worked closely with the NSA. The clearance he held was in danger of being withdrawn because of all of his antics of drinking and being high. Fortunately for him, he had a manager who knew a lot about serious drinking and drugging problems. She gave him an ultimatum to go away and sort it out or don't come back. Austin felt very fortunate. Many people don't succeed. The reward of all of this effort was to be able to live a life which wasn't a perpetual endless cycle of trying to kill himself. It also allowed him to reach for happiness and contentment. To someone with an addiction problem, those were meaningless and foreign words.

Undercover

Right now, in this group of hackers, he was posing as one of the six elite hackers ready to implement Håvard's plan. As Austin was turning the corner he looked back at Lisa and she had a notebook opened with the letters, B.S.H. and the number 8. She had this in large letters and the notebook was tucked under her arm but viewable from where Austin was. He turned back and Håvard was looking at him turning his head back to the front. Håvard's face looked like he was waiting for an answer from Austin. He just shrugged and said, "I'm just enjoying all of the scenery here at this conference. What?"

Håvard stressed, "OK, '*Z3bra-m9er*' this is no time to mess around. We all need to execute this **flawlessly**."

"Sure, no problem. Don't worry I'm focused on the task. Sorry, I thought she was hot," he quickly recovered.

Håvard addressing him by his online name, was unusual. Saying this here, which is a public place, is usually not done by hackers. In a closed space or online, it was acceptable to do. His alias took several years to build, so it was something he didn't wanted to be carelessly *outed*.

Once they reached the lobby of the Hynes Convention Center, Håvard went outside to catch a cab to take him to his hotel away from the center. No one in the group actually knew which hotel it was. Håvard booked all the hotel rooms for each person on the team. Austin was surprised but he went with it. He waited about 10 minutes and he saw Lisa walk into the lobby of the hotel and head over to the elevators. She still had her notebook under her arm with a page of the notebook visible. This time in big letters she had written 811. Austin was hoping she would keep up the ruse. She disappeared into the elevator to take her to the 8th floor.

He had no idea what spies Håvard might have in the lobby waiting for something exactly like this. He waited about 5 minutes, and he made his way to the bank of elevators.

Three minutes later he was knocking on the door of room 811.

"Who's there?"

"Fat-ass," he responded. This was the last insult she used on him during the coffee and orange juice fight they had.

Lisa opened the door with a big smile. She ushered him in and gave him a big hug.

"It's been a while since we last talked. How are things going? Still keeping yourself clean and sober?"

It was nice to see someone who knew where he had bottomed out. "yes, still trying to not kill myself with drugs or booze. Yourself?"

"Life is going good right now. Keeping busy helping companies reinforce their IT security. It never gets dull. Still going to meetings too. Ten years last month."

"That's fantastic. Great job! Thanks for understanding the signal downstairs. I didn't want to complicate things with this new boss I have."

"Sure, no sweat. How long are going to be here," she asked him?

He still needed to be vague with her. It wasn't so much as he didn't trust her, it was actually the reverse. He said, "I think I'm going to be here for most of the conference. We should go out for dinner some night, if you have time?"

"I'm having dinner with my brother and sister-in-law, or soon to be sister-in-law tomorrow night but how about Wednesday?"

He was hoping all of this stuff with Håvard would be done by tomorrow night, so this would work for him.

"Sure, sounds perfect," he grinned at her.

They continued talking for the next couple of hours, falling right back in the routine of conversation they shared when they were struggling in those first days and the withdrawals.

Lisa told him about her last client was the town of Portsmouth, NH. She described how the town was trying to establish themselves as being very forward linking and converted most of the US dollars into crypto currencies for most intra-town transactions. At first, people fought against it, but the town was also mining for bitcoins. They created a town wide fund which each resident was able to get a piece of."

"Yes, I think I did hear about Portsmouth being crypto friendly."

Lisa continued, "It started to go very smoothly until someone started stealing the crypto currency which was being mined. It all came down to the town treasurer. It turned out to not be the treasurer, of course that would be too easy. He did have an eleven-year-old boy though. This little boy found a way into the account of mined crypto, and he purchased a massive expensive tv, and a fully loaded XBOX. It was the trash man who figured it out. They weren't recycling all the cardboard boxes. When the town investigated, his son admitted what he had done. I laughed for two days straight after I finished the job for the town."

After they chatted for a little bit, he excused himself saying he still had some work to do tonight. He promised to have more time on Wednesday for dinner. They hugged again and Austin went out to the elevators and took it back to his room, several floors above.

He worked in his room for the next several hours fulfilling his part of the plan. Håvard wanted the three cell towers in the vicinity of the Hynes Convention center to shut down and block all cellular and data traffic from every device in the vicinity at 1:00 P.M. The hack was also supposed to block all devices except the devices Håvard carried and also the devices for his phone and the other five team members. Austin also added an additional 8 devices. It was important for those devices to not be blocked and be able to use the cell towers.

It had been a long day, so he turned in about eleven. Tomorrow was going to be a tense day with all the machinations needing to be executed smoothly.

Chapter 14 - Tootsie Pop

To attempt to advise conceited
people is like whistling against the
wind.

- Thomas Hood

The next day 10:00 AM

Austin met Håvard and the rest of the team
in the main lobby of the Convention center.
Today was supposed to be the biggest day of the
conference. Many speakers were lined up to
present different technical sessions all
throughout the day. At noon time, the enormous
showroom floor was opening up for all the
vendors who were planning to have a booth area
for their respective products. To say there was
going to be little traffic was a gross
understatement.

This was the sole reason Håvard had picked
this time and place to test out his plan. Over the
past two days, an army of people went into

many different little supply closets scattered around the 176K square feet and stocked and filled each of those supply rooms with case upon case of bottled water. These cases of bottled water were all previously sealed and contained a special water originating from a company called, Gullfoss. Gullfoss, or Golden Falls, is one of the more iconic waterfalls in the southwest part of Iceland.

Gullfoss had an exclusive contract with the Hynes Convention center to be the only supplier of water bottles for this event. Gullfoss also provided about 250 water stands, which could be filled with ice and a never-ending supply of Gullfoss water bottles scattered around the convention center.

When Austin heard of the extent of Håvard's plans, this didn't sound like a test run, but a full-on attack of a city with the most collateral damage possible. The good news was all of the nanobots wouldn't activate, until it received a special signal. If no signal was sent, the nanobots would leave the body in a day or two naturally. Austin knew Håvard was motivated more by money than killing. He wouldn't put it past Håvard to throw a wild card into the mix. Still, from what Austin had seen and known about him, money was a bigger motivator for Håvard than anything else.

The plan for today was to let people in the convention center come in and enjoy the sessions and walk around the showroom and mingle with all the companies and vendors in over 500 or so different booths. All of these booths were setup in several rows across the showroom. At every 3rd booth, a water stand was setup for people to grab a bottle of water if they were thirsty.

At 1:00 PM, the fireworks were going to start to go off. Most conferences like this one, contained long wide hallways which gave people access to the many sessions going on in rooms on both sides of the hallway. Similar to walking into a movie theater and accessing the room playing the movie you wanted to see.

One of the rooms at the end of the hallway was marked as RM 113. This room was the session room which Håvard had rented for his invite only session. The room was a medium sized room probably half the size of a room in a movie theatre. At the far side of the session room, there was another door. This wasn't marked to tell where it went to.

This door did open up to another room, which was probably half the size of the session room. Also, at the opposite side of the room was a door which opened to the showroom floor. This door was marked on the inside and outside with a sign saying RM 213.

In the room marked as RM 113, Håvard had approximately 50 chairs setup all facing three cameras on tripods. In addition, two large spotlights with light diffusing boards to soften the sharp light of the spotlights for the cameras.

Next to Austin, Håvard was looking at his cell phone for the time to click over to 1:00 PM

Håvard said to him, "Ok let's get the show started. Try and use your cell to make a call."

Austin knew the shutdown of the cell towers was on a timer. At 1:00 PM, they would all flip to reject any device trying to establish a cellular link to the three different towers. There were 15 devices that wouldn't be rejected and seven of those devices Håvard gave to each person on the team. Austin added an additional 8 devices he entered in last night which Håvard didn't know about. Austin, nonetheless, took out the cell phone out of his backpack and tried to place a call to a couple of locations. He tried calling the Boston Sheraton Hotel which was right across the street. He then tried to call an address far away. By doing this he was making sure the cell towers wouldn't connect his device. None of them worked and he got the same result of No Service.

He looked at Håvard and said, "the cell towers are down."

Håvard took his cell phone out and sent a text message to Austin on the phone Håvard modified. He received the text message as he normally should.

"Great. Let's get ready to receive some guests," and pressed send to another text message to the other five on the team.

Vaguely, in the distance he heard some people murmuring their frustration with the cell service. Håvard looked at Austin and smiled. Then he did the unexpected.

"You stay here, I need to go out for 2 minutes. Stay here and make our guests happy. I will be back soon," Håvard said absently leaving Austin stunned. Something is up, he thought to himself.

The door opened in the session room, Hydro and Homer were gently guiding two people into RM 113 and seated them in the back row of chairs. The people looked flush and pale. A piece of tape was put over their mouth and their hands were put behind them interlaced with plastic zip ties. The way their hands were affixed to the chair it would be almost impossible to stand up.

For the next thirty-five minutes, each person on the team brought with them one or two people who looked like they were very sick. Each time a person sat down their hands were affixed to the chair.

When all was said and done, everyone sitting seemed to be very relaxed and comfortable. The last guy who came in through the door to the showroom was Batman. He wasn't escorting anyone, and Austin didn't see it until too late. He walked directly to Austin and before he knew what was being done, the guy stuck a needle into his neck. The pain from the needle in his neck felt a little surreal.

It felt like he was watching things in slow motion. He knew it was the same thing everyone else in the room was given. It was a strong narcotic. In some small way he felt sorry for himself. He was probably one of the few people in the room who was familiar with this drug and could appreciate it. Austin had used it daily in his younger days. He might have a stronger tolerance than the others. Damn, who was he kidding, he thought. The cursing in his head got stronger and stronger as he started to succumb to the effects of the drug. He was also pissed off. He just lost a very long stretch of years getting away from this stuff. There was movement off to his right.

Hydro, the tall Icelandic, came in from the main corridor of session rooms, and brought a girl with blondish hair. She looked like his friend Lisa. He thought am I dreaming? He looked at her and could see the surprise on her face when she saw him. He smiled a goofy smile and regretted doing so. It was the drug acting on him. She was tied to a chair right next to him, in the front part of the room.

Meanwhile, outside of these enclosures people were oblivious to what was happening in these two rooms. You could hear people talking and normally walking though the showroom to visit different vendor booths. On the other side of the session room where all the people were ushered into, people could be heard outside just normally talking and walking to different sessions being conducted.

Many people tried to use their cell phones but all of them couldn't get any reception or signal from where they were located. Many people, just shrugged, thinking it was because they were in the large showroom or the convention center would have bad reception. Maybe reception would be better outside. Some people walked to the front of the Convention Center to try to get a better signal. No one understood or knew a way to fix this. These problems were minor compared to what was being done inside the enclosed room of 52 people.

Austin looked at Håvard and the rest of the crew he had worked closely with over the past few days. He just couldn't comprehend what was happening exactly. It felt as if he was on a time loop which was delayed by a minute. His brain was shouting inside to think and figure this out.

Håvard came over to Austin. "CutiePies, I'm disappointed in you. I thought you were a part of our team. I wouldn't have known it if you hadn't gone to the 8th floor to visit your friend here. Or at least be smart enough to leave the phone I gave you in your room on the 12th floor".

Håvard looked at Lisa, "Miss Harris, I really am disappointed in you as well. Don't you think I didn't know who you were? You have blocked several of my attempts to gain access to companies who were so rich it was really a shame watching them spent their money on such foolish things. Your skills are very good, but mine are better. Eventually, I was able to gain access, but then again, you blocked access from inside. Let's just say I did gain access and took millions from those foolish companies."

Austin looked at Håvard. It was very difficult for Austin to concentrate, but he was able to say, even though it was somewhat slurred and drug-affected, "Sixes, what are you playing at here. Why did you bring all of the other people in here, if your problem is with me? Let the others stay out of this."

Håvard turned sharply on Austin and bent down to be inches from his face and spat, "You still don't get it do you. Look at all of these people. What do you see in common with this group? I'm only going to give you 3 guesses and then one of my friends will break your finger. Every guess will cause a finger to be broken. I do hope you're a good guesser."

Austin turned and looked at all of the people tied in place to their chairs. It looked to be about an equal number of men and women. He quickly counted. It was 26 men and 24 women. Is this the answer, did one of the henchmen make a mistake? He decided to go with it and said, "There are equal amount of men and women."

"Hmmm aahh, NO!" Try again."

Think Austin, think. He kept saying in his head, which wasn't helping in the least. Everyone looks older than he is. Yeah maybe this is the answer. He said to Håvard, "They are all older than 35?"

"Come on Zebra. Really? That is your guess? No! One more guess."

Lisa started to come around, saw what Håvard was doing. She asked, "Can I take a guess?"

Håvard's glaring grey eyes rounded on her. "If you think you know the answer go for it, but if you're wrong, we are still going to break one of his fingers and also as a bonus to you, Pickles, one of your fingers will be broken. Are you still in?"

Pickles was her online moniker. She was surprised Håvard would know this. She looked at Austin, he shook his head no. Lisa was undecided what she wanted to do. If she was wrong, her finger and Austin's finger would be broken. She didn't care so much about her finger, well actually she did, but she also didn't want to be the person who guessed incorrectly and would cause her friend unthinkable amounts of pain.

Before she could finish those thoughts, Austin said, "Sixes, I hope you have a nice place in Iceland to hide, because I will hunt you down for as long as it takes. My guess is they are all part of one of your companies you have hacked into."

Håvard paused for a second or two and thought about it. Austin was partly right, but it wasn't 100% correct. He looked at Austin with the puppy like eyes, and said, "OK, you guessed incorrectly, but it was still a good guess, but I'm sorry it's wrong. By the way what hand to you write with?"

Austin thought quickly and told him he used his left hand to write with. Håvard motioned to one for the other Icelandic guys, Hydro, and he came over to the camera. He took it off of the tripod it was on and he came closer to Austin. Hydro was going to film Austin's finger being broken.

Håvard looked at Batman, the biker guy, who came over to Austin and half smiled and half grimaced.

Håvard said to Batman, "Use his right hand. I'm sure he just lied to us. Most people wouldn't want their writing hand compromised so break his right hand."

From his side, Batman, brought up a decently sized hammer and crashed it on Austin's right hand. The hammer smashed his ring finger which was being held in place.

The piercing cry of Austin was muffled by a handkerchief stuffed into his mouth just before the hammer came down on one of the fingers on his right hand. His finger started bleeding immediately and looked horrible. It was in an unnatural position.

Lisa was beside herself with fear as she saw the guy who was called Batman, bring the hammer down on Austin's finger. She knew Austin was lefthanded. The only reason she knew this was because, she was also lefthanded.

Håvard looked at the both of them in the chair. He said, "Ok I think now would be a good time to take a little bit of a break."

"Please take CutiePies and Pickles to the other room while we film the next part."

He motioned for the other two people who haven't been part of this yet, Bleu and Homer, to bring Austin and Lisa, into the other room, RM 113, which was empty.

Both Austin and Lisa were roughly grabbed by Bleu and Homer. For looking older than she probably was, Bleu was very strong. They cut the zip tie holding them to the chairs. The both of them were then, half dragged, half stumbled to the other room which was empty. Austin and Lisa were each given a new booster shot of the tranquilizer. Everything went fuzzy and they both passed out in a heap in the corner of the room.

In some respect, both Lisa and Austin, had a unique advantage here. They both held a high tolerance for drugs or alcohol. Make no mistake, they are both very high and loopy, but this is child's play for these two experts.

Lisa was probably the first one to start to rouse a little. She was trying to focus on what the situation was. She saw Austin, next to her on the ground. She used her foot to lightly kick Austin's leg. He wasn't coming around. On her second kick he started to come to. He was confused at first, but like Lisa, he was trying to take in the whole picture.

He looked at Lisa and she half smiled. He remembered her face from way back in time. This was the same face he had seen when they were both in line for coffee and were throwing coffee and orange juice at each other. Austin didn't miss this face, but the one thing he remembered about this look she had. This was her game face. She was ready to fight, kick, scratch, or slug anyone in her way.

Good, Austin felt in a similar mood. He looked around and saw none of Håvard's group of hackers watching them. He heard voices coming from the other room. It sounded like loud crying.

Lisa looked around the room also and she paused for a second as if in thought. Spontaneously, she rolled toward her left side, so she was face to face to Austin. She whispered to Austin to reach into her right pocket and grab a whistle she had in her pocket.

This was a very strange thing to ask him. A whistle isn't going to be very helpful. But he figured she probably had a good reason for doing this.

He said, "So is this how kids are getting friendly with each other now?"

"Stop it. Behave. There is a whistle in my pocket, and it's important," she scolded him.

He reached into her pocket and grabbed the whistle. Doing this sent his pain synapses on fire. His finger was smashed horribly, the pain emanating from this was nearly overwhelming.

Lisa rolled back over and was able to move in a way he could hand her the dog whistle. She also was flexible enough to just barely bring her knees to chin and be able to move her hands from behind her to being in front of her. Austin saw this and could smile a little through the pain.

He didn't understand what exactly what she was going to do with the whistle. It looked like it was just an ordinary whistle. No, wait. It looked like a dog whistle.

Lisa held up her hand while she blew continuously into the whistle. Obviously, he couldn't hear what the sound was. Perplexed. Why the dog whistle? When her fingers stopped counting to 10, she took the whistle out and took a deep breath. She adjusted the whistle tube slightly. Next, she counted with her fingers to three. She did this same count three different times. Three short toots, then three long toots, and finally three short toots. In Morse code this means S.O.S.

Once she was done, she smiled and said, "I just sent out an SOS to my brother. Hopefully, he will understand what I sent to him."

"How did you do that?"

"One little security tool I have been developing in my spare time is a program I wrote which can be attached to a drone. The dog whistle can remotely start the drone and it will respond to certain signals I can send with the whistle. It doesn't matter if we are in this area. It won't need Wi-Fi or cell service. The ultrasonic sound can go through the building and find my antenna on the drone. It will take off and fly to the nearest cellular tower with a signal it can establish a connection with. My brother is in my emergency contacts. Hopefully, he will receive the SOS and the GPS location of where we are. I hope he will call the appropriate authorities to help us and the rest of the people in the next room."

"That is incredible. You are really fantastic at this cyber security stuff"

"Thanks," and then she enacted a scene like she was going to barf.

She then said, "Hey wait a minute. You called the pale guy with tats 'Sixes.' Is his online name 6Ix6S! x?"

And then she asked quickly, before Austin could speak, "He also called you by the handle, 'zebra miner'. Is your online handle, Z3bra-m9er? You and he were part of the Ashley Maddison hack, weren't you?"

Lisa was absolutely stunned when Austin nodded yes. He could tell this was something personal for her. She tried to get up and move as far away from him as she could.

As she was doing this, Håvard and the guy with the denim-leather biker jacket called Batman, entered the room. Håvard wasn't happy. With the help of Batman, he half carried her into the other room. Before she was carried away, she looked at Håvard and spit in his face. She spit at him a second time before the other guy punched her in the gut.

Austin was left helpless on the ground. He desperately wanted to help his friend. She thought he had betrayed her. The facts are very different, and she didn't know the whole story. He was angry and exasperated with a feeling of futility. Austin had to be able to make this right.

Chapter 15 - King's Ransom

To begin,

Begin.

- William Wordsworth

Ingrid was on a train about 15 minutes south of Boston. She thought she heard her cell phone ring, but it was just the ringtone she had setup in her contacts. It wasn't a call, but it was a text message from Lisa with a number she didn't recognize. Sometimes, Stanley incorrectly configured his cell phone to forward any calls to her phone. Every time he does this, he also mistakenly forwards any text messages to her.

There wasn't any reason to get his text message alerts, but the forwarding of his phone calls was sometimes important. Not often, but occasionally, she would get a call needing Stanley's attention. Ingrid was in the best position to be able to know where Stanley is and would be able to get a hold of him.

The text message read:

Stanley: If you get this, then something is wrong. I would not send this unless it's necessary. Call my cell phone as soon as you get this. Included are the GPS coordinates of where this was sent out.

Ingrid immediately called Lisa's cell phone. It rang for a couple of seconds, and then the automated announcement of *the subscriber isn't available, please try again later*. She called Lisa's phone a second time and still got the same message. Now she was starting to get a little concerned. She called Stanley. She got her own voicemail, forgetting Stanley set his cellphone to forward all calls. She called the landline of his office and of the house. No one answered. She left a detailed message on both his office email and the home voicemail system. Her train was just coming into the South Station terminal in Boston.

She used an app to give her exactly where the GPS coordinates were of the phone, she assumed, sent this. The coordinates pointed to the Hynes Convention Center. GPS is usually pretty accurate and will normally give you an approximation of about 30 or 40 feet. In the city it might be a little more than 30 or 40 feet.

When she got off the train, she went outside and grabbed a taxi to get her to the Hynes Convention Center. It was just about 2:00 PM when she got out of the cab. She tried to follow the GPS directions, but she got no signal anywhere in the lobby of the convention center. The cab driver and also several other people were complaining about no service or no access to the internet. Almost thirty seconds after she entered into the center, she heard an audible click of every door with access to the outside. She recognized this sound. Her lab at work had a lock like this.

Her building had electromagnetic locks. Some electromagnetic locks can be a fail-safe lock, or it can be a fail-secure lock. The Hynes Convention Center most likely contained a *fail-safe* lock since it's open to the public. In the event of a fire or some other emergency, the exit doors would allow people to leave the building.

The sound Ingrid heard was exactly the same sound of an electromagnetic *fail-sure* lock in her lab. In this case, it was locked to prevent unauthorized access. However, if someone is in the lab at work and power is lost, the lock would still hold effectively locking the person in the lab. In this scenario, her lab had an override button inside so someone could free themselves if they needed to.

All at once, the noise died down and everyone stopped speaking. Every person changed at the same time. Off to the side, she heard one person say very loudly, "What the …" The last word was left hanging. A look of peace and calm appeared on his face. In fact, everyone's face took on this look. Cold shivers went up the back of Ingrid's neck. Something was wrong but she couldn't understand why or what. This is like a scene from one of those classic movies, like *Invasion of the Body Snatchers* or *The Host*.

She was the only person in her vicinity who wasn't sharing this look of peace and calm. Not knowing what to do, she took on a face of calm and peace. She wasn't feeling peaceful and calm. Not at all.

Over a loudspeaker, a woman spoke and told everyone to go to the huge showroom on the second floor. She decided she would go upstairs to the showroom. Maybe she could find out more information about what is going on here.

Everyone moved to the escalator to go to the second floor. Everyone was heading to a set of 4 wide doors to enter the huge showroom. Three people were standing by the doors. They were giving everyone a bottle of water. Also, next to the doors were the water stands filled with ice and bottles of water. It was apparent to Ingrid, whoever was doing this wanted everyone to have a bottle of water in their hands. Everyone was being directed to the back part of the showroom floor.

Ingrid took the bottle of water, but in every direction, she looked there was a sign with the logo of GullFoss Icelandic water. Ingrid took the bottle of water she was given, but she was smart enough to know something was in the water to make them act like this.

Ingrid tried to remain calm and wear the face everyone else was wearing. She caught sight of a man about twenty feet to the left of her, who was doing his best to exude calm and peace. He wasn't doing a good job. He made a quick decision sensing there was something wrong here. He abruptly turned around and started to walk against the flow of people streaming into the showroom.

It took only a few seconds, but a new person was walking toward the man. When the other guy reached him, he grabbed his arm and dragged him off to the side. What am I doing here, Ingrid thought? Now it seemed like she was trapped.

The forward movement of the mass of people she was walking with stopped. Two men, one with a black biker jacket, started to walk among the group of people in a zigzag like pattern. The other man was doing a similar thing in a different part of the crowd. Both of these men were holding a cell phone out in front of them.

What Ingrid now saw was just surreal. Ingrid watched this trying to keep her face neutral. It was like someone tamping down on some grass or weeds. Everywhere they went, all the people around them just sat down. Neither of them said anything. They both walked with a cellphone and held it up about face level. Everywhere they went all the people near them just sat down. One of the guys was coming near to Ingrid. Everyone around her was starting to sit down, she followed suit, so as, not to draw too much attention.

As she was lowering her body down to a sitting position. She got a look at how many people were in the showroom. It looked like it was about 500 people in this area of the showroom. She suspected on the other side of the showroom there was probably another group who were also sitting down.

Ingrid felt trapped. It seemed like a no-win situation. If she gets up, she will get pulled off to some other place. Her instincts told her it wouldn't be a nice place. If she was going to do something, she would have to do this without being seen by those two men who walked through the crowd. She wasn't worried about the people who were in a stupor. They most likely couldn't register anything else except peace and calm.

Ingrid noticed a door in a closed off room. If she was going to do this, then she needed to do this now. She stood up, took her cell phone out and held it in front of her, like the guy she just saw doing this. She didn't run, but she walked very quickly to the door which she hoped would lead out of the showroom.

She arrived at the door, opened it, and stepped inside. She thought she got away without anyone seeing her or stopping her. When she turned around, she saw a young, handsome guy, lying down on the ground. His hands were behind his back held together by a zip tie. He was conscious and saw Ingrid come in. Now she was really confused. Who is this person on the ground? He saw Ingrid and whispered something to her.

She couldn't hear him, so she came closer.

"Hi. Can you help me?" he asked.

Ingrid came closer and saw his face. It matched the situation. He wasn't calm or peaceful but a little pissed off. She could understand the being pissed off part. If she were tied up in this fashion, she wouldn't be happy either.

"What is going on here?"

"There is a guy in the other room who is very dangerous to you and also the people in the room over there," he motioned with his chin to the door on the opposite wall of the room.

Ingrid was still trying to process all of the information being thrown at her. A young guy is in an empty room, tied up. Outside of this room are 500 people acting like sheep. She said, "Well this is the thing. I came into the building and everything appeared normal and then all the doors locked. I don't mean lock with a key I mean lock by an electromagnetic lock."

She paused a second and started to fish in her pocketbook for her keychain. Then she continued, "Someone over the loudspeakers told everyone to go to the showroom floor. Something happened though to everyone. They all stopped talking and became like robots. Their faces totally devoid of any kind of emotion or expression. I just followed them in because my friend sent a text saying she needed help. She also sent coordinates of where she was."

He interrupted her, "Who is your friend? She couldn't have done this anywhere near this building. Unless …"

"She was trying to send it to her brother, but his call forwarding is on. So, I got it when I was on the train. Who is this psycho you are talking about?"

She could tell he was getting a little annoyed by her questions. She found her keys and on the keychain was a little Swiss Army multi-purpose device. This little device had a little mini screwdriver and small knife. She used this to cut the zip tie behind his back.

She gasped when she saw his hand.

Austin anticipated this when she went to cut the zip tie. "The guy in the other room is using the people in this building as hostages unless he is paid a large sum of money."

"Why aren't you effected like everyone else is?" Austin said. He saw the water bottle in Ingrid's hand and said, "Don't drink the water! Did you drink any of it?"

"No, I didn't but they gave a bottle to each person in the group I was following into the showroom. They're very focused about making sure everyone had one. Why? What's going on here?" Ingrid insisted.

Austin smiled, "Is your friend's name Lisa Harris?"

"Yes, how do you know that?"

Austin was still shaking the narcotic off which was still in his body, but slowly dissipating.

"What is your name? My name is Austin. Do have a cell phone?"

"My name is Ingrid. Yes, I have a cell, but I can't get a signal. Everyone else is also having the same problem. No one can get in and no one can get out."

She gave the cell phone to Austin. He looked on the side of the phone and was able to extract the SIM card in Ingrid's phone. Ingrid was about to stop him doing this, but he seemed like he knew what he was doing.

Austin reached into his pocket and pulled out a new SIM card and inserted this into Ingrid's phone. He quickly called someone and turned away from Ingrid and talked in a hushed voice to someone else. It sounded like he was calling the police or something.

He turned around and faced Ingrid. "Ingrid, this person in the other room is from Iceland and he wants to use things called nanobots in your water bottle to change people. He has found a way to be the puppet master of anyone who drinks it."

This was getting just stranger and stranger. "Austin is this person's name Håvard Evans? I'm supposed to marry Lisa's brother in 3 months. This guy Håvard caused a car crash which crippled her brother Stanley and deeply affected Lisa. Who did you call?"

He nodded when she said Håvard's name and then said, "I have a special way in through the cell towers. I don't think they will be able to get inside the building if the doors are electronically locked. The person I spoke to will get all the correct people to help us to free these people. Telling me about the electromagnetic locks helps a lot. I told the person I spoke with about this and they will probably cut the power so they can open the doors, hopefully."

Chapter 16 - Lights, Camera, Action

Defending Our Nation. Securing the Future

- NSA Motto

Lights, Camera, Action

The narcotic Lisa was given, was still in her body, but as Austin thought, she was in a better position to handle this due to her previous life of using these kinds of narcotics

In the next room, the 50 or so people were all sitting, in several rows of chairs. If someone were walking by and was looking in the room, they would think everything was perfectly fine. One exception to this was everyone was displaying the exact same expression or to be more accurate, the lack of any expression. If the people in the chairs didn't have their eyes open, she would incorrectly say everyone was either asleep or dead.

In the front part of the room, there was a chair on a little raised platform to simulate a stage. On both sides of this stage were two video cameras pointing at the chair. In the back portion of the stage was a blue partition being used as a background for the cameras. Also, on each side of this stage were two spotlights.

Lisa was roughly pushed into a chair in the first row. Her hands were quickly zip tied to the back part of the chair. On the stage, a middle-aged man with black hair with little wisps of grey was sitting in the chair.

Håvard walked over to a young girl. He started asking her questions and she gave quick nods. Lisa couldn't hear them from where she was sitting. She then went over to a little folding table where about 6 computers were laid out with several monitors. When she sat down, she started typing into the computer.

There was no writing on the board, just a steel grayish blue color. The girl sitting at the computer table gave him a thumbs up. He started talking into a small wireless microphone attached to his shirt.

Now Lisa was able to hear him. He said, "If you're watching this then I want to stress the facts here. This is a live broadcast and is very real. This broadcast will continue for the next hour. Unless money is paid to the address, you're looking at below."

Here he paused to look at the girl at the folding table with the computers. She gave him a thumbs up. Supposedly, to reference the bitcoin address and a QR barcode was showing up correctly on the video which only she could see.

He then continued, "If the money isn't put into this account, then this man will die. We have an additional 50 people who are in line to share the similar fate. Every hour after this, another person will be killed. After each hour it will be doubled. The price to stop this will also double. Without further ado, let's begin the show."

Håvard took out his cell phone and opened up an application and started to press several buttons. Almost, immediately the man sitting in the chair started to moan and cry out in pain. Small bits of blood started to come out of his nose and his ears. No one in the room registered anything expect the peaceful and calm exterior. For the next 60 minutes, the man's internal organs started to fail from a lack of blood flow. The nanobots in his body were rewiring veins and arteries in his body with new veins and arteries.

Typically, this might not be a problem if you were to have a bypass system to keep the blood circulating to any other organs which weren't being rewired. As a result, the staccato ordering of destruction and then construction would cause excruciating pain and then he would be fine for a few minutes. Then the whole process would happen again. Sometimes blood would seep out of different places in his body. His ears, nose or mouth would start to bleed and then stop. The man was crying out in pain. No one besides Lisa reacted to this.

She asked Håvard to please stop. Whatever effects from the narcotic she received was quickly dissipating due to the overwhelming shock of what she was forced to watch. She could only barely tolerate to watch this. At the end of 60 minutes of watching this Lisa was in tears. She begged him to stop.

He motioned to the girl behind the computers and she shook her head yes. Håvard moved his hand left to right as in a cutting motion, to signal to stop the live feed. The girl froze a still of the guy in agony. The still picture of him was shocking. Lisa assumed the cameras were being broadcast on a website with a live feed.

Håvard pulled his cell phone up and pressed a couple of buttons on the phone and the man on the chair, let out a deep breath. Miraculously, the man's expression changed. Lisa had a keen eye for this, so she could tell the man's brain was flooding his system with endorphins to assuage the pain. His body also seemed to stop bleeding and his skin was starting to show a healthier complexion color.

Håvard now turned his attention to Lisa. "How did you like this little show we are putting on. See this man is now in no pain and his body is fixing itself. This little feature we are displaying here is probably going to replay out all over the globe after tomorrow. Now, *Pickles*, it seems, you're a fan of mine and have been trying to track me for several years. Why is that?"

Lisa said, "It seems you have all the cards here. Why don't you figure this riddle out? If you knew the answer then maybe you would understand why I have been looking for you for so long."

A third man in the last row of chairs stood up and walked over to someone. Lisa couldn't see who the person was. She couldn't see what this person, *Hydro*, was doing. She couldn't turn around far enough. directly, Lisa couldn't see who the person who they were getting from the last row. In her peripheral vision, she sensed movement behind her and was starting to come into sight.

Lisa's shock and sorrow felt like being hit with a sledgehammer. The man called *Hydro*, was pushing a wheelchair to the front of the room. The man in the wheelchair was Stanley. How is this possible? Stanley was brought up to the stage to sit opposite the other man in the chair. Stanley's face was wearing the same expression of calm and peace.

"Maybe this will help jog your memory," Håvard snarled.

Stanley was wearing the same blank expression on his face. She knew if he was going to survive this, she would need to break him out of his delirium. The man in the chair who was crying out in pain earlier, kept oscillating between pain and no pain by his brain chemistry turned the pain receptors on or off. The damage to his veins and arteries were real, it was just the nanobots were changing the man's brain chemistry.

Lisa's anger was building in her. She was still stunned by the sight of Stanley. She screamed at Håvard, "Haven't you done enough to my family! You killed my mother and my father! You killed my sister! You crippled my brother! Haven't you done enough damage to my family?"

Apparently, Håvard didn't know anything about the car crash so many years ago. He momentarily looked confused.

"Håvard, please don't do this. I beg you, please? What are you going to do to my brother? Please don't hurt him?"

"Ok, but you're wrong about the rest of your family. I didn't kill anyone. I also didn't cripple your brother here."

"Håvard, you really don't know anything about the car crash you caused when you flew out of the 7-Eleven 24 years ago? Honestly, you don't remember 24 years ago. You got into a fight with a guy at the 7-Eleven store near Logan Airport?"

Håvard paused for a second, trying to recall what Lisa said to him. He vaguely remembered it, but he decided to not admit it.

"Ms. Harris, you're wrong. I never was at a 7-Eleven store."

Lisa had an idea, "Håvard, why don't you ask my brother yourself?"

"Maybe I will do exactly that."

He brought out his cell phone and pressed a couple of buttons. Stanley's face and demeanor took on a more natural form. He looked confused, but he saw Lisa and smiled a little bit.

"Lisa, what is happening here? Where am I?" Stanley asked.

"Stanley what game were we playing right before the car crash??"

Both Stanley and Håvard had a confused look come on their faces. Stanley figured it out quickly. They loved to play kick ball when they were younger. He was facing Håvard. Håvard assumed he was in front of a crippled paraplegic. Stanley stood up quickly and kicked him in the groin. He wasn't expecting this, and he doubled over in pain. Stanley kicked Håvard in the face very hard. Blood started to come out of his nose. Lisa yelled at him to get Håvard's phone. Stanley reached down and plucked it from his hand.

Stanley ran over to Lisa while he was pulling his house keys out of his pocket. Like Ingrid, he also had a multifunction tool connected to his keychain. He pulled out the small knife and was able to reach Lisa and cut the zip tie.

The Icelandic guy, called *Hydro*, came over to Stanley and Lisa in a menacing way. He knew the cell phone was the key to all this. Stanley tossed the cell phone to Lisa once her hands were untied. Lisa pointed the cell phone at *Hydro* and told him to stay back or she would hurt him badly.

It was a ruse on Lisa's part, but it had the desired effect. The girl who was at the computers started to come over to Lisa. Lisa held up the cell phone and threatened to use it on her also. The app was still running on the cell phone. Stanley walked over to *Hydro* and around his belt there were several zip ties. Stanley grabbed a couple of them. He grabbed the man's arms and tied his hands behind his back with the zip tie. Stanley turned to do the same thing to Håvard. Håvard wasn't there.

Stanley looked for him and saw him running over to the back of the room where the girl had been sitting at the computers. She was furiously typing in a few commands onto a laptop and then disconnected it from the plugs she had it hooked up to. Stanley saw her and Håvard run out of the other door marked as RM 113. The both of them disappeared into the crowd in the session room hallway. They were both able to escape in the chaos.

Hydro, still with his hands zip tied, tried to run out of the other door leading to RM 213 with access outside to the showroom floor. When he reached the door, it opened from the other side and several people started to stream into the session room.

Lisa watched this as almost 30 people in black and blue wind breaker jackers with big letters, saying FBI or NSA. The FBI agent nearest to the man trying to escape through the door grabbed him and forced him to his knees. Several NSA and FBI agents now filtered in. Austin came into the room and went over to Lisa.

"Lisa, I'm so sorry about this, but I didn't have enough time to tell you fully about this guy. I was able to get my job back after I straightened out and got sober. I was working for the NSA. I couldn't say anything to you because I was undercover. I almost got Håvard, or *Sixes*, as you know him, back when he did his stunt on the *Ashley Madison* website hack. He disappeared the second he got paid and he didn't leave us any trail to find him. I'm so very sorry."

Lisa said, "Let's not do this now. We can talk later."

Ingrid came up to Lisa and gave her a big hug. "I'm so glad you're ok. You had me worried, after your text you sent to me."

"Ingrid, I sent the text message to Stanley?"

"Stanley has his calls forwarded sometimes. I received it on the train when I was coming in. I couldn't get a hold of you or Stanley, so I came here."

Ingrid now saw Stanley up near the podium. He noticed she came over to give her a huge hug.

Stanley asked, "What happened? How did I get here? The last thing I remember was driving here and parking in the parking lot near the hotel. I received a text message about 1:30 from Lisa to meet you in the lobby of the Boston Sheraton Hotel."

Lisa squinted her eyes a little as she said, "I think Håvard spoofed my phone. I never sent a message saying to meet you in the hotel. It had to be Håvard."

Austin was listening to this and added, "There was a period of time maybe 30 or 45 minutes. Håvard left me in the room alone. This is probably when he went and got you."

"I went into the lobby and last thing I remember was taking a free bottle of water in the lobby and then ending up here."

Ingrid added, "yeah they were very weird about everyone drinking some of the Icelandic water call GullFoss. Do you think he had the water spiked with our nanobots?"

Stanley nodded his head in agreement.

Austin continued, "There were 6 people and Håvard involved in this scheme. They were all using special code names that Håvard assigned to each of them. Not really sure why he did it this way, but this is the way Håvard wanted it. The guy, *Hydro*, also worked with a woman named *Bleu*. Their focus was on making sure everyone had only GullFoss water available to the people here. They did something to spike it with the nanobots."

Lisa added, "I saw many places containing marketing materials for GullFoss water all over the place yesterday and today. Everywhere you turned it was displaying a sign or a stand with cold water. I would have drunk some of it, but I had some coffee in the morning and that was about it."

Austin continued, "In addition, there were two others called, *Homer* and *Batman*. They were responsible for all the props and work with the staff here at the Convention Center to make sure everything went correctly. The FBI has those two in custody. and also, *Hydro*. The girl who was by the computers, was called *Edie*, and she escaped with Håvard and *Bleu*."

Lisa asked, "So what was your name and part of all this?"

Austin smiled saying, "My name was *Carbon*, and I was in charge of shutting down the cell towers near here. The NSA removed the changes I put in to affect the cell towers. The code I put in, was to let only the phones Håvard gave to everyone work and make calls or receive them. Everything else would be blocked or get a *no signal* response. I added those phone ID's into some code which was set to execute at 1:00 PM today. I also added an additional 8 devices and those devices were owned by the NSA and FBI agents here today. This would let them call into or call out of the area and not be affected by the code I put in to block most devices."

Austin still had Ingrid's phone. He asked, "Ingrid I still have your phone. Can you give me about 4 hours to make sure no backend viruses came back at your phone after I made the call to the NSA?"

"Sure, no problem. Do you need the unlock PIN?"

With a crooked smile said, "No it's OK. We can test it without the code." Austin belatedly realized he might have said too much. In the NSA, breaking into or bypassing the security of a cell phone was an everyday activity. In spite of this, he added, "Don't worry I will be overseeing this so your data and personal information is safe and won't be looked at by anyone other than me. Promise."

Ingrid didn't really think about the security of her data. She never kept anything really personal or embarrassing on her phone. So, she wasn't worried in the least bit.

Another guy with a blue NSA jacket, a little older than Austin, came over to ask Austin some questions. He was holding the cell phone

Håvard had given to Austin. This phone contained a special application which would be able to deactivate any of the nanobots in his body so he would be immune to the effects of them. He showed the other agents the application and how he could deactivate the nanobots.

The deactivation can also be turned off on the people who were affected today. They would do a similar thing they did earlier today. Just walk through everyone and broadcast a deactivation of the nanobots.

Austin pressed the button in the application and the guy still sitting in the chair with his hands zip tied behind him, suddenly reacted. His expression changed from calm and peaceful to confused and irritated.

Austin said it uses Radio-Frequency Identification (RFID) to deactivate them. Austin gave the phone back to the man and said anyone within 10 to 20 feet would be affected and would deactivate the nanobots.

MD HANLEY

Ingrid kind of innocently asked, "If this signal is broadcast out to anyone in the area who had active nanobots, would now deactivate them and will be flushed out of the body in a normal process. Right?"

Ingrid knew very well what would be happening. She suspected correctly Austin knew more about Stanley and Lisa than he was showing right now. It wasn't hard to figure out Stanley should have been wheelchair bound. So why was he standing? She played coy and didn't bring the issue up.

Lisa did follow her line of thinking also. Stanley should have all of the nanobots stop working in him. Why is he still standing up?

Lisa mentioned to Austin and the other NSA agent, they should be careful with the man on the stage. Deactivating those nanobots could cause a lot of damage if they were in the middle of repairing or fixing his arterial systems. She suggested he be taken to an area far enough away from the RF-ID signal and to be medically checked out.

The NSA agents had taken possession of the cell phones from *Hydro*, *Homer*, and *Batman*. They took the man on the stage to a safe area and a doctor was called to attend him. The agents started to walk through the session room for the 50 or so people all zip tied to their chairs and deactivated the nanobots. Most of the people in the session room were confused and disoriented. Some were angry when they found themselves tied to the chairs. The NSA agents quickly went around and untied everyone. The other NSA agents were quickly moving through the showroom floor releasing them from the dreamy state of mind. Many were confused, but it was all containable.

Austin disappeared for a few minutes talking to a different agent who wore a similar jacket to the FBI, except his jacket had additional big letters, SAC, or Special Agent in Charge. The Special Agent in Charge was for all the agents, both NSA and FBI. After a minute or two he came back to Lisa. She could tell he didn't have great news. Håvard had escaped from the building. The girl who was at the computers, at the last minute when she was typing quickly into her computer was to turn off all the security cameras in the building and the surrounding areas. She was also able to unlock all the doors which were electronically locked.

She unlocked all the doors almost at the same time one of our agents were about to try to break through the thick glass in the doors. They didn't have to break the door because all the door unlocked simultaneously.

Chapter 17 - In Plain Sight

Common sense is not so common.

— Voltaire

All of the agents who were a part of this operation, were very quick to squash any of this from the media. There was however, one or two people who did make it onto the news later that night. They were portrayed as computer nerds and probably high on some editable marijuana. They were very convincing. They really hyped up the fact it was a *hacker's* conference and implied maybe a hacker had *hacked* the conference people's minds. The person saying this burst into a fit of laughter as he thought about the pun of hacker's who were hacking the computer conference.

Lisa suspected it was actually a couple of NSA agents doing this. She was surprised this hadn't been a bigger splash than the two or three items being brought up in the local channel news. The NSA and the FBI were old pro's at this game. Hide and conceal was the name of the game.

As the day went on, they had no information on where Håvard and the girl called, *Edie*, had disappeared to. They sent agents to some of the airports to make the airports customs agents aware of these two fugitives Their focus would be planes going to Canada, Western Europe, and of course, Iceland. It was turning into a waste of time, but it was the most obvious way of leaving the country. The trains and borders were called to be on the lookout for the fugitives.

Lisa, deep down, knew Håvard was too smart to try to leave from the airport. There had to be someplace where he could hole up. Since Austin was part of a crew, he was the only person who could help the search for him. Håvard never came into the Sheraton Hotel which was next door to the convention. Whenever they were done for the day, Håvard jumped into a taxi or Uber to go to his hotel.

Pretty quickly, the FBI found that the credit card used to secure the multiple rooms was a bogus credit card. Austin was expecting this.

The FBI checked all the surrounding areas for any type of security video of Håvard. If they could find a decent picture of Håvard's face or of *Edie's* face, then they could do a facial recognition. They could also check several other security feeds outside of the area *Edie* had shut down. They were able to get a video feed of Håvard from the subway station of the MBTA (Massachusetts Bay Transportation Authority) for the Prudential stop. This subway stop was right next to the Prudential Center.

For some reason, Lisa suspected the video was fake. Why would he go into an area he knew would have tons of video camera's? It didn't make sense. She asked Austin if she could see the video feed.

"What's up? Do you think he did something to the video feed from the subway?"

"Would you? I wouldn't go into an area where I knew I might be spotted by a security camera that records almost every part of the MBTA?"

"Yeah, it does sound like it would be an amateur move. It might be a move he wants us to believe. Let me get the video we have," Austin said.

In about 3 minutes, he came back with a laptop and the video feed all cued up. She watched the video with Austin. They both said almost at the same time, "This is fake!"

The video Austin replayed showed a good quality video of a subway car coming into the Prudential Center station. They could watch him coming into view and then boarding the subway with *Edie* at the same time. The reason this was a fake video was because the video they were looking at showed a blue subway car coming into the Prudential station. The subway should have been a green subway car.

In Boston, the subway cars who serviced a specific set or line of stops were usually referred by the color of the subway cars. In Boston, there are basically four different main subway lines called Green Line, Orange Line, Red Line, and Blue Line. There is also a smaller service line primarily to support the airport and it is called the Silver Line.

Lisa asked if the NSA or the FBI have searched all systems and not just the obvious ones near here. She knew the NSA have a lot of tools for ways to get into other computer systems or networks. They would have the ability to get video of cars going through an intersection, speed traps, ATM's, and other businesses using security cameras. Looking through all the information would be a huge amount of time. The NSA has several ways they can streamline the search.

Austin said, "I know you have your own, let's say non-conventional, ways to get into foreign systems. The NSA also has some additional non-conventional ways to get into systems You probably already know this, so I won't insult you by saying these are secrets. However, you have to promise to forget about them existing. There are 3 ATM's in the area which we might be lucky to catch some images.

For the next couple of hours, they scoured all video they could get their hands on. None of the video showed even a hint of the two showing up. This was discouraging. Lisa got a call from Ingrid.

"Hi Lisa, how is everything going over there? Stanley and I are done speaking with the FBI and NSA. We are going to stay in the city tonight. We got a room in the same hotel you're in. We were wondering if you wanted to go get something to eat?"

Lisa was a little torn on this. She wanted to talk to both Ingrid and Stanley about what happened here today. She looked at Austin and he overheard Ingrid asking about dinner and he motioned for her to go. She told Ingrid she would meet her in the lobby of the hotel in 10 minutes.

Lisa made plans to meet tomorrow morning for coffee or breakfast with Austin. He said he would call her if anything changes or with new information on the whereabouts of Håvard.

Lisa met Ingrid and Stanley in the lobby and went over to a little bar and restaurant in the hotel. After they ordered their food, Lisa looked at Stanley and said, "Stanley what happened today? Why were you able to continue to stand and walk? You had an altered look and expression, like everyone else. I don't understand why when he deactivated the nanobots you were able to still stand, then kick Håvard. By the way, it was an awesome kick!"

Ingrid jumped in and commented, "Lisa I think I know what happened. The nanobots in his system, have been gradually releasing themselves, over the last few weeks. I would want to have some medical tests done, but I think Stanley's spine isn't being run by just nanobots. They were at first maybe, but now, if I'm correct, the nanobots have fabricated real spinal cord tissues and real vertebrae to correct and replace the damaged areas in his spinal cord. This is actually what it was designed for."

Stanley said, "Lisa, we need to be kind of quiet about this. It wouldn't be received well if the director of research went from being a paraplegic to an able-bodied person with the full use of their legs. This could also be perverted by many people who want to use this breakthrough for cosmetic surgery, or other non-disease specific uses."

Ingrid followed up with, "These little *stem* cell printers have an ability to be used against some of the most horrific diseases that humans haven't been able to cure. Can you imagine, a world where cancer didn't exist? Or a world having no cases of AID's, or the flu, or really anything? I can see this also extending the life-expectancy of humans to become centuries long. This is where it becomes a problem. This treatment has to be free for everyone. If it isn't free, then only the wealthy will be able to afford to get this treatment. The greed and corruption potential are astronomical."

"The other side of the argument is also what Håvard was doing today. He was ransoming the lives of people today for money. Can you imagine if this was used as a weapon to indiscriminately kill foreign leaders or people in power? It would change history in the world forever," Lisa said.

"Ingrid, how did Håvard activate the nanobots which were in the GullFoss water?"

Ingrid replied, "Good question. I was thinking about this earlier when I saw the other people in his little group were walking around to a crowd of people and they were holding up their cell phones. When they came close to the people, they just sat down on the floor. I didn't drink the water, so I wasn't affected by this. I think the cell phones they had were sending out a signal to activate the nanobots. I don't have enough information to find out if it was a Radio Frequency, or RF ID, signal to the nanobots in each person to cause them to sit down. I would need to look at the phone from the one of the people the FBI rounded up."

Lisa started to say she would ask her friend Austin if she could get one of the phones. She was interrupted by a large crash of plates and glasses.

The three of them were so intent on their discussion they didn't notice what was happening to the people who were in the bar and restaurant with them also. A waiter was coming out of the kitchen with a tray of food on his shoulder. He collapsed with the large heavy tray and then sat down on the floor.

A little boy was tugging at his father's arm and crying when his father just sat there with the same calm peaceful look she saw earlier. Everywhere people just stopped and sat on the ground. Outside there were sounds of cars screeching to a stop, Horrific sounds after the screeching with the unmistakable sound of two cars crashing. In a split second, everything in the hotel became still. Almost as if time slowed to a stop, Lisa and Ingrid watched everywhere people were, they just stopped and sat on the floor.

Lisa looked at her brother, and she could also see the look he wore earlier today. Ingrid saw this too. She shook Stanley hard with no effect. Ingrid didn't have her cell phone because she gave it to Austin.

Lisa pulled out her cellphone and called Austin.

He picked it up on the first ring. He said, "Lisa is everyone around you stopping and just sitting on the floor?"

"Yes, what is happening over there?"

Austin quickly replied, "Anyone in the building from earlier today were all evacuated earlier. Two agents drank some of the GullFoss water and are affected. The rest of the team is ok and didn't drink any of the water. How is your brother? Is he ok?"

"No, he isn't. He is the way he was earlier along with everyone else. Blank expression of calm and peaceful. It's creepy, but he seems ok."

Austin said he would be right over and to stay where she was.

Chapter 18 - Checkmate

A good listener is a good talker with a sore throat.

— Katharine Whitehorn

Pandemonium was happening all around them. Lisa and Ingrid just looked around completely stunned at what they were seeing. Stanley was right next to them, sitting motionless and staring with vacant eyes. The little boy two tables away was tugging at his father's arm and getting no reaction from him. This lack of reaction just sent the boy into a fit of wailing. He didn't understand what was happening to his father. Every time he pulled on his father's arm, the more frightened the little boy was. Everything in the restaurant area was becoming eerily quiet.

Lisa saw Austin coming through the lobby door. He made eye contact with Lisa and walked quickly toward her. He saw Stanley with the blank expression. He sat down next to Lisa and opposite to Ingrid and Stanley.

He looked at Ingrid and asked, "Ingrid, I need to know everything you can tell me about these nanobots. I saw Stanley earlier today, and I saw him stand up and kick Håvard. I don't believe he was able to do this just from the GullFoss water alone. Help me understand what was going on before this today?"

Ingrid looked at Lisa. She could see on her face, she wasn't happy with Austin's question. Lisa answered before Ingrid could answer him.

"Austin, what are you implying here? Ingrid and Stanley aren't the bad guys here."

Austin expected this reaction, especially from Lisa. He countered, "Lisa, I am very aware of what happened to your brother. Your family. I know Håvard caused it. We have trusted each other with all the demons we had to fight to get here. Please, trust me now. Anything we can do to stop Håvard is all I want. Nothing else, I promise."

Ingrid looked at Lisa. Lisa was angry, but she nodded her head a little.

Ingrid understood the reluctance of Lisa. The situation had to be corrected. She might have some answers to help fix it. Ingrid started to explain how the nanobots worked and how they printed out template *stem* cells to fix areas of a body. She described how Stanley had accidentally injected himself with the nanobots.

She explained how the process needs to start. The first thing the nanobots do is to go to an area that isn't working correctly. It is able to go there with pinpoint accuracy. Once the nanobots get there, several things start to happen. The first part of the process is to deploy the nanobots payload. The payload are millions of what we call *factory* cells. Each of those factory cells creates millions of 3D printers. Now, each of those 3D printers is able to **print stem** cells for the area that isn't working correctly. If everything goes correctly you can have billions of 3D printers running through your body. Stanley is the medical part of this research and I am the mechanical part of it.

Austin said, "Ok, I think I get it. You said Stanley was walking before this. This didn't happen overnight I assume."

"Yes, this all started about 6 months ago. It has been slowly happening. We were assuming, real tissue and real vertebrae were being created by Stanley's body. A lot of the muscles Stanley needs to walk have atrophied and make him very weak after just a little bit of standing or walking.

Austin asked, "Did Stanley ever get into this same state of mind which everyone seems be under the influence of?"

"No, he never had this look on his face. A lot of the work on spine from the nanobots mostly happened at night. It makes sense to fix his spine when there is very little activity of the part being fixed. Today is different though. It seems to be going into the brain and overloading the body to be catatonic. All of the body autonomic systems seem to be working correctly, breathing, heartbeat, eyes blinking etc. One thing I saw earlier today was the people working with Håvard were walking through all the people on the showroom floor and were holding up a cell phone. Everywhere they went everyone just stopped and sat down. I sat down too, but I did this only to blend in. I think those cell phones were broadcasting a signal and triggering the nanobots into action. Do you or the FBI have any of those cell phones?"

"Yes, we have three of them. I shut down the cell towers earlier today. How do the nanobots get told to activate? Is it an RF ID signal being broadcast? Is it a cellular signal? Is it Bluetooth? How are these nanobots being activated?"

Something Austin said sparked a smile in Ingrid and she asked, "Austin, do you have my cell phone I gave you earlier? Also do you have a cell phone used by Håvard or his other people helping him?"

Austin was a little surprised by this question, but he replied, "Ingrid I still have your cell phone from earlier today. I also have the cell phone Håvard gave to me."

Ingrid was surprised by the last statement. She didn't know Austin was working with Håvard. She took her cell phone and went into her contacts list. After a few seconds, she found the contact she wanted to call. Before she pressed send, she told Austin she was calling someone at her work who could be trusted.

After Austin nodded yes, she pressed send. It rang twice before someone answered the phone. The person she called was an old colleague, Robyn Scott, or Ike as most people called him.

The first thing Ike said was, "Ingrid, what is happening to people. Everyone is just stopping what they are doing. Do you know anything about this?"

Ingrid replied, "Ike, we need your help. Do you remember when we had a problem 5 of the mice we were using just stopped and turned into statues? It seems like the same thing is happening here. Do you remember how we fixed the issue?"

"They were euthanized."

All the blood in Ingrid's face disappeared. "Ike, there must be another answer to this." Ingrid turned her face away from Austin and Lisa and spoke in a whisper, "We can't euthanize everyone affected."

"Sorry, I know this is a horrible thing to say and I'm not saying this is what we will do. I am just saying what I remember about the mice that were receiving an overload of neurotransmitters. They were causing their brains to be overwhelmed and saturate the reward and pain centers of the brain. It happened very quickly and when it did happen it was a glitch in the software forcing it to go into an endless loop. It would stay in this position until they were removed from the body or the body was unable to keep them functioning. What we need to do is to reboot the nanobots somehow. Where are you right now?"

He told Ingrid he would contact her in ten minutes. There was something he wanted to look at first.

Ingrid relayed to Austin and Lisa what Ike told her. She purposely didn't mention anything about euthanizing people to fix this.

Almost exactly ten minutes passed and then Ingrid's cell phone rang. She answered it and Ike asked her to put him on speakerphone.

She put him on speakerphone. Ike said, "Ingrid you mentioned Stanley is also affected by this right?"

"Yes"

"Bear with me here. I am going to play a sound at a certain frequency. I will keep escalating the frequency until you notice a change in Stanley. Ok, I am starting now."

For the next 2 minutes, nothing but silence from the cell phone. The RFID, or Radio Frequency Identification signal, Ike was broadcasting through the cell phone were radio frequencies in various ranges. These frequencies were too high to hear. After two minutes, Ingrid thought maybe they had dropped the cell phone connection. Then out of nowhere Stanley's expression changed. For the briefest second, Ingrid could see Stanley's eyes move. She told Ike to stop.

Stanley's face took on a normal expression and life came back in his eyes. The little boy near them stopped crying softly. His father's face became the one he knew was his father again. All around them people were looking around and they were all confused why they were sitting on the floor. The little restaurant was silent only moments before and was now alive with people talking and picking up broken dishes or cleaning up drinks spilled.

Ike was still on speaker phone. He asked, "What happened over there?"

Ingrid replied, "Ike, yes it worked! What was the frequency you emitted when you stopped?"

"I stopped at the 2.4 GHz frequency. Anything at this high frequency will reboot all of the nanobots. Once they are rebooted, they will exit the body naturally. How is Stanley doing?"

Stanley answered, "I'm confused but I feel pretty good though. It's a very weird feeling. Please don't do it again."

Ike said, "Ingrid I am going to send you a file which has the code to emit this frequency. This frequency is very close to the 2.5 GHz Wi-Fi bandwidth. If this can be emitted across all wi-fi access points and can also be uploaded to the cell towers to get a bigger range."

Austin said, "Ike, I can get it to the cell towers. Is this something you can send to Ingrid as a file? If you can I will upload so it will be broadcast to all the towers and all devices in the range of a cell tower."

"There is also one other thing I am seeing here. There's another signal which is broadcasting near you. It isn't exactly the same frequency, but it's very strong. When I first turned my oscilloscope on to broadcast a frequency to you, I had to douse out the signal it was receiving. I can tell you where it is coming from though. What exactly are the coordinates of where you are calling me from? I think I can tell you where it is originating from."

"Wait, you mean you know where the person who is broadcasting this is right now? They were doing this from a cell phone earlier today. Can you back trace this to locate where the cell phone is right now?"

Ike excitedly said, "Yes, I can. Ingrid can you give me your exact coordinates of where you are right now?"

Lisa jumped in first and gave Ike, their exact coordinates.

"Ok, hmm. This may sound a little strange, but the coordinates of where this signal is broadcasting is exactly where you are at right now. This doesn't make any sense."

Silence from Ingrid's phone, and then Ike said, "Wait a second. Ok, yeah, this makes sense. If you are on the bottom floor of the Boston Sheraton Hotel, then the signal is being broadcast from your location. But this is where it's a little strange. The signal is approximately 120 feet above where you are at now. Does this make any sense?"

Austin said, "Yes it does. This means it's broadcasting from the 12th floor of the hotel. I've a suspicion I know where it is being broadcast from. Håvard made a reference to know exactly where my room is in this hotel. Ike thanks for all your help in this."

"I was glad to help out. Ingrid let me know if you need anything else from me. Thanks," and Ike hung up.

Austin was on the phone with his boss. When he hung up, he looked at Lisa and said, "I suspect Håvard is waiting for me to go back to my hotel room and is waiting there for me. There is a squad of FBI agents coming over here right now and we are going to go into my hotel room. Please stay here for now. I will let you know what happens."

Lisa said defiantly, "No way! I'm not going to sit here and just watch this. He killed my family and I need to see this through. Austin you aren't going to stop me. I need to do this."

"Lisa, I understand. My boss will never agree to this. Go to the elevator now and go to the 12th floor. I will have to make up something for my boss but go now!"

Lisa leaned over and gave him a kiss on his cheek. Before Ingrid or Stanley knew it, Lisa was gone.

"I need to go and stall my boss for two minutes. Ingrid can I borrow your phone again? I want to bring this upstairs and send this out so if anyone else is affected this will turn it off."

"Sure, we will wait here."

Austin's boss and a hoard of FBI agents swarmed into the hotel lobby. Austin went over to his boss and told him Håvard was in room 1244. The group of agents split off into three groups. One group headed up the stairways to the 12th floor. Austin and his boss and a couple of other agents went into the next elevator. Three agents stayed in the lobby of the hotel.

12th Floor Room 1244

Lisa wasn't sure what she was going to do when she got to the 12th floor, but she tried to be positive and hopeful that she would know what the right course was to follow. Right now, her mind was a maelstrom of thoughts screaming for attention. The louder thoughts were echoing people in her past who would say, *dig two graves for revenge, one for the other person and one for yourself.* These sayings about revenge and resentment were physically storming into her thinking right now. With everything in life, we are always presented with choices of how to decide the course of our fate. Everything Lisa thought about in her life, whether right or wrong, always boiled down to a choice of **doing what she wanted to do** and **doing what she should do**. The "yin or yang", "black or white", "good or bad", "fair or unfair", "honest or untruthful" and so on. Always an opposing course of a decision to be made.

When she got off the elevator, she turned to the right and was facing a wall with signs pointing to room numbers to the left and room numbers to the right. Room 1244 was in the hallway to the left.

Lisa walked down the hallway toward room 1244. She was hoping to find a little room containing an ice machine. If there was one, she could hide in there until after Austin and the FBI agents broke into Austin's room. She needed to see this out.

She had just stepped into the little room for the ice machine when she heard the ding of the elevator stopping at this floor. In a minute she saw Austin, and six other agents with guns walk by her hiding spot.

The plan she assumed was for Austin to open the door to his room as normal and the rest of the agents to rush in and apprehend him. It didn't go exactly as planned.

She heard noise coming from down the hallway. A door shut and 3 shots fired. Lisa peeked around the corner and saw the unbelievable happening. There were two bodies lying face down in the hallway. Each of them was wearing an FBI jacket.

She came out of her hiding spot and ran down the hall to Austin's room. She saw the two agents, lying on the floor.

What she saw in the room, was unbelievable. Håvard's was standing in front of Austin with a gun pointed at his head. Another agent was pointing his gun at Håvard telling him to release Austin.

It was a stale mate.

Lisa was at the opening of the door and saw that one of the agents had a gun at his side. She quickly bent down and picked it up. She really hated guns. The agent opposite to Håvard assertively told him to let Austin go.

"Never. Kill me if you want but think of how many people were under the influence of my nanobots? Massachusetts is a tiny state. Think of how this will be if there are 300 million under this control. What then?"

"We will find out how to shut them off like I just did," Lisa said.

Håvard was a little startled but he definitely didn't show any concern now with two guns pointing at him. He looked at Lisa and spit out, "You are wrong about this *Pickles*. You are very wrong."

He reached in his pocket quickly and pulled out a cell phone. "All I have to do is to press one button, and it will make every one's brains become fried."

As he was saying this, he raised his arm with the cellphone, the second FBI agent in the room, fired his gun twice. The first shot hit Håvard in the shoulder causing the cell phone to drop from his hand. The second shot was to his chest. The bullet hit Håvard's midsection just as Austin was ducking to get out of the way.

Almost in slow motion, Håvard fell to the floor. One very strange thing happened as he fell to the ground. He grabbed his arm and pinched his skin just underneath where his arm met his body. This would be in the same place most people have their lymph nodes. It was a feeble attempt to grab his arm out of the way of the bullet which hit his midsection. The damage that Håvard sustained was too much. The second bullet, hit him in the chest, piercing his lung and his liver. It was a deadly blow and soon after this, Håvard Evans was dead.

The two agents at the entrance to the room, were both wearing bullet proof vests. They were sore but still alive and physically fine.

Chapter 19 - Escape

The cure is worse than the disease

The sound of the gunshot was deafening. The man who shot Håvard was just standing there with a gun in his hand with tiny wisps of gun smoke coming out of the cylinder of his gun. As Austin was diving out of the way of the other FBI agent's gun shot, he looked at Håvard's face. He thought surely, he would be surprised. No, it was not surprise it was a very small smirk. To Austin, it seemed as if Håvard knew he was going to be shot tonight and was accepting it. This left Austin with a troubling unsettled feeling. His brain quickly countered this thought with a questioning feeling. Normally when the brain cannot logically make sense of what your eyes see or your senses are feeling, you question. Austin was pretty sure he saw something, but again maybe he was wrong. The brain usually wins this argument and will discount it as an anomaly.

He heard Lisa starting to hyperventilate. Big racking breadths in, and big sighs on the way out. Austin could see she was holding one of the other agent's gun. Slowly he approached her and asked her to release the gun and hand it to him.

The moment she gave him the gun, she broke down and started crying. Austin sort of expected this. This person lying dead in the room was the person who caused a lot of pain and death for Lisa. Ending this part of her life so suddenly was overwhelming for her. It was natural and Austin knew from his own experiences, the best thing to do is to let it run its course and let the body and mind adjust themselves. It would take a few days or even weeks to come to an equalization of these events in her brain.

For the next few hours, several people were called and brought in. The medical forensic expert needed to look at Håvard's body and determine the cause of death. The coroner came in and took his body away to a morgue. In the next few hours, Lisa was able to give a complete statement of all the events of the day. Once this was complete, she told Austin, she was going downstairs to her brother and Ingrid. Austin asked if he could see her tomorrow. They agreed to meet at the hotel for lunch.

One hour later

The coroner had the body of Håvard on a stretcher and he wheeled it to the elevator. He took this elevator to the sub-basement level of the parking garage. A black Chevy Suburban SUV pulled up to the elevator area so the stretcher could be easily loaded. The large SUV, with blacked out windows, exited the garage silently. If anyone asked, they would be told this is a Mortuary Ambulance. While the SUV was enroute to a house in the suburbs outside the city, one person in the back of the vehicle, *Bleu*, was washing the wounds with some alcohol wipes. The person sitting in the driver seat, *Edie*, was holding a cell phone up and punching some buttons into an app. The app she was running was almost up to the point where she needs it to be. The driver of the vehicle pulled into a long driveway leading up to an exceptionally large house set way back from the main road. Homes like this are rare but they are really amazing to look at up-close. *Edie* pulled the black suburban into one of the bays in the 4-car garage.

Everyone in the SUV jumped out and they all knew what they were expected to do. *Bleu* and *Edie* pulled out the stretcher of Håvard's body and brought it into the house. Just off the entry way was a room which was being used as a workout area. There was plenty of room to move around in.

Edie walked over to Håvard with the cell phone in her hand and pressed the button to activate something. She took out a stethoscope and placed one end of it to his chest to listen for his heart. At the moment, this was all they needed to do. She could faintly hear a heartbeat. She smiled. Ah ha! The nanobots Håvard released from the capsule he broke right before he was shot. These new nanobots would start to repair the damage the two bullets did to him. These nanobots were slightly different. Once activated they could never be deactivated. They would also swim around his body and correct and stop the normal aging process in his body. In a month he will be a new person, stronger, more resilient, and invincible. He will stop aging and he will not die. He knew many people with many sinister interests who would pay an extremely high price for this power.

These nanobots could give life and they could also take life.

Chapter 20 – Sleeping Beauty

Doctor to patient:

"I'm waiting to see how many "LIKES" my diagnosis gets before I share it with you."

- The Speed Bump by Dave Coverly

One Month Later

It took many weeks for Håvard to heal from the bullet wounds he received at the Sheraton Boston Hotel. The scenario at the hotel was something he had anticipated happening. He had planned for the Mortuary Ambulance to retrieve him from the hotel if anything happened to him. Luckily, *Edie* and *Bleu* were aware of these plans.

He was brought to a large secluded house in Brookline, Massachusetts. It was far enough away to be out of the scrutiny of Boston and private enough so no one would notice the comings and goings of the people staying at this large house. Håvard rented this house in Brookline for two months. It was expensive to rent, but it afforded him the privacy and seclusion he needed.

When Håvard was younger, actually much younger, he always loved playing chess. He had a knack to look ahead and envision all the possibilities of the next move. Actually, his mind typically worked to think of the next 7 to 14 moves ahead, for almost all possibilities.

He remembered his grandfather, Ingvar, teaching him chess. Those early days playing chess with his grandfather were ruthless and memorable. Håvard needed to look and think about each of his next moves. It wasn't just one or two moves ahead it was 5 and 6 moves ahead. Each of those 5 or 6 moves contained another set of 5 or 6 moves ahead of those. Every game his grandfather would win, which was always, he would then mock him for it. Taunting him. Calling him weak and "not worth anything". At 7 years old, this was a brutal lesson to learn, but one he was forced to learn well. He finally beat his grandfather at a game of chess when he was

9. Håvard started to act like his grandfather was to him. He mocked his grandfather about how easily he had won the game. For a man in his late seventies, his grandfather had a strong left hook. Finally. Harvard was knocked senseless and left on the ground with a broken bloody nose. His grandfather refused to play chess anymore with him. It was the last time he spoke to his grandfather before he died 3 years later.

Now as if in a chess game, he realized that this part of his plan contained the greatest risk for him. He needed to be able to trust his crew to execute the next part of his plan. He would be in a very vulnerable state, so he needed to make sure the people he assigned to this part of the plan were able to execute it flawlessly. He hated these scenario's because he had to trust people. For most of his life he was left disappointed when he trusted people. However, Håvard felt confident in Bleu and Edie. They would execute his plans like he asked them to. He felt sure of them. He thought they would do what he asked because they were both Icelandic. He was playing the Icelandic card, so he hoped this would grant him a little extra respect.

Before coming to the conference in Boston, they all flew to Canada. They met in the airport and were going to take another plane to go to Boston. It would help to hide their travel details a little more. While they were waiting to board the plane, he spoke to them both about a possibility of one possible outcome.

"One possible scenario of this trip is a tiny possibility of someone getting hurt. I'm not saying it will happen, but I want to make sure you understand what should be done if it does happen. I have details about a house near Boston we could go to if we need to lay low, or if we need to recuperate. I also want us to have cover stories which won't arouse any questions. Bleu you will be my younger and smarter sister. Edie you will be my adoring daughter."

Bleu started to cackle in a fit of laughter. Edie didn't really know how to respond but she smiled, nonetheless. It was much later that

Håvard would realize the position he had put Edie into.

Two highly skilled nurses arrived an hour after Bleu called them. A husband and wife who were registered nurses came as recommended to be very discrete and would have the proper credentials to take care of Håvard. Bleu gave them the cover story Håvard asked her to provide. This would help to sell anyone coming in to help as a safe cover story. This would also help to make sure she was involved in all the decisions of these nurses. Håvard told her to let them do their work, but make sure you are being told exactly what is being done.

The first day was important to have a quick response. Tony and Angela as they were known to Edie and Bleu, quickly administered I.V. fluids, cleansing the wounds properly, and intubating Håvard so his body could be receiving oxygen at the appropriate levels. They introduced powerful antibiotics to the IV drip he was on. This regimen of antibiotics would help him to keep any infections at bay for the moment. Another bag of a saline fluid was hung to help with any pain or dehydration. They were told to assess the damage. Håvard provided a name of a highly skilled surgeon, who would be discrete and be able to perform any procedure to assist in his recovery.

In the first couple of days Angela and Tony took x-rays and attended to his body to reach a stasis point. The x-rays Angela and Tony took showed he would need to have a skilled surgeon to perform two procedures to assure his recovery. The surgeon would perform the surgery the next day.

Håvard had damage in two areas. His shoulder was damaged in the typical way a bullet damages anything in its path, exploding into the muscle and bone. The bullet was still inside Håvard and would need to be taken out. The surgeon could place a pin in his shoulder to allow him to recover the use of his arm quicker. If the pin wasn't inserted, he may recover successfully but it would take a fair amount of rehabilitation.

The orders Bleu and Edie were given, and which were also known by the two nurses, were to address his health as the priority and not the rehabilitation. Håvard was very clear in his instructions. Patch what could be patched temporarily and remove any bullets or shrapnel. Angela and Tony both knew they were being highly paid for this, so they were compliant with any plan Edie or Bleu wanted to have done.

The surgeon would also perform a procedure to repair the damage done to his intestines, and his spleen. After discussing the plan for the operating procedure, Angela, the nurse, assertively told the surgeon this would be a temporary surgery to help him to get strong enough to see his physician in his homeland. She was smart enough not to tell the surgeon he was from Iceland.

On the morning of the surgery, Angela and Tony were in the makeshift operating room sterilizing the equipment needed for the procedure; and also, just making sure everything was in place. All that was needed to be available for the doctor.

The operating room door had a little glass see through portion at the top of the door. Bleu knocked on the door to get their attention and motioned for the nurses to come outside to talk to her.

"Sorry, to interrupt the work you are doing. I know I have mentioned this before, but it's very important we are all on the same page with this procedure. The surgeon, Andy Kauffman, called me a few minutes ago and said he would be arriving in about an hour. He also mentioned you had spoken to him about his requirements for equipment and anything else he would need for this to take place today," Bleu said in a matter of fact way.

Angela nodded her head and said, "I spoke with him yesterday and I have all the equipment and materials he will need. We were just doing some last-minute wiping down and sterilizing the room before he arrives. I feel we will be ready for just about anything the doctor will need."

"Ok. Good. I'm glad to hear it. I apologize for this, but I just want to make sure the doctor doesn't do anything extra on this surgery. The only thing he should be doing today is to make my brother, ready to travel in a few days. His injuries will be addressed by my brother's doctor at home. Tony as I understand this, you will be handling the anesthesia, and Angela you will be assisting the doctor. Is this correct? I want one of you to be in charge of this operation. I need someone to be able to make sure the procedure the surgeon does today is only the necessity for travel. Would this be ok?"

Tony spoke before Angela could say anything, "Angela should be the one to do this. I have seen her tell doctors many times they are wrong, or that something they were doing was wrong. She flashes those sexy eyes and the doctors just melt before her. This is why I married her."

"You know that isn't true. I'm just smarter than some of the doctors is all."

Bleu smiled and said, "Thank you both. You have both been great through all this. If this all goes right, I'm sure my brother will add a little bonus in this for both of you. Angela, anything goes wrong in there today let me know right away. Ok."

As expected, the doctor was a little put off by this, but this client was paying him 4 times higher than the price he asked for. This large amount was paid to ensure his "discretion" and for the privacy of his patient. The same was also true for Tony and Angela.

One curious thing the surgeon did was to take several vials of blood before the surgery started. He easily pocketed the vials. He took blood samples only to take a closer look at his blood work later. He said to himself he was only doing this "to cover his ass".

Over the next several days, Edie and Bleu, watched over Håvard. It was almost 10 days after the shooting, when Håvard started to come around and began to stay conscious for a little while at a time.

The intubation tube in his windpipe was something Håvard wanted to be taken out. Very uncomfortable. It took an additional two days for Håvard, to start to regain enough strength to try to get up and walk around for a little bit. He wasn't trying to push himself, but he started to feel a nervous energy. He smiled to himself about this. This was a direct result of the nanobots working on his body.

His appetite was phenomenal. Eating 3 times a day was an adjustment for his body, but it did respond. His injury to his intestines started to feel more normal each day. He was able to remove the tubes taking care of his body fluids while he was recuperating. He could start to feel his midsection was working normal again. He was able to move out of the little makeshift hospital room and into a normal bed.

He discovered a strange side effect of the nanobots. His shoulder was healing well. He was using some weights and physical therapy tools to strengthen his arm and his shoulder. What he saw happen was the muscle development in his right arm was about 10X more rapid than it usually was. In only about 4 days he saw his shoulder and arm become much stronger. He didn't think it was any different than just a normal healing process. Then one day he noticed something strange when he came out of the shower. The mirror showed his right upper body was larger than his left side.

When he tested this the next day, he found the arm where he was shot was able to lift far more weight than the shoulder which wasn't shot. It was strange, and Håvard knew he would need to be mindful of this. He started to adjust a routine of exercising both arms to equalize his body muscles.

The next part of his plan was to contact a couple people who he knew from the darknet. They would pay a phenomenal amount of money to gain access to the nanobots that he could sell to them. For this he would need to get access to a computer so he could start to build up a machine and create some custom-tailored packages for these very powerful people. These people would pay almost anything to achieve the power of life and death he could give to them. In essence, this was the final leg of the long term planning that Håvard started so long ago.

Edie was a savant at technology. She had the ability to assimilate complex projects and break them down to their individual components. He gave her a list of specifications needed to create a new work machine. All the necessary files and source code were stored in a remote cloud machine he could access.

For Edie, this was fun. She would spend Håvard's money and get him the most powerful computer and laptop which would be an improvement from the machine he used before he came to Boston.

Almost like a scene in Pretty Woman, where Julia Robert's tells the Rodeo Drive store clerks, they made a *huge mistake! Huge!* when they turned their nose's up at her the day before. Julia Roberts says this in a dramatic way by showing her arms laden in shopping bags from very expensive stores.

Edie could identify with this character. In a lot of ways, people have always discounted her as not being attractive and not having any intelligence. She looked young. She was filled with anxiety about talking to other people. Håvard was probably the only person who really treated her with any respect, as an equal. She could pretty much hack anything and make a computer do things which would seem impossible. She appreciated this respect in many ways he wasn't even aware of.

When he got all of the equipment Edie had acquired for him, he started right away in building his new machine. Edie did an exceptional job in exceeding the specs he gave to her. He would need to make sure she was rewarded for this in a meaningful way. It took almost a day to complete setting up his new pc and laptop. He also asked Bleu to go out and buy 5 cellphones with very specific technical details. It took him about 3 days to totally get his equipment all set up. Now the fun part starts he thought to himself.

He retrieved his contacts of the correct people to sell this technology to. His hope was to alert a few of these people that he knew from the darknet. There were 6 people he reached out to find out if they would be interested in the new power that he could provide with the nanobots. His offer was to give the ability to indiscriminately kill someone they wanted to remove. Dictators and Generals would love to get this. The other option was to extend the lifespan of some people to about 150 years. The 150 years was the control he put into it so that they would eventually die.

Of the 6 queries he sent, he received an answer from two right away and said *thank you but no thank you*. This was fine and he appreciated the quick response. The next two people he heard back from said they would be interested in this capability and asked what the price for it would be. One person said yes immediately. The other person asked for 48 hours to give his response. Håvard agreed to this. In 48 hours, he heard back from that person, and their response was yes, and they would pay the price asked.

Now the last two people, gave him a response and it was extremely repugnant to him. They tried to negotiate with Håvard. This wasn't a smart play on their part. Negotiating meant he was trying to take advantage of them and thus this is exactly what they were doing to him. They were trying to take advantage of him. His offer was pretty straightforward. *Here is what I can provide* and *here is what it will cost.* Your choice was a simple, *yes* or *no*. He would take care of them soon enough.

Right now, he wanted to create the two different custom tailored nanobots to give to these clients. One of the clients wanted to be able to extend their life for many decades, but they were infirm and would likely die in the next 5 years. This request was easy for him since it was already designed to correct malfunctioning cells in the body. He added some additional checks into his nanobots to make sure this client would attain his physical health quickly. He also decided this person would get a little gift since he responded so quickly and would pay his required fee. He decided to deduct 20% of the fee he was charging and asked him to donate it to any charity he wished. He contacted the client and told him his package was on the way for him. He packaged a cell phone with his custom code on it to activate the nanobots in the bottle of Gullfoss water he included.

When the customer first activated the app on the phone, it would take him to a Bitcoin exchange to deposit Håvard's fee. Once the fee was received it would send an activate code to the phone app and then it would activate the nanobots in the bottle of water. He sent this out overnight to the customer.

Now the second client wanted a way to kill a dictator in one of the South American counties. Even though the messaging between them was encrypted, he knew who this person was. It was the son of the dictator in question. This client was specific and wanted the victim to feel extreme pain.

Pain and torture weren't really very effective. At least, this is what Håvard thought. It wasn't really difficult to create this solution for his client, since he was repeating what he did with the nanobots he used at the Hynes Convention Center. He would need to tweak the nanobots a little and compile a suitable candidate to give to the client. Although, this would satisfy the client, Håvard didn't like this. It was effective but it wasn't efficient.

It was the 15th day since he created the mayhem at the Hynes Convention Center. He completed his work for his new clients and in 2 days he would have nearly 150 million USD in Bitcoin. As much as he loved crypto currency, he wanted to make sure all his eggs weren't in the same basket. He would spread this money around many different commodities with a nice mixture of dependable safe returns, moderate risk returns, and high risk returns on his money. Diversify was the word he was looking for in his mind.

These last few thoughts felt strange to him. Diversify? Torture? Charity? He asked himself, "where is this coming from? This isn't my usual way of doing things?"

As he was musing these thoughts, a gentle knock on the door. He turned and saw Edie opening the door.

She asked, "How are you feeling tonight? Bleu is making a nice salmon dish downstairs. If you want, I can bring you up some? Also, did everything I got for your computer and laptop work out OK?"

Håvard beamed, "Yes, it's better than OK. I'm very impressed with it. Thanks for doing this for me."

Edie smiled and then realized she was beaming about his compliment. She felt embarrassed a little.

"What about your equipment? Were you thinking of upgrading your PC or buying something else you have been wanting?" Håvard added.

This question seemed to surprise her a little. She started to say something and then shook her head no.

"I'll tell you what. Think about this tonight and then let me know. We will be collecting some money soon for the work at the Hynes. Were you and Bleu planning to sit down for dinner? If so, I will be down in a few minutes."

Edie was visibly excited. I think she let out another smile before her brain told her she was talking to someone. Quickly the smile disappeared and was replaced with a more normal expression of her face.

"I'll tell Bleu. She was hoping you would feel up to coming down to eat with us."

She turned and walked out of the room before Håvard could say anything else. This conversation with Edie was a little puzzling to him. He felt he was acting normally, but his mind was screaming at him. Something wasn't right. He just couldn't put his finger on what "**it**" was.

He turned back to his computer and sat there motionless for a minute thinking he needed to do something else. It was just agonizingly slow before he could make the decision to stop working for today.

Later that night, they all went out to the back of the house where a beautiful deck wrapped around a large part of the rear of the house. The deck had a large jacuzzi off of the swimming pool. Off to the side was a set of comfortable lounge chairs set in a semi-circle around a blue crystal firepit. It was a little cooler tonight, so they decided to sit around the firepit, and Bleu had brought out some authentic Icelandic Reyka vodka. They sat around the firepit, discussing the windfall of all the money coming, the others who were caught, and how they had pulled off a great plan and a great escape.

After a short while, Bleu and Edie decided to turn in and call it a night. Håvard said he would be in soon himself. He sat in the glow and warmth of the firepit for a while thinking about how his body was changing. He felt physically fine.

Something Lisa Harris, or her online username as Pickles, had said to him before her brother kicked him. There was something else about what she said which he just didn't understand. She mentioned, he was the one who was responsible for killing her sister, her mother and father, and for crippling her brother. The thing he couldn't piece together was about her brother being crippled and wheelchair bound. He was in the wheelchair and this makes sense if he was indeed crippled. So why was he able to stand up and kick him in the face and the groin? That doesn't seem like he is crippled! Why would she say these things?

Håvard thought back to the day she mentioned about him and the 7-Eleven store. His brain slowly started to remember that day so long ago. The other guy was trying to steal money from him by using the same gas pump. After Håvard started pumping the gas, he let if fill while he went into the men's room to change clothes. The other guy in the truck was using the same pump to fill his gas tank too.

This meant he was giving the guy a free tank of gas.

It all started to come back to him now. He used the restroom to change into the disguise that he needed to use to clear customs in Boston. He drove out of the 7-Eleven parking lot and nearly hit another car that he pulled out in front of. He also remembered that he had looked in the rear-view mirror and saw that the car had crashed into a ditch. This is probably what Lisa was referring to. Well he needed to get out of Boston fast and he also thought the person who was driving the car should have been more aware to see his car coming. They were at fault not me. Yes, this is something he cannot take responsibility for. No way!

It had been a long day and he was pleased with the progress he had made with selling his new toy to make a ton of money. No one was really looking for him right now. He was on the mend and he was looking forward to living his life with these nanobots. He would never die. He would never get sick. He literally had an eternity to do whatever it was he wanted to do.

On this final note for day, Håvard went inside and went to bed.

Chapter 21 – The Off Switch

"Having a beard is a good way to make your face more susceptible to Velcro."

- Demetri Martin

After the Hynes Convention

In the weeks after the episode at the Hynes Convention Center, it felt like things would start to go back to normal. Lisa decided to stay with Stanley and Ingrid for an extra week. It made sense, Stanley and Ingrid are getting married soon, so there was ample opportunity to help Ingrid with the planning and crossing things off of an endless list.

Austin and Lisa's relationship status took a definite right turn and started to head off into a more serious relationship. When they were back in the early days of getting sober, handling just normal living and normal life without substances was phenomenally challenging. A relationship was out of the question, back then.

Today it was very different. They shared a lot in common and they both made each other laugh.

Lisa made a trip back to LA to get some more of her gear and then come back to Boston in a month. On her flight back to LA, she started to think about the whole whirlwind of events happening in her life recently. She has been focused on this epic search for the person responsible for so many different events in her life. Her search for Håvard was now over. Technically it wasn't over because he escaped. However, one detail that seems to be missed by most, was the search for this girl. There was a good picture of her in the subway system. Both Austin and Lisa knew the picture was spoofed because it was the wrong subway servicing the Hynes Convention center. The picture of the girl wasn't altered, and it was a recent picture of her.

She had to come from somewhere. The somewhere is critically important because it was almost impossible to not leave a trail somewhere in a person's past or record interactions with other people.

Another thing which was absolutely surreal to her, was her brother, Stanley, is walking now. In fact, yesterday they went to a local park and they ran a mile together in one of the trails near it. Running! I don't think I will ever get over that. She smiled to herself.

As she got closer to LA, she started to put together a list of things she needed to take care of when she got back to her apartment. She needed to pay some bills. Some of her clients have been sending her some email with technical questions or new work they want her to help them with. She was glad she had stayed with her brother for an extra week.

She really didn't want to jump back into work now. She was thinking how great it would be to stay in Boston longer than just the one week. So, what is keeping her locked into LA?

The answer seemed so obvious. She was astounded she didn't realize this before. She doesn't need to be in LA. She was renting an apartment and she was paying a lot of money for it and it was tiny. She doesn't really have a huge social life. She mainly hung out with people like her who were trying to get through good times and bad times while trying to maintain their sobriety. They are good friends, but it doesn't mean she would lose them if she left LA. There is nothing to keep me in LA.

The only reason she came out to LA five years ago was because a couple of large companies she did consulting for were in the LA area. It made sense at the time. Now, not so much. Why can't she move back to Boston? She decided right then and there on the plane back to LA. She was going to start the process of packing up and relocating back to the Boston area.

When she got off the plane and arrived back at her apartment, she started to make a list of the items she would need to do, if she was serious about moving back. She went online and started searching for available places to live. Access to the city. Access to beaches. Access to Stanley and Ingrid. On and on she went and after several hours, she looked down at her to-do list of crossed out items she solved.

In a couple of hours, she found a couple of potential apartments with a good location to the city and decent rental price per month. Boston area is typically not cheap, but LA is much more expensive, and you get a lot less for your money. She set up several appointments with a few realtors to show her a couple of apartments when she returned to Boston next week. Her mind was made up at this point. She was going back to Boston.

Stanley and Ingrid

For Stanley and Ingrid, life started to come back to normal. Stanley's secret was now out. People now knew he could walk. A couple of days after the incident with Håvard, Stanley called his boss, Ed Bruinter. He wanted to talk to him before he went into the office on Monday.

It was very unusual to call his boss on the weekend. When Ed answered, he asked him if he could meet him somewhere and talk about an important fact of his work. He said he was at his son's soccer game and it was just finishing up. His wife was at the game also, so she would be able to take their son home when the game finished.

They decided to meet at a coffee shop. 45 minutes later, Stanley met Ed at a local coffee hangout. After they sat down with their drinks, Ed asked, "Stanley this is very unusual to call a meeting like this unless it is important news. I'm glad you called because my son's team were getting pummeled by the other six-year old's soccer team. So, what's up?"

Stanley knew how Ed worked with his staff. No BS just tell me the facts. Stanley said, "Ed you must have heard about a little incident which happened at the Hynes Convention Center earlier this week? There is a lot more information than what was told on the news. You need to know more of the details."

Stanley hesitated a half a second, but Ed prompted Stanley, "Stanley out with it. Good or bad we will figure it out."

Stanley shrugged his shoulders and said, "Ok but promise you won't freak out."

Stanley was in his wheelchair. He pushed back from the table and then stood up. Stanley was watching Ed's face going through a myriad of changes. Finally, he just said, "Holy Shit!!"

"Wow! Ok, *walk* over to counter and get me a straw. If you can do that I will be really impressed."

Stanley did as he was asked and then sat down in his wheelchair again.

"You weren't kidding last week when you were talking about changing the face of medicine. Ok, let's start at the beginning. How did this happen? I need all the details. I mean this is great but there are going to be a lot of questions. We have to make sure we get behind this. The presentation you made last week, was brilliant by the way. The board was very impressed. We need to be careful in how to respond to any questions of this incredible thing."

It took almost 2 hours, 2 coffees, and 2 bathroom breaks later, Ed's wife interrupted the discussion. She was calling him to ask if he would be home for dinner or would be getting something to eat outside. He said he would be home in a little bit.

"Stanley, it's going to take me a day or so to figure out what to do. Can you do me a favor? Both you and Ingrid shouldn't come into the office for a couple of days. I just want all of us to make sure this is communicated consistently. I'll talk to Ingrid's boss about having her taking a couple of days off. Don't worry, staying out of the office is just to let us coordinate communication on this. Both you and Ingrid aren't in trouble or anything. If anything, we are going to need the both of you more on this for the future steps.

I still can't believe you are walking?"

"Phew I'm glad you said this last part about staying on the job. I swear this was an accident. My fault is I didn't tell anyone sooner. The guy who organized the whole thing at the Hynes

Convention Center was a man named Håvard Evans. The NSA were actively looking for him. My sister Lisa has also been looking for this guy for the past ten years. It actually was a good thing Lisa and Ingrid were there at the convention center. Ingrid and another person she worked with are really the ones who actually corrected the problem Håvard caused."

Ed held up his hand to signal Stanley to stop and then said, "Stanley can you imagine what our world would be without some accidents in science? Those are the miracle breakthroughs! We wouldn't have Penicillin, TEFLON, Microwaves, plastic, Velcro, and so many more. It is a tragedy if we don't learn from our mistakes. Hey do it again, please? Walk over to the trash bin and toss my coffee cup out."

Ed was all smiles when Stanley returned to the table. Why does everyone want me to walk for them, Stanley mused.

Ed laughed and said, "I still can't believe this. Don't worry though. I'm 100% in your court on this. I'm going to go home and eat some dinner. I will call you in a day or two to let you know where we're going with this. I suspect this doesn't even really need for us to do anything. This will blow over and now we can learn how to split off the work into a couple of projects. I also appreciate being upfront with me on this. By the way, it was a good idea to bring Phil to the meeting with the board. I heard a couple of them tell me they liked him a lot."

5 months later

Stanley's boss Ed was true to his word. It turned out no one really knew anything about what happened at the convention center. Even though this lasted for several hours, no one remembered they were in a catatonic state of mind. It seems like everyone had turned the tape recorder in their brain to off. When everyone was released from this state of mind, there was a lot of confused people. How did they get to this place in Hynes Convention Center? No one really knew. Most people just thought they went down a wrong corridor or something.

The one really interesting piece of information was about the man who was on the stage and Håvard was having many of his veins and arteries all being removed and recreated *'while the plane was still flying'*, so to speak. The man had some serious heart issues. He had a triple bypass two years previously. This and any other surgeries he had on his heart were now gone. His heart and the arteries and veins going into and out of his heart were all rebuilt. The doctors checked him out thoroughly. Thankfully, they were working for, or under contract by the NSA, so no leaking of information would happen. He did have one issue of a vein in his left hand which needed a simple operation. The vein didn't attach to the corresponding vein in the hand. Surgeons were able to fix this quickly.

New Address - Boston

It took Lisa a total of 3 weeks to fully move back to Boston from LA. She was very glad she had made this decision. Her relationship with Austin felt right. It was different than a new relationship where it is all about discovering new things about the other person. Everything was new and unexplored yet.

This wasn't the case for Lisa and Austin. They knew each other for a long time. They had developed a very strong trust bond. Relationships as a general rule must have this. With a new relationship it is built from the ground up. Her relationship with Austin already contained a trust bonding. Hell, the first words she ever said to him was "You Asshole." It was at this point where Lisa needed someone else to help her get through the hell she was in those few days of detoxing. Austin also needed the same help.

When they both got through such an awful time, they had a new understanding of each other. It wasn't anyone or anything hurting you but your own body and mind! Not really sure when it actually happened, but the feeling of being hurt and kicked from inside your body feels a lot like *betrayal*. So, the overwhelming power of wanting to escape; to escape life; to escape pain; to escape responsibility; and to escape just living contained very little power to keep dominating your life. This is the place where Austin and Lisa had already built a strong bond of trust. Being in a relationship would help make it even stronger. It felt right.

Stanley and Ingrid are going to get married in a week. Lisa was so happy for Stanley and Ingrid. She really loved both of them, maybe even more than they knew. I'm Everything in her life seemed to be going so well. She tried looking for Håvard, but she really lost a lot of interest in doing anything further. Austin and the NSA kept a look out for him, but like he did on the Ashley Maddison hack, the trail was cold.

It kept nagging at her to follow through on the search for the other girl from the camera on the subway platform. She knew this would be a potential rip cord to open everything up. She was positive it would generate new leads to find him, but she really lost the drive for this. Let sleeping dogs lie.

Andy Kauffman

In the last 5 months, Andy Kauffman has been a very busy man. He knew when he performed the patch up job on the guy in Brookline, there was a lot more to this than just making him travel-ready. He was very glad he had taken the three vials of blood from the man. Andy didn't understand how these nanobots were being created but he knew this was an absolute miracle technology.

Several years ago, Andy setup a private lab for himself. He did this so he would work atomically and do any research he wanted. He could spend as much time as he wanted. It was pricey so he still had to make a living. Once in a while, an opportunity to perform a procedure to repair or patch up a wound on someone would come to him. These types of procedures required no questions and no authorities to be alerted. His discretion obviously would come at an expensive price. The businessmen he dealt with did not care about that so much.

Businessmen or not, if they paid well then, he was happy to do it.

Most of those procedures were very simple for him, he could do it in his sleep or even blind drunk. One surgery he performed, he was actually quite drunk from drinking Russian Vodka with a "not so nice" Russian businessmen. Everything was a complete success and they paid him very well.

He got another colleague of his, Dr. Bruce Atwood, to help research this new discovery Andy found in those vials of blood. Bruce was equally as brilliant a researcher as he was a surgeon. They both knew they would need to replicate these nanobots. If they could find a way to do this, they would be able to cure so many diseases and *really* change the face of medicine. They were able to cause the nanobots to generate the *stem* cells, but they had to force them to go through the cell mitosis, or cell replication. Normal cell mitosis would start as one cell and then it would split in half to become two cells, the two cells become four cells and on and on.

They had everything which Håvard started with. They could duplicate the blood samples but the one thing they were missing was the cell phone and all the modules Håvard worked on and changed. So, under the covers, the 3D Printer Factory's and the 3D printers stayed *on* and just kept reproducing and making more and more cells in the body. Håvard's phone would also tell the nanobots to make 3D Printer Factories and 3D Printers which were specifically made to print out *stem* **stop** cells. Once the signal was sent, then all the nanobots would deactivate and be released from the body naturally.

Neither of the two surgeons knew anything about the cell phones to turn them on or to turn them off. The only thing driving them in this research was to replicate the amazing things they were seeing happening in the lab animals. The monkey and the rats and mice were literally growing a new limb if one of the limbs was amputated. They were seeing mice or other test animals with different types cancer, being cured overnight. They didn't realize it then, but if they had tested this further, they would have seen one incredible error. The nanobots never stopped making 3D Printer and *stem* cells. They never turned off.

Andy and Bruce had reached a pivotal point in their research, so they decided to stop for a week. Bruce had several outside commitments he needed to honor so he would be away for a week. Andy told Bruce this was a good idea since they had been working incredibly long hours researching. A week break would give them more energy to hit it fresh if they stopped for a little bit. It was a well-deserved break and also a change to both clear their heads.

Bruce wanted a break and he also wanted to make sure he could squirrel away several vials of their replicated nanobots. He didn't tell Andy anything about this because he wanted to have his own private stash of their research. Bruce was certain Andy was doing exactly the same type of thing. Bruce's daughter was getting married in Iceland, so he really did need to leave for a week to attend to that. He had no choice since he was the one paying for all the costs of wedding ceremony.

Andy has no intention whatsoever to stop. He made some plans to accelerate this miracle discovery. Andy planned to dive even deeper into different ways he could sell this. Where does he start? Big Pharma? Big Tech? Big Biomed – **no!** Absolutely not that route. He would be found out in a second if he was connected to this.

He invited a woman to dinner that he knew was in charge of one of the bigger venture capital companies in the Boston area. At one point they had a thing going on many years ago, but it ended up being a parasitic relationship. She wanted what she wanted from him physically and he wanted the exact same from her. It was mutually agreed to be just an on-off type of thing.

They did stay in touch, however. Sometimes she would call him to ask his opinion on some new technology, or a new pharmaceutical. One that was being looked at seriously. She also knew he had few scruples and didn't mind crossing the line once or twice. She introduced him to a couple of Russian businessmen who required his medical expertise and also most importantly, his discreteness. He told her about his new discovery, and they discussed some possible options to make a lot of money. She said she had someone in mind, and she would contact him.

Unfortunately, he wasn't prepared to have a visitor come to his home the next day at 6 AM. It was a person who his friend was connected with. He knew this man as Valentin. He worked for him once and it had not been a successful procedure. Several years ago, he desperately needed him to deliver a baby from his girlfriend, but she was shot. The reason she was shot was because his current wife didn't know about the girlfriend or even about the baby.

The girlfriend recovered, but the baby didn't. In some way this person, Valentin, felt Andy owed him something. Every six months or so one of his men or even sometimes it would be Valentin himself, would come by and demand money. It wasn't unusual for Andy to have several thousand dollars in his safe in his bedroom. He also kept stored in this safe several very special Russian vodka nips. Valentin demanded two things, $2000 and two samples of the stuff he told his venture capital friend about.

It always annoyed him when this guy would come over like this. Valentin would insist he follow him into his bedroom to wait for him to get the money from his safe. The one in his bedroom was his *'safe'* safe. It usually contained around $2000 and he also put in six Russian vodka nips injected with the nanobots inside the safe.

When he opened the safe in front of Valentin, he saw the money and he also saw several of the little vodka nips. There were six of them. Valentin wanted all of them.

Andy was smart though. He actually had two safes. One for the possibility of anyone trying to rob him would only get about $2000 or maybe $3000 tops in this safe. He kept the big money and the big investments in another safe. He has been siphoning away many different drinks which contained the new nanobots and putting all of those in his other hidden safe.

He told Valentin only a few milliliters contained plenty of nanobots. Each bottle was approximately 50 milliliters, so he really didn't need the six, all he needed was one.

Valentin didn't like this answer. He punched Andy in the face, grabbed the 6 vodka bottles and all the money ($2300) and left Andy on the floor of his bedroom.

Andy smiled even though it hurt to do so. He had plenty more. This also told him his friend in the venture capital firm was in deep debt to them. He wouldn't be calling her again. He got up off the floor and flopped on his bed planning to go back to sleep.

It felt like an eureka moment. His face hurt like hell. Why not use some of pesky little nanobots to help him heal his face? In ten minutes, he was sitting in his kitchen with a hot cup of coffee and he injected 40 milliliters into his coffee and drank it down. It didn't real have any type of taste so mixing it with coffee didn't seem too bad. Once he was finished, he went upstairs and plopped on his bed again and this time he did go back to sleep.

Chapter 22 – The Mulligan

I'm not a schmuck. Even if the world goes to hell in a handbasket, I won't lose a penny.

- Donald Trump

In the months following his escape from Boston, Håvard still had to worry about the 4 people who were involved in his crime and were being incarcerated. He created a special cocktail for Homer, Hydro, and Batman, who worked with him and knew a lot of details about him. He could not allow them to continue being held by the FBI. Eventually, he figured, they would crack and tell a detail which might allow them to come after him.

He was successful in terminating them in their sleep after they were given a bottle of Gullfoss water with loads of nanobots. It wasn't too hard to bribe a prison guard to smuggle the water bottle into the prison cells of the 3 people they were supposed to give them to. Of course, the guards were curious and tasted the water first to make sure it wasn't some drug or other thing. The saying *curiosity killed the cat* was never truer at that moment.

Unfortunately, this also had a huge side effect on the world outside the prisons. Cell mates of the inmates who died used the Gullfoss water which was left to use for prison wine. The cities and towns around the prisons were slowly starting to die. Many of these were categorized under 3 different types of death. Aneurism in the brain, heart stoppage, and total and complete removal of veins and arteries in sections of the deceased bodies. The last death was suspicious.

It rose up to different levels in government. The CDC, FBI, and the NSA were called to comment on any cases which might be familiar causes of death. The NSA was the only one organization who recognized the death in a similar case and responded to the inquiry. This was a similar to a case involving a man in Boston, who was tortured by Håvard Evans.

Austin heard about this and he was brought into a meeting with a couple of people representing various departments in the government. Their suspicion was very high of an attack would be sent to Austin in some type of innocuous way. Not very different from someone sending a mail package with Anthrax powder. Everything that came into contact with Austin or was sent to him was checked.

It didn't take too long, but eventually he received a coupon for a free bottle of water at one of the vendors in the area of the NSA campus. Austin went and used the coupon to get the bottle of water and gave this to the task force. They found billions of nanobots in an activated state waiting to act on its biological host. The vendor said he was sent a case of 150 of these water bottles to help his sales. Someone mysteriously sent out 50 coupons to various government offices. The vendor didn't know anything about it. All he knew is he had more people coming to him for this water looking to buy it or use a coupon to get the bottle of water. His traffic of customers was higher every day for this promotion. The water bottles were Gullfoss Water from Iceland. He gave out almost 50 just this week alone and probably 100 bottles in total.

Global Pandemic

Around the world, people started to die very suspiciously. Some were deaths of a total heart stoppage, and others were brain aneurysms in their sleep. Both of these were hard to finger and find a commonality. The veins and arteries rebuilding themselves was starting to pop up in several different areas of the world. Boston and the entire northeast of the United States contained people who were infected, and it was killing hundreds of people daily. Europe had a large cell breakout in the areas around London. Iceland also popped up as a large concentration. In two months, this *sleeping death*, as it was called, had killed almost 50 million people. Several countries were hit the hardest. USA, Iceland, Russia, and China were the largest ones hit with this *sleeping death*.

Most countries all contained similar causes of death. Iceland was singled out as one which had an additional type of death cause, an overproduction of *stem* cells. It was incredibly difficult to detect whether a person had this happening in their system or not. The over production of these cells continued until the body couldn't assimilate or eliminate these cells. It seemed as if the body worked its way to death.

All the organizations looking into were the World Health Organization (WHO). United States Department of Health and Human Services (HHS), Centers for Disease Control and Prevention (CDC), NATO, and several more were starting to mobilize different task forces to look for a way to solve this emergency health crisis.

10 Months after the Hynes Convention Center

Håvard was sitting on the back porch of his new house overlooking a stunning horizon with every color imaginable. The house he was in was large but not so large as to attract unwanted attention.

His life has significantly changed since he was able to create some customized packages for several powerful and incredibly rich clients who would pay him anything he wanted. He was smart about it so his price was an expensive one, but he didn't want it to be something his clients would feel buyer's remorse over. He learned this the hard way.

In a commercialist society, trust and honor, got lost among the lust for more. The best course is always to honor a commitment. Even if the honor is from a person who is in the business of killing people or helping them to cure or extend their life. If he agreed to a contract to produce a cocktail of nanobots, his loyalty was always to the first contract. He would not double cross the buyer even if it meant he was offered more money than the first contract. If he agreed to the first contract, then he wouldn't break that bond. This was one rule he would not break, ever.

One month after the DEF-CON 2020 conference, they were ready to fly back home to Iceland. Håvard was driving and Edie was in the front seat and Bleu was sitting in the backseat. On the way to Boston's Logan Airport, Håvard drove by the 7-Eleven where Lisa said he had caused their car to crash. It was on the way to the airport, sort of. He stopped at the 7-Eleven to get some gas. He was only there for a few minutes, but it seemed as if Edie was really disturbed by being here. She stayed this way for the whole time they were on the plane heading back to Iceland.

He didn't understand why she was so disturbed. He asked her if he had done anything wrong. He looked to Bleu for help, but she wouldn't give him any help. Everything had been going so well. He didn't understand why she was so upset. When they arrived in Iceland, Håvard got in his car to go back home to Kópavogur. Both Bleu and Edie lived on the eastern side of Reykjavik, near a town called Lágafell.

They planned to get together later in the week for dinner. It was a nice time of year before their long winter would be upon all of Iceland. Plans to meet in the following week didn't happen. It wasn't until, three weeks after they were back to Iceland, he received a message from Edie. The message was cryptic and was sent via an old school form of encryption. The message was easy to decrypt, and it was very terse. She asked if Håvard could meet her in Reykjavik at a busy coffee shop and a popular hangout. He agreed to meet her the next day at 11:00 AM.

Edie

When he walked into the noisy and busy coffee shop the next day, he spotted her in the corner sipping a cup of hot chocolate. After they greeted each other with a hug, they sat down to talk. He knew Edie needed to work up to telling him something was on her mind. Surprisingly, she was very direct and didn't really need any prompting. She looked at him in the eyes and asked, "Håvard do you know who my mother was?"

Wow! Where is this coming from and where is it going, Håvard thought quickly. He thought about it a half a second and then said, "No. I don't think I ever met your mother. Why?"

In a very measured voice, "No, not yet. One more question. The 7-Eleven store we stopped at on the way to the airport in Boston. Did you recognize the area near this store?"

Håvard started to get a little nervous about where these questions are going. "Edie, this is sounding like you are setting me up. No, I won't answer your last question until you tell me where this is going."

"OK, have it your way then. I am done with this and done with you!" Edie got up from the table and was about to leave before Håvard asked her to stop and to sit down again. Reluctantly she did sit down again.

She drew a deep breath and said, "Håvard when I was seven, I was given up for adoption.

My mother got sick and she died from pneumonia. I grew up near the area by the 7-Eleven store. I had friends and my school, and everything changed almost overnight. The woman who adopted me was related to my mother in some way and I was carted off to Iceland to live with her. My adopted mother was not really a good parent. She was callous and vain. Everything about me growing up and the unbelievable changes we have to go through in our teen age years were bothersome to her. For whatever reason she adopted me for, after a while she got tired of it and left me alone to sink or swim."

Once more she leveled a question to him like she was a sniper looking through her scope for the target. She paused and pressed the trigger to shoot the question to Håvard, "So once again I am going to ask you, who was my mother?"

"Edie, I'm sorry but I really *do not* know who your mother was. The 7-Eleven store was something that happened a long time ago. I went to Boston to do a particular hack for a company. On my way back to the airport, I stopped at the 7-Eleven and I got into a fight with one of the other people at the gas pump. The girl, Lisa, at the DEF-CON conference, she said I crippled her brother. The bloke stood up and kicked me in the face. You saw him do this to me. She was lying."

"Did you know a woman named Izzie who lived in Boston?"

He thought for a second and it did sound a little familiar. He said, "It was a long time ago, but I think I remember someone by that name. I met her about 2 years **after** the episode at the 7-Eleven. She didn't mention anything to me about her having a baby. Wait... No, that isn't possible."

"Håvard, whether you want to admit it or not, you are my father. You met my mother **before** the confrontation with the man at 7-Eleven. It was not **after**."

Håvard didn't dare interrupt her. His mind was buzzing like crazy to remember details from a long time ago.

She continued, "You left me all alone for all those years. I really needed some adult figure or anyone to help me during those years growing up. Did you even know? Did you even care?"

"I found out who you were a few years ago when the horrid woman tossed me out on my ass about 60 minutes after I turned 17. I used computers to survive by hacking banks or corporations. I became very good at it too. When this woman who dragged me to Iceland died about two years ago, she told me something on her deathbed. She told me she was going to leave me with nothing except a name, Håvard Evans. She also told me you knew from the beginning Izzie was pregnant, and you did nothing," Edie finished with a sad and tortured voice.

Edie just got up and left Håvard their speechless. He never saw her again. She died six months later when her body died from overproducing *stem* cells and overwhelmed her body. He wouldn't have known about this until he got a message from Bleu. It was a video message which he thought was unusual. She

spoke strictly in Icelandic tongue. She looked
horrible. Bloodshot eyes, stringy hair, whatever
blue that was in her hair was gone, not bathed
in a while, and definitely not slept. Her voice
was ragged and sounded so tired.

Her message was:

*Håvard ef þú ert að fá þetta þá er ég
líklegast dauður. Þetta er Sjálfvirk
boð sem verða send ef ég dey. '
Nanobots ' eru að drepa allt fólkið í
heiminum. Allir sem ég þekki eða
hvaða fjölskyldu ég hef er dauður
núna vegna þess að þú klúðraði
mannslíkamanum. Edie lést í apríl
sem er sjö mánuðum á eftir DEF-
CONráðstefnunni. Hefur þú komið til
Reykjavíkur Nýlega? Bærinn er að
deyja. Götur sem hlaðnar voru með
ferðamönnum og íbúar eru allir tómir
núna. Íbúafjöldi í heimalandi okkar
er helmingur af því sem það var áður
á ráðstefnunni í Bandaríkjunum.
Landið okkar og landsmenn okkar
eru að deyja. Ef þér er annt nokkuð*

um Ísland og fólkið þitt, gerðu þá eitthvað til að stoppa þetta. Annars muntu deyja einn í þessum heimi.

Translated into English:

Håvard If you're getting this, I'm most likely dead. This is an automated message that will be sent if I die. The 'Nanobots' are killing all the people in the world. Everyone I know or what family I have is dead now because you messed up the human body. Edie died in April which is seven months after the DEF Con conference. Have you come to Reykjavik recently? The town is dying. Streets loaded with tourists and residents are all empty now. The population of our homeland is half of what it was before the conference in the United States. Our country and our countrymen are dying. If you are concerned somewhat about Iceland and your people, then do something to stop this. Otherwise you will die alone in this world.

For the first time in Håvard's life, he felt an overwhelming horror. It was unmistakable from what Bleu said, there was no one else to blame. Except himself. He caused this. He wanted to live forever. He wanted to always be healthy and not die because of a frailty or something trivial like a car accident. He insisted every day for absolute control of his life and his actions. For the first time in his life, he didn't know what to do.

At first his mind has been so conditioned to find fault in others or seize upon a frailty it started to put up a struggle saying to himself it was all not true. He couldn't possibly be responsible for this. Every argument his mind could think of, was quickly squashed as not true. He killed a girl who was his daughter and he didn't know it. He knew people were dying but he was aloof from the mundane world issues and problems.

And why not? He lived comfortably, he could go anywhere or do just about anything he wanted to do. He also relied on no one. Why shouldn't he be entitled to this? Silently in his mind he heard the lone thought repeating over and over, you don't control life or death!

For the next six torturous days. He had a battle raging inside of him. He was starting to get close to the borders of insanity. Every single time, he thought he could justify his actions, they all fell silently on the ground like a toppled house of cards.

At the end of these long and agonizing days, he finally knew what he needed to do.

Chapter 23 - Forgiveness

"End? No, the journey doesn't end here. Death is just another path, one that we all must take. The grey rain-curtain of this world rolls back, and all turns to silver glass, and then you see it."

—J.R.R. Tolkien, The Return of the King

Delayed in Reykjavik

Håvard was able to get a flight to Canada, but it was constantly being delayed. Almost 24 hours later he got off the large Boeing 757. There was a total of 17 passengers on the plane which could easily handle 210 additional passengers. He was flying to Montreal and then getting on a different plane from Montreal to fly to Rhode Island. From Rhode Island he would drive to Boston and check into the Boston Harbour Hotel. This is a good location for him to get anywhere in the area pretty quickly.

He was still concerned about going through customs, especially in Boston. He has several impeccable ID's with the various disguises he uses. It can sometimes be a real pain to accomplish this change, but no one has ever questioned him even once He has been using these disguises and ID's for the last twenty years, so he must be doing something right.

He felt awful leaving Iceland. Bleu was correct. The streets of Reykjavik were nearly deserted. His aircraft delays were the result of just not enough people on the plane. The same was true in Montreal. Luckily, his flight left on time. But Rhode Island airport and the highways driving into and out of the city were nearly deserted. No one was traveling. He saw about 40 or 50 cars on the highway with him. Usually, at least how he remembered his many trips to this area, it was always several hundred cars on the road.

The entire trip from Iceland to the USA was a constant battle of endless condescension and contempt for his life and the actions he has committed. He came here for a purpose so now he needed to not procrastinate and just get this over with.

He spent a large part of the night doing a lot of research for all the information he would need to accomplish his task. Tomorrow was going to be a long day. It was now Wednesday, hopefully if everything goes correctly, he will finish this by Saturday.

Thursday - Lindsey

The next morning, he got up early and walked around the city. He forgot how robust and exciting the city of Boston was. Like anywhere else cities have their own peculiarities or ways they treat people. It was nice day out, so he took his time to enjoy the city and its people. Few people were outside today. There just were not enough people to go outside to have it be a noticeable thing.

Eventually, he went to Mass-General Hospital. He left a text message for his friend asking her to meet him. She confirmed shortly after he sent it to her. They agreed to meet at 4 PM at the local bar where he had originally met her. Boy, it was so long ago. At least, 25 years in total.

They have kept in touch at various times. He has asked her in the past to help sometimes, with one of his projects. She was the person who recommended the surgeon, Andy Kauffman and the two nurses. She also arranged for the funeral ambulance which brought him to the house in Brookline to recover.

That isn't to say he hasn't helped her in the past too. She wanted me to dig into the personal life of someone in her way for an executive position. She desperately wanted to advance her career at one of the large Medical Insurance Companies. Håvard brought things to light which were supposed to be private but were now put out in a public way. Any indiscretions her rival had done in the past, were now public.

Her competitor got attacked and was vilified; so, her competition for the job disappeared and she was able to get the position easily.

Håvard now needed her for an even more sinister job using her medical help. They met and had a nice time having dinner and some light wine. They laughed about things in the past and she also discussed the somber subject of the *sleeping death* which was raging around the world. She gave him some even more unsettling news about the amount of people who were dying everywhere. The doctors couldn't understand why this was happening. It was very difficult to diagnose. People around the world would fear and dread waking up each morning, or to be more exact fear not waking up each morning.

One good thing came out of all the sickness. It was happening globally. A new ritual started to happen every morning all around the world. People were waking up each morning and just celebrating life. They were alive. Their family was alive. This wasn't just a curt nod to the heavens it was a party. A real-life party with balloons and confetti and sometimes presents for different family or friends. The presents were just small tokens, nothing like a Christmas or Hanukkah. Maybe it was a child drawing a picture the night before and giving it to his parents the next morning. Or a sweet candy for a child. Viral videos of this were sweeping the world.

The videos were amazingly funny sometimes, children and animals so innocent also joined the celebrations. It was hard not to share in their joy. Hard to imagine 7.8 billion people were truly, honestly, and profoundly happy they were alive. But it was true and real.

Sometimes the morning celebrations were woefully sad. They would wake up and not all of their family would make it through the night. Even death of loved ones, friends, or neighbors were a call to our humanity as a whole. To be compassionate; to be empathetic; to understand; to be caring, in all those times.

For Håvard to watch these celebrations was troubling, but he saw the videos she pulled up on her phone. Now he needed to come to the heart of the reason why he called her and needed her help.

"Lindsey, I called you today because I have a situation that I need your help with. I would need you to help me on Saturday if you have the time available. Do you have any time on Saturday?"

"Saturday, I am going out with some friends on Saturday night, so I can be available most of the day on Saturday. So, what did you have in mind for this help?"

Håvard said nonchalantly, "Lindsey, you and I go way back but this is a very delicate matter. I trust you totally. This thing is something personal to me and it has to be done by someone I can trust. I promise to you this isn't illegal. You will not have any type of blowback on you. I will pay you a ridiculous amount of money and I might even throw in a deed to some land I own. Do you think this could be something you would be able to do?"

Lindsey face didn't change one bit to give him a clue as to what she might be thinking. She was a very good poker player. She responded, "First of all, of course I will help you. We have a long history together. You haven't told me yet what it is you want me to do? Is it maybe a gunshot wound or something worse? You are kind of scaring me. I can't commit to something I don't know about or can be prepared for."

Håvard expected this response. Originally, he thought about just going to any doctor and pay his way to accomplish what he needed to. However, he did trust Lindsey more than anyone.

"I know this is a lot to take in with almost no details. Lindsey I won't hurt you or put you in an impossible position. You will understand this all on Saturday, I promise. Please bring your medical bag and pack it with stuff you might need for a suture, drawing of blood, or some minimal investigatory work."

Reluctantly, Lindsey said, "Ok I will bring my field bag of medical goodies. So, how much land are we talking about? And how ridiculous an amount of money are we talking here?"

They laughed and kissed a little like they did so long ago. She wanted to go back with him to the hotel, but he politely said tonight wasn't good but definitely after this Saturday. He smiled and winked at her. She wasn't too put off from his rejection. They never really had exactly the right chemistry for a relationship. She liked and enjoyed him as a faraway foreign friend.

Håvard took a cab back to his hotel. Tomorrow, he needed to go to the bank. The morning was going to be busy but hopefully he would be done around midday.

Saturday 7:30 AM

A large navy-blue Lincoln SUV pulled into the driveway of Stanley's Harris's house. The driver got out of the car and went to the front door and rang the doorbell. The driver talked to the woman who answered the door. She listened and nodded her head a few minutes after the driver explained he was only here to pick her and her husband up for a celebratory party of a close friend of theirs.

The driver went back to the SUV and waited about 20 minutes before Stanley and Ingrid came outside and got into the SUV. They had no idea where they were going.

Stanley asked the driver, "I'm sorry but what is your name again? You said this was being arranged by a close friend, do you know who?"

The driver replied as politely as possible, "I'm sorry sir. I was only given the instructions to pick you both up and to also pick up one other couple. I was then told to drive all of you to the waterfront area of the city for a morning party. This is all the information I was given."

Ingrid and Stanley looked at each other and neither of them knew what to say other than ok. The next stop was to a familiar house. They both recognized it as the house Lisa and Austin were renting. Lisa answered the door and when she saw Stanley and Ingrid she agreed to go for the ride. Austin was out this morning for an early morning meeting that he had at the field office in Boston.

The driver was told to pick up 4 people and to bring them to the waterfront. Lisa said she would call Austin and have him meet them there. The driver was satisfied with that. The mystery of this early morning trip was kind of exciting. In the last year there had been so much death, the morning parties were always a nice start to a day. This morning party was at a level unheard of. The morning parties were usually personal and with loved ones. There was a lot of love in the back of the SUV, so it does kind of made a little sense.

Lisa's cell phone chirped, and she got a text message from Austin. He would meet them at the waterfront at Rowes Wharf. She told the driver this and he then sent a message to whoever it was who organized this party or whoever was the next person to guide them through this *clockwork orange*.

Ten minutes later, they met Austin out in front of the Boston Harbor Hotel at Rowes

Wharf. The driver directed them to the back of the hotel where there was some tables and chairs for people to sit and enjoy some coffee, or enjoy the waterfront. The driver left them and said a blond-haired man, named Albert would be with them in just a minute. Stanley just looked at everyone rather stunned. None of them knew what was going to happen. Lisa and Austin felt apprehensive about who the person showing up would be. Is this some form of a reincarnation of Håvard?

As the driver said, a blond-haired man in his mid-forties approached them. He was a little overweight, but he had a thick Australian drawl. He said his name was Albert, but everyone called him 'Lefty'. He was older and looked a little frail, but an immediate physical risk wasn't apparent. He directed them to a very expensive and elaborate looking yacht tied up to one of the docks. When they boarded, there was another woman on the yacht. It seemed as if she was waiting for them. Neither Stanley nor anyone else recognized her. She was polite and professional, and introduced herself as Lindsey.

After some introductions went around 'Lefty' or Albert said it was time to depart. Stanley stepped in front of him, blocking his way to the back of the boat.

Stanley irritated now, peevishly said "I'm not going anywhere until you tell us where we are going."

Austin also stood up and said the same thing.

Lefty trying to calm everyone down saying, "We are going across the Harbor to Georges Island. I was told to bring you all there for a special event. The person who organized this elaborate plan with the driver to pick you up, and the yacht, told me only to get everyone to Georges Island. That is all I know. The only way to get to the island is by water. If you open the cabinet there down below, you'll find some champagne, a few cans of cold soft drinks, and some cheese and cracker to nibble on if you want.

Stanley looked at Austin, not really sure what the next move would be. Austin was also thinking the same thing.

Austin turned to everyone and said, "Don't touch anything. If there is something wrong with the champagne or the cheese and crackers are laced with anything. Don't touch anything."

Lindsey looked at Austin and said, "Oops I have already had one glass so far and also several pieces of cheese and crackers."

She looked at Lefty and said, "Did you do anything to the Champagne or the cheese and crackers?"

Lefty put on a look of sincere honesty and said, "I swear to you on my daughter's soul, I have done nothing to anything being served. Would it ease your mind if I have some Champagne or some cheese and crackers?"

Austin immediately said, "Yes it would. If in 10 seconds you don't drink some champagne and eat some crackers or cheese, then we are going to get off this ride right now."

Stanley looked at Lisa and her body language said, "Yeah honey you go!"

"I'll do anything you want me to do. I swear I didn't tamper with it. Look," and he grabbed a class and filled it with champagne and gobbled up some crackers and cheese.

Stanley asked, "Why is this on Georges Island? I mean it's a nice park and is the location of the 19th century Fort Warren. From history it's interesting but it's just a tourist attraction now. I don't see the connection to all of us. I haven't been there since I was a kid. Lisa, do you remember when we went there once with Mom, Dad, and Maureen? You were so seasick that day."

"Yes, I do remember it. It was a fun day, even though I was puking over the side of the boat almost the whole time. I can't drink champagne, so I pass anyways."

Austin, Stanley, and Ingrid all passed on champagne and cheese and crackers.

Lefty went to the back of the yacht, turned the motor on and gradually pulled away from the dock. Slowly, they entered into the Inner Harbor section of Boston Harbour. They saw Georges Island in front of the yacht as they steadily made their way across the Boston Harbor.

Lefty said they would be there in about 10 minutes. He heard a beeping below deck and asked everyone to hold their questions for one minute. He would be back shortly.

Stanley looked at Austin, and said, "I really don't get this. What the hell is this all about? Then to Lindsey, "Are you sure you know nothing of this? We are here so if you're trying to get our attention, well guess what? You did!"

Ingrid sensed the irritation in Stanley's voice, and he was close to exploding. Stanley took a deep breath and tried to slow down and not let his frustration get away from him.

A person came up from below deck from where Lefty had departed. The person walking up the stairs wasn't Lefty. It was Håvard without the disguise he used to become Lefty.

Everyone's mouth just dropped to the floor. Håvard looked at Lisa and said, "Please don't spit on me again. All I ask you is to please give me 5 minutes to explain this and everything else."

Austin exploded and grabbed Håvard's arm. Håvard's arm was like a cement pole. Håvard looked like his body wasn't too strong, but his arm was unmovable by Austin. Håvard gently pushed him away.

"Please I beg you. Please hear me out. This is an incredibly important moment to you all and it is incredibly important to the world. I am very, very, serious. Our decisions here today are happening in the gravest of circumstances. The stakes are that high. This meeting today has a global implication to it. Our species is at a breaking point at this moment. We are soon going to be extinct if the sleeping death isn't corrected and reversed. I'm not using words callously saying the implications are of the global kind. Please 5 minutes."

From the side of the boat, Lindsey said, "Håvard you had me fooled. I didn't even realize it was you, honey," and she laughed.

"Håvard you have already caused me and my family so much pain. You can't do anything more to hurt me," Lisa growled.

Stanley stood up and faced everyone, "Lisa's right he can't do anything to hurt us. The damage is done. I am willing to hear him out for 5 minutes."

Everyone eventually agreed to this. Håvard stood up and addressed Stanley and Lisa specifically. "I have committed many crimes in my life. One crime is nothing compared to the crime of the power of life and death. Lisa and Stanley, what I am going to say to you may be hurtful, but I must. If you all agree I will start. There are a lot of details that must be explained. I will stop and let you ask questions if you have any at any point. OK?"

A deep breath and then Håvard said, "25 years ago I came to Boston to do a hack job on a company that my client was competing with.

Lisa and Stanley, it was my car which jumped out of the 7-Eleven on the day of the car accident. I was the cause of it. I know this accident took everything from you both in a split second. The accident I caused took your mother Maria, your father Julio, and your sister Maureen. I have nothing I can say or do that will change this."

Lisa was about to say something but as Håvard suspected, bringing up this sad memory put her close to the edge of her feelings. He very gently looked into Lisa's eyes saying, "Lisa, I'm responsible for this, and there is no doubt about it."

He paused for a second. Lisa's head was down looking at her lap. She lifted her head up and nodded her approval to continue.

"This was my first trip to Boston, and I met a woman on this trip. She got pregnant and had a baby. I never knew she was pregnant. Ironically, this baby, my daughter, moved to Iceland after her mother died when she was 7. She was adopted by a woman in Iceland and she grew up in a town only 20 minutes from me. She grew up there and I didn't even know it. She was also part of the nanobots hacking at the DEF-CON conference. Austin you would have known her as Edie. Edie died 4 months ago. It was from the *sleeping death*."

Håvard grabbed a can of Ginger-Ale from the cabinet where the champagne was chilling on ice. "God, this American Ginger-Ale is such shit. Ick ok, sorry. Do you want me to continue? There's still a lot more to tell you, but if you have questions, I'll answer them."

"No, everything you have said is all stuff I know. Well not about your daughter. You admit you killed my mother, my father, and my sister. Lisa has been doing all the hard work tracking you. You aren't saying anything new to me. So, no I have nothing to ask," Stanley said a little irritated.

He looked at everyone and resumed his story, "Austin, this next part is for you. You totally fooled me with the *Z3bra-m9er* online personality. There were seven people involved in the DEF-CON hack. Homer, Batman, and Hydro. As I understand it, this is when things started to go a little off the rails. They died in their prison cells. I was afraid of them saying anything or giving details that would lead back to me. I was the one who orchestrated having them drink GullFoss water loaded with nanobots. Somehow, and this what I'm not sure of, is how the nanobots got out of the prison. I think it is probably that someone else drank from the water bottles I sent to them. Maybe one of the guards, I'm not sure. If they did then they were also infected.

Austin, you never did get the bottle of water I tried to get to you. Right? The NSA intervened? Never mind. Now, the fact you're in the NSA and a part of a global system of resources, will help."

Another sip of soda as they were all waiting for him to continue.

"Ok, now Austin you were one of the seven who successfully made it back from the conference. You weren't hurt. The only people left from the job were Bleu and Edie. As I said earlier, Edie died of the *sleeping death*. Her body was overwhelmed with nanobots hyper creating *stem* cells. Bleu also died from the *sleeping death*. Over 150,000 people are dead in Iceland now. This is about half of the total population of Iceland and 99% of them died from the *sleeping death*. How many people worldwide have died, 50 million? It doesn't really matter of an exact number but it does matter that everyone will die in the end."

Håvard paused and Ingrid asked, "So the sleeping death is from your modified nanobots? If this is true, then mass murder doesn't even begin to describe this. Those nanobots won't shut off. Believe me, we have tried thousands of tests to change this and turn them off. All of those tests failed. I made those nanobots and you turned them against humanity! That makes you one of the evilest people to ever live in my book."

Now Lindsey who has been listening quietly asked, "Håvard, why did you bring me in here today?"

Håvard looked at Lindsey and said, "I'm getting closer to the answer to your question. Give me just a minute more of your attention. Ingrid you are correct about being a mass murderer but not really 100% percent evil. Here is where you can start to see where I am going with this."

He looked around and was still holding their attention and said, "Ingrid I am very selfish, not evil. I tried to take on a power that should never be done unless there is more thought about the prevention of altering a simple law of nature. Everyone is born and eventually everyone will die. In my case, I have tampered with the nanobots so I will never ever die! I will be the last person on the earth at the end of time. I will not die, **ever**. Now this is where I am trying to get to. Lisa let me ask you one question. Don't look at anyone else, just look at me. If you possessed a way to kill me, a gun, a button, or whatever you desire, you could kill me, and it would be intentional, would you do this if I gave you a way to do it? Even after all the torment and pain I have caused you personally, would you do this?"

"Håvard, the decision over your life or anyone else's, isn't mine to make. The only life I can choose to not kill is myself. This is an absolute and it doesn't matter how I look at it. I don't have the right to decide life or death."

Håvard now turned to Stanley and asked, "Stanley, I have the same question for you. I know you were trapped in a wheelchair because of the car accident, but I am guessing the nanobots have changed this?"

Stanley's face took on a calmness and introspective look and said, "Yes the nanobots did help this, it wasn't intentional. Now, if I had a chance to kill you right now, here? My answer would be the same as Lisa. I won't make the choice of life or death. I can only make a choice for my own life."

Austin, Ingrid, and Lindsey said it would probably be the same choice for them as well.

Austin did add, "Håvard everyone must account for the crimes they commit. We are all held responsible for this. If it weren't so, our entire civilization would break down. Everyone must pay in some way or another."

Håvard continued, "Yes, you are right in this. I also knew that if I gave Lisa and Stanley a choice to end my life, the answer would be no. So here is the critical piece. The *sleeping death* is caused by me in some way. Lindsey, I think the surgeon last year who patched me up took some of my blood and did some tinkering. This caused the type of *sleeping death* Edie died of. The printers and the factories never turned off. They just keep going in an endless cycle of reboot. The body keeps getting more and more *stem* cells until the body can't function anymore. Before I modified the source code, which was stolen from Robyn Scotts, or Ike's, computer, the nanobots acted in a similar way. All we need to do is to turn the nanobots off and they will leave the body. No more sudden heart stoppage, or brain aneurysms, or artery and veins being rebuilt. All those people with the overactive stem cells will stop. It will bring their bodies into a stasis in the natural way."

Håvard looked at Lyndsey this time and said, "Honey, I am sorry I lied about us being together again, but in order to do this effectively and correctly then I will need to die. I don't mean like poison me. It's basically a reset, or a CTRL-ALT-DEL, on the nanobots in my body. Once those nanobots are told to turn off, they can be used as a sort of anti-body to cure or make immune the nanobots. Do you see what I am saying here? I can cure the *sleeping death*. In order to do this then I must die."

Stanley scratched his chin and was trying to wrap his brain around the new information. "Wait. What do you mean by saying you won't die? It's not possible. If you jumped overboard and sank to the bottom, your body and organs will die. Your brain will stop."

"You would think so, wouldn't you? No, my body is constantly creating and destroying cells. It always maintains an equilibrium everywhere in my body. If my organs started to suffer, like in the case of drowning, my lungs fail. They will constantly be recreating lung tissue. I have thought about this for a while.

Another nanobot must tell other nanobots to die."

Håvard noticed they were drifting a little bit. He went to the back and motored a little more in the water to a point they were at before.

When he came back, he said, "On my phone I have many things to do this effectively and efficiently. There is an app on my phone which last year we used as an override to make people at the conference calm and relaxed. Ingrid you saw many of them walking through the crowd outside in the show room floor. All the people with me on that job, just walked near the people and they all sat down. None of my crew were affected. They walked through the crowd and were immune to the call to be calm and relaxed. Well, my phone contains that same over-ride."

He reached into his pocket and showed them his cell phone. He thought to himself that pausing right now wasn't good. The next steps need to be done before he chickens out. His voice was getting a little raspy from talking. He grabbed another soda can and satisfied his parched throat.

He continued, "But there is an additional module which over-rides the over-ride. Pressing one button will force all nanobots to deactivate in my body. The nanobots being deactivated is not telling them to leave the body. Another nanobot has to the nanobots to die. Once that happens, they will leave the body. The nanobots are the only thing that can tell another nanobot to do this. Ingrid this is why your tests failed. This will efficiently make me die. Lindsey, I need you to take 4 vials of my blood before I die and 4 vials of blood after I die. All of these vials need to be given to Austin and Ingrid. Austin, after Lindsey pushes the button to deactivate and kill all my nanobots, they need to be placed in the public tap water around the world. With some countries it's going to be difficult to get their compliance, but this is the vaccine to the *sleeping death*."

"Stanley and Ingrid don't abandon this research. It's very important, and it will cure so many diseases. I am sending each of you different document packages. Lindsey, the details of the money I promised you and the property we talked about will be sent to you. If Ingrid will verify her email, I will send everything to her." Ingrid looked up to see that he had the correct e-mail. She nodded her consent.

"This is just a safety measure. Ingrid you will have the vaccine, as well as Austin. I am giving you both all the source code and any documentation I can think of about the nanobots and exactly the steps I followed."

He turned to Lisa and Stanley, and said, "Finally, Lisa and Stanley, I'm sending you documents with instructions of how to access a very large trust fund divided between you. It will be yours to do whatever you want to do with it. The source of this money was from some truly evil people. Donate it. Live lavishly. Do whatever you want. I can't ask you for forgiveness and this isn't a way to settle the score. I cannot change what is done. I can only ask you for forgiveness when I can forgive myself. I'm not ready to do this. There has been too much blood spilled. I hope what happens next can be a start of a process to put a stop and reverse the course we are heading down."

Håvard downed the last of the Ginger-Ale and grabbed the bottle of Champagne and took a long drink out of the bottle. After he put the bottle down, he looked at Lyndsey and said, "Lindsey, honey can you get your medical bag of tricks and take some of my blood? I have to do this now before I change my mind."

"Just kidding," he said as he looked at Stanley and Lisa.

Lindsey went over to where her coat was and pulled a large Med Kit out. It contained a variety of items for cleaning wounds, getting blood, or stitching a cut. She grabbed some gloves and some alcohol swabs, and she grabbed 8 vials for blood. She took a pen out and labeled each vial as **H. Evans Before #1 of 4** to **H. Evans Before #4 of 4**. She labeled the remaining 4 vials the same as she did the first 4 but she marked them as after, **H. Evans After**

#1 of 4 to **H. Evans After #4 of 4**. She inserted a needle into one of the veins in his arm and filled the first 4 vials of Håvard's blood.

Håvard looked at Lindsey and asked her to give 2 vials to Austin and 2 to Ingrid. After she did this, he took out a cellphone and said, "Lindsey, I'm not sure how you feel about doing this, but this will save countless lives so you must do this for me."

He added, "Shit I forgot to ask? Does anyone know how to drive a boat?"

Everyone nervously laughed at that. Austin said he had done some sailing a long time ago, but if not, he would contact the coast guard.

Finally, Håvard said, "Everyone, I guess this is goodbye. Please follow my instructions. I know you are all the right people to stop this pandemic. Austin please make sure this gets out. Create a cocktail of this vaccine and dump a little bit into every reservoir or well, any water source anywhere else humans are living so they aren't at risk of the *sleeping death*. Another thing, I really like this morning party thing. It really gives a good reason to just stop and appreciate family and all the little things in life. Just wake up and greet the day on your terms. I like it."

He handed the cellphone to Lyndsey and said, "Goodbye everyone. Ok, Lyndsey, press send."

Lyndsey pressed the send button and an error occurred.

"Håvard it didn't send, I don't think I can get a signal out here."

That just sent Håvard and everyone else into hysterical laughter.

"I can't even die with a dramatic ending!"

Everyone kept laughing at this and for a moment it broke the tension in the air.

Lisa looked down at Håvard. She tugged Stanley's sleeve to have him look also. Håvard's eyes were closed and he wasn't breathing. Austin, Ingrid, and Lyndsey also looked and realized Håvard was dead. Lyndsey took out her stethoscope and confirmed that he was indeed dead. Lyndsey took another four vials of blood and gave 2 vials to Ingrid and 2 vials to Austin.

Everyone on the boat hugged and they knew this was the start of a new era in the world. Håvard was right. Decisions here today were going to have a global impact.

THE END

Also, by MD Hanley

Bit By Bit

Quantum Mind

Humility: A Spiritual Way of Life

Watch for more at my website

http://www.mdhanley.com/

or

https://www.hanleyadamspublishing.com

Thank you for reading Carbon Copy! I hope you enjoyed it as much as I enjoyed writing it. If you did, I would be grateful if you could take a moment to leave a review on the site where you bought this book, or if you want to go to https://www.goodreads.com and share any thoughts or information you would care to leave about this book. Reviews are incredibly helpful for authors and also help other readers discover new books.

Thank you for your support and happy reading!

MD Hanley

Did you love Carbon Copy? Then you should read

Bit By Bit

Here is a sample of his book,

Chapter 1 - Gary McKeown

As witnesses later recalled two small dogs waltzed into the dance studio, grabbed the cat and waltzed out

- The Far Side by Gary Larson

200 miles east of the Australian coast.

It's 6:30 AM in the South Pacific Ocean about 200 miles from the east coast of Australia. This early in the morning, there's a breath-taking view of the South Pacific Ocean with the sun climbing ever higher and becoming warmer. The surface of the ocean had what looked like dozens of tiny little mirrors reflecting back to the sun. A familiar tug of war between the sun and the South Pacific Ocean that's been going on since the earth was first formed. The sun continuously beats down on the ocean surface and the response of the ocean is to reflect back to the sun. At the end of each day the ocean and the sun call a truce until the next day. The salty smell of the ocean is strong and pungent. This salty smell is not unpleasant, but it hints there is nothing between the boat and Australian coast.

The triple decker diving boat rocks gently on the water, anchored to a point in the ocean above the S.S. Yongala shipwreck site. Among most scuba divers, the Yongala is one of the premier dive sites around the world. The SS Yongala was a passenger ship out of Melbourne heading towards Cairns, Queensland in 1911. On the way up the coast they ran into a severe cyclone and sank. All passengers and cargo were lost. Over the years, the Yongala has become an artificial reef and the home of many species of fish and beautiful coral formations. The wreck sits in an area of sandy shoal about 120 feet underwater at about 4 miles west of the Flinders reef.

The warm sun feels great compared to two days earlier in Boston where a cold winter had a 'Kung-Fu' grip on New England. Gary McKeown is 48 and physically in good shape. Gary was never the type to go to the gym religiously every morning and lifting huge weights to attain huge muscles. Gary had always liked working out but his attitude toward physical strength was very pragmatic. If he was hanging on the edge of a huge building, would he have the strength to lift his body to the roof or safety without having a huge issue? Could he also do the same if someone was injured and he needed to carry them on his back? Yeah, he figures he could do that but that's it. People at the gym he belongs to are the 'gym rats' getting their bodies ready for the apocalypse and would need the strength to carry eight people on his or her back to get to safety. To each his own, I guess.

Gary starts to think about the events that got him here. He had almost cancelled the whole diving trip when he got a call about 3 hours before his flight out of Boston. His friend Ben Costello, who was supposed to come on this scuba diving trip, told Gary that he was in the Emergency Department. He was on a ladder doing some of the last-minute things that his wife had asked to do when he had fallen and broke his leg.

With the prospect of canceling all his plans and staying home over the Christmas Holiday, Gary's business partner, Roger Tillson, mentioned that he might be able to help Gary. Roger still stayed in touch with a mutual friend, Barry Parker, who they both knew from their Northeastern College fraternity. Roger said that Barry had been pestering him to go scuba diving with him so Gary agreed to let Roger see if Barry was available.

In fifteen minutes, Roger walked into Gary's office and announced that he was the great miracle worker. Roger said he had to call in huge favors. Use some of his contacts with the airlines, use favors owed him. He had to use his amazing negotiating skills to be able to miraculously pull this off. Roger had bought an American /Qantas Airline round trip airline ticket for tonight's flight out of Boston, got all the Visas that were needed, booked a cabin on the Spoil Sport diving boat Gary and Ben were going to take. Unfortunately for Barry he had to fly coach and share a cabin with one of the crew.

Gary smelled something wrong here. How could all this be done in 20 minutes? Even if it wasn't last minute, it still took a while to book all of these things. At the last-minute Roger was able to book an American Airline/ Qantas Airline coach ticket to Brisbane Australia and then a 3-hour flight north to Cairns, Queensland? And even more surprising was to get a spot on the seven-day scuba diving boat, Spoil Sport. Obtaining all the tickets and visas for this was done in the space of about 20 minutes?

At first Gary thought something was not quite right here. If feels as if Barry already had airplane tickets, visas, and a reservation on Spoil Sport. Even though he was suspicious of this, he was really looking forward to this trip. Reluctantly, he agreed and packed up any papers he was currently working on. He would look at these when he came back. The next 10 days was going to be a great way to just relax and unplug for a while.

Gary went out to the dive deck to see the sun rising. He loved this time of day. Peaceful and calm. The quiet and calming factor of the dive deck is like a house of cards. Undisturbed. No one has broken the silence yet.

Pretty soon, there's a buzz of people going in every direction on the lower diving deck. Some of these are the Spoil Sport diving boat crew. The rest of the people on the deck are the passengers who were there for one thing and only one thing, scuba diving. All sizes of people were here, big, small, tall, or short. The amount of neoprene was obviously abundant!

Almost everyone on board is going on this dive, except Barry. He has not shown up on the diving deck yet. Most people are sitting on one of the three rows of benches. Underneath the bench is a bin that holds all their scuba gear, snorkel, masks, diving fins, weight belts and diving computers. Behind each person is one scuba tank attached to their BCD (Buoyancy

Compensator Device). Each tank had been filled earlier that morning with Oxygen, or an Oxygen Nitrogen mix.

On the left and right of the dive deck are a short set of stairs leading to a flat platform, only about a foot above the surface of the ocean. This is where they can put their fins on and jump into the ocean. At the back of the dive deck is a chalkboard that displays the information for their dive. On it is written various depths of the different parts of the dive sight. One of the dive crew starts to get everyone's attention and proceeds with the diving brief.

Whether it was an Oxygen, or a Nitrox mix, it was very important that they be certified to use the right mix. Each carried its own life-threatening ramifications from Nitrogen narcosis or Oxygen toxicity. Incorrectly using the wrong mix can have dire consequences.

Like most scuba diving boats, they have two hard fast rules. Initial when you leave the boat and then initial it when you come back on board. The other rule they have is what they call, 'Peace on the Reef'. This means look all you want, but don't touch. The Great Barrier Reef is one of the world's most beautiful treasures and some of the reef formations take decades and decades to grow that way. Humans can ruin this wonder of the world very quickly and it needs us to respect it and not destroy it.

Since Gary has never dived with Barry before, it was really important to be reading from the same page when they are diving. Over the years Gary has learned the hard way that some people are very safe to dive with and others are not. Gary and his friend, Ben, always approached diving with safety in mind. Gary had not dived with Barry before, so he wanted to make sure they were using the same hand signals. He stressed how important it was to dive as a team. Don't wander off 50 yards away from your dive buddy. What if you have a problem with the tank etc.? If someone gives you thumbs up that doesn't mean 'Ok' but means to ascend. Checking your tanks air supply and communicating when it's half empty and when it is a quarter tank left.

Keep checking your dive computer for how long it is safe to stay at a certain depth. Always, always do safety stops. Stop at 60 feet for 3 to 5 minutes, stop at 30 feet for 3 to 5 minutes and finally stop at fifteen feet for 3 to 5 minutes. If you don't follow these safety stops then you are not allowing your body to release the nitrogen from the various parts of your body and muscles. Gary would rather abort a dive for safety rather than push the envelope just to see something interesting.

This is the first dive which Gary and Barry are scuba diving together. Immediately, Gary could tell that Barry's diving experience was little to none. If you took a vacation to the Caribbean, there were many hotels that would give you a quickie 3-hour scuba dive class and you would mistakenly believe that you had your official scuba diving license. What you received from the hotel was not a PADI Scuba Certification but was a recreational diving certificate. It was only valid at their hotel, and it only allowed you to go to a depth of 30 feet with a certified diver.

It was still light out and the visibility was good. They swam out to the guideline that was about 20 yards from the boat. They slowly released air in the BCD to allow for a gradual descent. Going down slowly helps to equalize the pressure that builds up in the sinus passages. As soon as they descended about 5 feet, Barry just dropped like a rock and let out all of the air from his BCD to help him descend quickly. When Gary reached the same depth and swam over to Barry, he could tell that Barry had a lot of pressure pulsing into his temples and sinus's tissues. When this occurs, you can do one of two things, stop descending or pinch your nose and try to blow air out of your nasal passages. This is called the Valsalva technique. This will help to equalize your eustachian tubes in your inner ears and releases the pressure that builds up. Depending on a person's physiology, some people have a great deal of trouble while others do not.

Gary thought Barry's behavior was a total rookie mistake. He got Barry's attention and asked him if he was ok. He asked him by putting his hand to his nose, as if he was going to equalize the pressure, and then gave an OK signal as a question to see where Barry was. Barry shook his head to say 'no'. Gary said in hand signals, stay for 3 minutes and if the pressure equalizes then they would continue the dive. If not any better, we would ascend to 60 feet and again wait a couple of minutes to see if it corrected the pressure he was feeling. Barry decided that he would just do what he wanted and grabbed the guideline and pulled himself quickly up the guideline.

On his way back to the surface he pushed a girl who was descending, out of his way. As he pushed her aside, he ended up getting his hand under her regulator hose, that connects to the air tank, and yanked it out of her mouth, as he moved his left arm up the guideline. She was a seasoned diver, so she recovered quickly. As Gary ascended to follow Barry, he reached the diver that Barry just bumped into. He tried to pantomime an apology to her. She nodded and accepted his apology.

Later in the morning Gary, and most everyone on the boat, is hoping to do a dive before lunch. Gary is starting to get annoyed that Barry has not come out to get ready for this dive. If Barry didn't show up soon, Gary was going to ask one of the other divers if he could tag along with them on their dive. Gary is partly hoping that Barry doesn't show up for the dive, which would be a blessing. As soon as he was thinking this, Barry stumbled down the stairs to the diving deck.

Shortly after the dive brief, everyone started putting their scuba gear on and trying to get in the water as fast as possible, maximizing their dive time. One thing about scuba diving trips, they follow a consistent pattern of dive, eat, and then dive some more. Generally, you can get anywhere from four or five dives a day. Most conversations people had with each other on the boat were generally about the type of fish or coral that they saw on the last dive, or a hope that they would see it on an upcoming dive.

"Hey, are you up to doing this dive?" Barry asks.

Gary replied, "Yes I am. You're going to love seeing the Yongala site. Now we are doing a regular air tank dive so hopefully we can stay down on the Yongala wreck for at least 45 or 60 minutes. Also, let's just take our time descending to about 110 feet."

Gary had all his gear on and waited for Barry to put on his equipment. Once he had all his gear on

Gary asked, "Ok Barry can you do a scuba gear check for me?"

Barry looks confused asking what Gary wants him to check?

"Never mind I'm pretty sure that my gear is on correctly. Let me do a gear check for you." Gary starts to go through the gear checklist on Barry's gear. This checklist is something that you learn at the very beginning of your lessons for scuba diving. Gary checks for any tangles in his primary regulator and also his secondary regulator. He also checks that Barry's air tank is turned on and open. Gary checks Barry's dive computer and checks that his BCD vest is on correctly and that his weight belt has the proper amount of weights.

Now they are all set and wait patiently to get into the water. When it is their time, they go down the stairs to the flat platform which will allow them to put on their fins. There is a crew member on the platform with a clipboard that each diver needs to initial at the beginning and end of their dives. The crew member also checks that their air tank is fully on. Gary initials the clipboard and hands it to Barry. Barry was hoping for this to happen, it didn't happen earlier. Now that Gary put his initials down,

Barry crossed out Gary's initials and initials in the space next to his own name. By doing this he effectively makes it seem as if Gary did not go on this dive.

"Barry let's just take our time on this. We need to stay together and not wander off. We also need to be clear on the hand signals."

Barry says sarcastically, "Ok Gary, I get it. Come on let's go down there".

Barry and Gary swam over to the guideline that they will use to descend. They both started to slowly descend down to the ocean bottom. As they descend, pressure builds up in their sinuses and they must clear this using the 'Valsalva' technique.

Barry was dropping like a rock and not equalizing. Eventually Gary caught up with him and Gary could tell he had a problem with the pressure build up in his ears again. Gary mimicked Barry to pinch his nose and blow out. After doing this about 4 times, Barry gave him a thumbs up. Wrong hand signal. Thumbs up means go to the surface. Gary mimicked the ok hand symbol which is where you make a circle with your thumb and index finger. Once again, Barry did a thumbs up signal. Gary shrugged his shoulders to indicate that he did not understand. Barry did the 'Ok' symbol realizing why Gary was confused. They continued diving and exploring the reef.

The SS Yongala ship is just amazing. There is every type and size of fish and coral outcroppings. Everywhere you look there is something interesting to see. The boat is tilted to the left and you can see all the compartments and rooms on the ship. The rule that we were told by the crew was not to go inside the ship or to touch any of the fish or coral outcropping.

Gary was looking at a fantastic coral formation at the bow of the ship. Barry swims toward Gary and does not stop his momentum so he bumps right into Gary. Now, Barry is stepping on the coral formations and breaking them off. At one point, he is stepping on parts of the boat and breaks it off.

Gary is mortified and pissed off. Enough of this guy. Now Barry is chasing a grey reef shark swimming away from the boat, Gary is able to catch up to him and motions him to go back to the Yongala. Barry shakes his head 'no'. Barry reaches over to Gary and pulls his mask off. Gary is surprised and pissed. Once Gary exhales and replaces the water that was in his mask, he again looks for Barry. Barry is now another 50 feet away

Gary thinks why the hell would Roger go diving with guy? Gary catches up with Barry. It's only sand here. Gary looks for the ship, but the visibility is not great, but he is pretty sure if he back tracks, he will be able to find the ship. Barry points even further away from the ship. Gary says no and points behind where he believes the ship is. Barry looks at Gary with a big grin and then pulls his mask off again. As Gary is trying to clear his mask, Barry reaches over and turns Gary's air off. While Gary is dealing with his mask, Barry takes off his weight belt of 45 lbs. of lead, and puts it on Gary with the release clip in the back so it will be difficult to get off. And then Barry swims back to the ship.

Gary looks at his dive computer and it says that he has been down at 110 feet for too long. He was down here at this depth for an hour and twenty minutes which is 20 minutes longer than he should. Gary starts to have problems getting oxygen and realizes that his tank has been turned off. Gary tries his safety respirator, and it is still bad. Worry starts to creep in from the sides. Gary can't reach the knob to turn the air tank on. Ok well this is what you train for when you get certified. First you need to take off the BCD vest. Gary can't get the weight belt off because it is hooked around his BCD vest and the release clip is in the center of his back.

Nitrogen Narcosis is starting to envelop his body and brain. Gary has felt this before and knows that if he doesn't fix this soon and ascend that he will die. Slowly Gary can feel the different parts of his body start to shut down. As unconsciousness comes marching toward him, he stops struggling and uses whatever air is left. I guess Barry didn't totally turn off the air; Gary takes little sips of air. Unconsciousness wins and Gary stops struggling. Gary is trying to not go unconscious, but it starts to win. Just before Gary goes under, he sees a hand turning him over and taking off that bloody weight belt. His last thought was why did Barry do this? Was this Roger's plan from the beginning?

One of the divers on board the SpoilSport is looking for Gary to show him some the pictures he had taken on the latest dive. He asked one of the crew members, if Gary had finished his dive or was still under? He says, "No, Gary never left the boat."

The diver that was looking for Gary said he absolutely went diving. He saw him under water by the bow of the Yongala ship. This is worrying for the crew member. He looks at his sheet again and doesn't see Gary's initials. But maybe he forgot. Better safe than sorry. He tells the captain that there is another diver down there and all the other divers have signed in, except Gary McKeown.

Four divers from the crew check in all directions. The crewman, Steve, finds Gary and immediately puts his second respirator for Gary to buddy breathe. He turns Gary's unconscious body so he can remove the weight belts from Gary's gear. He takes Gary and makes a rapid ascent to the surface.

Next, Gary is being carried up on the boat and placed on the top part of the boat. The captain radios the EMT's and they are sending a medical helicopter. The captain asks the crew to clear all the sunbathing chairs and block the steps up to this part of the boat from other divers.

In about 30 minutes there is a medical helicopter landing on the top floor of the boat which is usually used for sunbathing. The medical team carries Gary from where he was laid down, on a stretcher, and then onto the helicopter.

Barry runs up to the helicopter and starts to get in. The first aid people said no way. Barry said that Gary was his brother and he needed to go with them. The guy in the helicopter grimaces and then nods his head for him to get on board. Barry is happy to be done with scuba diving. It bore him to tears. So tired of pretending to be really interested in the fish or the slimy coral. The only thing that Barry was thinking when looking at those fish was wishing he had a spear gun to shoot at them. The whole time he was underwater he kept thinking about what each fish would taste like.

They are about 25 minutes from Mater Hospital in Brisbane. After they land on the roof of the hospital, Barry follows them to the elevator to take Gary to the emergency department. Barry acts like he is following them there but stops at the intake desk to give the clerk Gary's name and insurance information. He also gives a contact number of Roger's cell phone. Barry asks her if there is a bathroom. She points to the right of the automatic doors to exit; Barry says he will be back in a moment. As he walks towards the men's room, he goes out of the emergency door as another couple is walking through the doors. Barry never makes it to the restroom.

Barry flags a taxi down and asks him to get him to the airport. Roger is going to be pissed that I haven't finished the job. The little bits he heard in the helicopter was that he was showing signs of an acute nitrogen narcosis coma. This new event may make Roger happy.

Chapter 2 - Lucy McKeown

"Watch out world

I am wearing my sassy pants today!!"

- Lucille Ball

Lucy McKeown, who is 49 years old, has always been in good shape and has a lean body to show for it. Her figure is highlighted with a head of fiery, red curly hair. She has dealt and worked with men who look at her and think that she can be easily swayed or intimidated. Make no mistake on that! Men have tried to act all superior making sure the little women will do what they want. She doesn't mind playing along if it gets her to achieve her goal. However, if you poke the bull then be ready to get the horns!

Growing up with her younger brother, Gary, there were some real knockout fights. He always knew how to get under her skin and push the right buttons. Gary has a special gift in which he has a nearly perfect, total recall of anything that he sees or reads. When they were younger, this could be infuriating. He would correct her about any of the slightest details, that she was describing to him or to someone else. Lucy remembers slamming many doors when she was a teenager.

Conversely, she knew the way to get him to *toe the line*. Maybe it was a maternal thing, but at times she knew that if she offered any comment toward the quality of their daily chores, he would just short-circuit.

She was almost nineteen and Gary was seventeen, when they both learned about the death of their parents. This was devastating. Every part of their lives turned upside down. This was a turning point for them. An unspoken truce developed. They were both hurt, as anyone would be. It became apparent that if one tried to hurt the other, then they were indirectly hurting themselves.

Lucy is usually a calm person and rarely gets very annoyed or angry. Today was not that day. She is feeling extra angry today! It's not that she's in a rush, or there was heavy traffic, she just felt mad at everyone and everything. Lucy turned on the radio and a popular song came on. She liked this song but turning it up really wasn't doing anything to improve her mood.

Lucy navigates her blue Subaru though the winding path to get to Ashwood, a long-term care facility. This is where her younger brother, Gary, was being treated as a patient. Gary had returned from Australia in a type of coma called an "anoxic" coma. This type is largely due to oxygen deprivation. Gary had been in this coma state for the last 2 years.

Lucy pulls into the Ashwood facility and the same thought keeps bouncing into her head. Why do they call it a *long-term care facility*? It's a nursing home. This is a familiar conversation that she has with herself every time she drives the 45 minutes to visit her brother.

Walking through the front entrance, she goes to the set of elevators on her right. On the ride up to the third floor, the feelings of anger and annoyance turn into a feeling of sadness and longing. She misses her brother.

When the elevator door opens, she walks over to the nurse's station. One of the nurses sees Lucy and pushes her chair away from the computer to face her. She can see the monitor the nurse was looking at and it was no surprise that it was her Facebook page. This nurse, Milly, was someone

Lucy usually saw when she came here every couple of weeks.

As usual, Milly is wearing light green hospital scrubs and white tennis shoes. One her chest she has a solid blue patch with a white tree in the middle and below the tree it says "Milly Howards, RN".

"Hi Milly. Have there been any changes on Gary's care that I should know about?", Lucy asks.

Milly pulled out Gary's chart, attached are several papers that show all of the blood tests, brain tests, and various care items like feeding, or changing his different linens etc.

"Nope. No changes since last time.", Milly said with a strong emphasis of "last time".

"Has the financial department contacted you? Betsy Richter came by earlier today and said that she needs to talk to you", Milly adds.

Lucy says, "*Nope*" trying to mimic Milly's last response to her. Why does anyone say "nope"? Saying just 'No' is a smaller word and conveys the same thing.

"You can give Betsy my cell phone number if you want."

As Lucy was walking toward Gary's room, she could hear each room's combinations of noise makers. Whir, hum, buzz, or beep. Each room added to the concerto that was being played for the long spotless white hall. It's kind of funny but also not funny. These monitors and machines helped each person's health in some unique way.

Even though it was only about 1 00 everyone seemed to be sleeping. From Lucy's point of view if someone died, Milly wouldn't probably detect that until the next shift came on for the evening.

This was frustrating that the staff didn't see the obvious minimum care they should be giving to patients. She doesn't need to get into the politics of the Ashwood facility, because she keeps on top of Gary's care. She must do this because if *she gave them an inch, they would take a mile.*

As Lucy rounds the corner and enters room 33C, she sees Gary in his bed, hooked up to several machines. Some to check blood pressure, another to give fluids, and others to administer various nutrients to his body. Lucy is not startled or shocked to see her brother like this. She visits Gary often, so she is used to this. However, it does make her feel very sad. She misses talking with Gary. She misses both the laughing and fun that they had always shared and also some of the arguments they would get into. But now is not the time for sadness or self-pity.

Lucy has a routine that she follows every time she comes to visit. She reaches into her pocketbook and brings out a notepad. She lists the things needed to be attended to by Ashwood staff. They have not given him a shave since the last time she visited. He should get a haircut. She walks to the end of his bed and looks at his chart. It's supposed to list anything that the staff has done for his care. She's not surprised to see several days with blank entries.

It annoys her when she sees this. It just highlights that Ashwood is not doing a great job taking care of him. She makes several entries in her notebook.

Lucy pulls out a bottle of skin conditioner and begins to cover Gary's feet, legs, and arms with this. She washes his face; pulls out a razor, bottle of shaving cream and a small hand towel and proceeds to shave the growing beard and mustache on Gary's face. Ashwood really doesn't like it when she does this. They are concerned with liability rather than personal care. The staff here only does as little as they can get away with. Next, Lucy takes hold of Gary's limbs and moves them all around and does little stretching exercises for his tendons and muscles.

After she had finished shaving Gary, and was satisfied with his clean-cut face, she reached into her voluminous pocketbook and pulled out the Stephen King book "Dead Zone". This was a book that Gary had read several times. Lucy never understood why he would reread a book since he has an almost perfect recall or eidetic memory. He said he just likes to go through the process of reading the story. The smells, the colors, the tastes, and the feelings conveyed by the author are a little different each time he rereads a book. She found it ironic that this book was one of Gary's favorites. The story is about a guy that's in an accident and ends up in a coma. The character wakes up after several years and discovers he has a new psychic power of precognition. Maybe Gary ironically had a precognition that he would be in a coma many years later after reading this book.

Lucy finishes the chapter she was reading and collects the things that she brought in with her and heads out to her car. When she passes the nurse's station, she talks to Milly about seeing if she could have someone give Gary a haircut and also to make sure that he was being attended to on a regular basis.

Milly says "Yup."

Lucy walks over to the elevator and starts to make her way out to her car. She was just opening the door to the parking lot when someone from behind her called out her name. She turned to face the person with the screechy voice echoing and reverberating in the large atrium.

"Ms. Hamilton, ah Ms. Hamilton? May I please speak to you?" That voice is Betsy Richter from the financial office. She always addresses Lucy with her married name. She had changed her last name back to her maiden name because it was a constant reminder of her husband, David, who died from cancer 12 years ago.

Betsy asks if she had time, could she come to her office to discuss the financial arrangements for Gary's care. Betsy has one of those super sweet fake personalities that was far from being sweet and far from being real.

Betsy said, "Ms. Hamilton, I have tried several times to reach you regarding the cost of your brother's care. I wanted to alert you that the cost for your brother's care has gone up substantially. Four months ago, the cost for your brother's care increased by five thousand dollars. The money that was being sent to Ashwood for Gary's care wasn't the full amount to cover his care.

Lucy was speechless. Since the day that Roger Tillson called her to inform her about Gary's scuba diving accident, he has been true to his word. She remembers it as if it was yesterday. Roger made a solemn promise to her that the cost for Gary's care would be paid, no matter what the cost.

"Did you speak to Mr. Tillson about this? He's the one who has been paying the cost for Gary to be here. I'm sure that he would be able to take care of this."

Betsy looked a little baffled. "Tillson? I am not aware of a Mr. Tillson being involved in the financial responsibility for your brother's care. I always assumed it was paid by you, cr that Gary had set up a trust account to provide for his care. Let me pull up the account and let's take a little *looksy*", Betsy said as she plopped into her chair.

After a minute or two, Betsy said "When your brother was first brought here, we received a letter from a company called Trinity Trust Holdings in Boston. They asked that all financial bills and statements be sent to an account at Trinity Trust Holdings. For the last two years every bill sent to this account has been paid for within one business day. For the past four months the bills were sent but the payment was only enough to cover the cost of his care before it was increased."

Betsy continued, "I am sorry about this, but we really need to find a solution. The current total for Gary is $22,575. At least half of it needs to be paid by the end of the month, which is in two weeks. If payment cannot be made, then I'm sorry to tell you that Gary will need to be moved to a different care facility. For the last several years all, patients that are unable to pay for the full amount of their care are sent to the state-run UMass hospital in Worcester."

Lucy knew the UMass Hospital very well. It's not a place where you would want to be a patient. There have been many stories about different doctors being sued and a high rate of patient deaths over the years. Many have given it a nickname as the *Death Hospital*. People go in, but they do not come out. It sent shivers up and down Lucy's back.

Betsy continued her rambling on about the cost of her brother's care. She said they could accept a credit card, a cashier's check; or if Lucy had a saving's account with enough money to cover at least half of this bill today.

Lucy is only half hearing Betsy. It was taking an enormous amount of energy to get control of the tornado of thoughts and emotions going around in her head. She just kept repeating in her head "that bastard! that son of bitch!" I knew I should not have given Roger any control over Gary's care. Who or what is this Trinity Trust Holdings company?'

She said to herself, stay focused. How can I possibly pay this off? And then it hit her all at once. First things first. Get my brother out of this place. She can take care of him better than they can. Why does Gary need to be here, really?

She and her husband were very good at saving money. Nothing extraordinary. A little bit here and a little bit there started to add up after a while. When David died, he left a lump sum of money for Lucy and the kids. This helped to cover bills for tuition and also to help pay down the mortgage. She felt the cruel irony of his love when anyone called her by her married name.

Why didn't she think of this earlier? She paid off the mortgage several years ago, so paying the money for this hospital was not something that she couldn't have. That's exactly what I am going to do. Busy with the paperwork, Betsy didn't really notice that she wasn't paying attention to her.

Then, Lucy interrupted Betsy in mid-sentence and said, "Betsy I do not want Gary to be moved to the UMass hospital. I will be going to the bank tomorrow, to get a cashier's check for the balance that is due. Please let me know the total amount that is due by 10:00 AM. I will have an ambulance take my brother from Ashwood at 2:00 PM. I would appreciate it if you could have all the paperwork ready for me when the ambulance is here. I will also need to know the address and phone number for the company that has been sending payments for Gary."

Now it was Betsy's turn to be speechless. "Ok, if you want any of the medical records for Gary then please let me know the name of the long-term facility that will be handling your brother's care."

Lucy looked at Betsy with a firm commanding face and said, "Betsy, I will be taking my brother home to live in my house. Honestly, it's just easier for me to give my brother the care that he needs. I am quite sure I can do as well if not even better than Ashwood have done."

Betsy made one last attempt with Lucy, "How are you going to be able to take care of Gary? How are you going to do that? You won't have any of the medical supplies or medical equipment that is needed. How will you transport him to your house? I have already called the UMass hospital and they said they would hold a bed for him at the end of the month. Ms. Hamilton. I really think you are making a big mistake. Also, I do not think that moving your brother is legal!"

That was a big mistake for Betsy. She assumed that this would be fine without Lucy's input. Betsy thought that tossing the veiled threat to Lucy about this not being legal would make Lucy comply. Nope, that is not going to happen. If Betsy wants to play this game Lucy thought, then I can also play with her.

"Betsy it is unfortunate that you did not include me into your plans for Gary to move to the UMass

Hospital. If you had consulted with me on this, I would not have agreed to it. So legally you are not allowed to move Gary unless I approve it. I am my brother's health care proxy and his legal guardian. This means that all medical decisions for Gary are with me. I plan to bring him home to my house, I can take care of him just as well, if not better than Ashwood has. I have a large room on the first floor of my house that will be perfectly sufficient for Gary's care. These are my brother's wishes when he asked me to be his health care proxy. So, if you could have all the paperwork done by 2:00, that would be perfect" Lucy said assertively.

Betsy was still speechless, it appeared she was having a hard time wrapping her head around this. Finally, she said, "Ok I will get the paperwork ready for tomorrow, but it will be tough to complete on such short notice. Do you want me to see if one of the Ashwood staff will be able to continue his care? They could stop by to help you on a regular basis."

It was difficult to contain her pleasure when Betsy said it would be difficult to get the paperwork done. Ha! Betsy had no problem cornering her and asking her for $22 thousand dollars payable in two weeks. Lucy responded, "No Betsy, I have been in contact with several different hospice organizations that are closer to me. When I spoke to them one woman came out and looked at where I would have Gary and felt that it was not a problem at all. In fact, she said that she would be able to provide a comfortable bed, like the ones used in hospitals, and provide any medical supplies or equipment that Gary would need. I think this will be a better situation for Gary". Lucy hated to tell lies but everything she just said to Betsy was a total lie. The look on Betsy's face was all that Lucy wanted. The cash stream that Lucy brought into this facility was now shut off.

As Lucy walked out to her car she was smiling. Why didn't I do this earlier? On the drive home she thought, now where the hell will I find a hospital bed for Gary? Her favorite song came on the radio, and she turned the volume up as loud as she could. Lucy was very happy, indeed.

Chapter 3 - Freddie

"Anyone who does anything to help a
child
in his or her life is a hero to me."

— Fred Rogers

One year later

The late July sun was overhead and felt great.
To Lucy, the air and the warmth felt like being
wrapped in her most comfortable robe and slippers.
The smell of pine trees and pinecones filled the air.
The squirrels at the border of Lucy's property were
just running back and forth dancing to their own
tune. Chasing each other and then running up a tree
and then immediately running down. Lucy never
really figured that one out, but it made her smile and
laugh each time she saw them.

Lucy was in a zone right now. Wearing her ear
buds and listening to an eclectic playlist of songs
booming from her old iPod. Lucy is wearing a big
white and red poker dotted hat. Apparently, it's the

new 'La Rive Gauche' to make yourself look like a red and white beetle. She doesn't care because the music is turned all the way up, and she is wiggling her butt to the beat of the music as she's tending to her garden.

The smells from her rows of tomatoes, zucchini, and cucumber plants are unique and distinct. The garden has a very musky and intoxicating smell. The soil is a strange color of deep dark brown. Almost black but not quite. The soil looks moist but not necessarily with water. It contains a rich amount of nitrogen, phosphorus, and potassium. Only the best for my garden Lucy thought.

Lucy is so content with her gardening that she doesn't notice the big white and black shadow coming up behind her. When Lucy turns, she sees Gary's 4year-old Great Dane, Freddie. He has dirt all over his nose and several bits of roses, sunflowers, begonia stems and flowers either in his mouth or on his black and white fur. Lucy can't decide to be angry at him for destroying her flowers or laughing at how cute he is. Freddie realizes that she likes the flowers he brought her so now she's going to give him a treat or play rip up flowers game with him. Lucy can't contain it and bursts out laughing. Lucy feigns with her right hand that she is going pat him and give him some affection. And then the left hand comes down quickly and starts scratching Freddie's belly and long neck. He falls for this every time. But that's ok, he likes it, and he gives Lucy a big, sloppy lick all over her face. Freddie likes this game.

Looking at her watch, Lucy realizes that she needs to go to the grocery store before her two boys come over for dinner tonight. She rushes inside the house and changes her clothes; grabs her wallet, keys, and phone; puts Freddie's water dish outside; and gets in her car.

As Lucy is driving to the grocery store, she thinks about what has happened with her brother since his trip to Australia. When Gary traveled, she always got a message from Gary of where he was. Gary had been looking forward to this diving trip for a while, so it would not be unusual for Gary to extend this trip for a few days or a week. Christmas and New Year in Australia occurred in the warmest months of the southern hemisphere. Lucy thought maybe he would stay longer because it was so far away.

After two weeks of not hearing anything, she started calling some of the people that might provide more information on where Gary might be. The first call was to Gary's friend and diving partner, Ben Costello. When she called his cell number it rang for a long time before someone picked up.

"Hi, is this Ben Costello?" Lucy asks.

"Yes, it is. Who is this?"

"This is Lucy McKeown, Gary McKeown's sister. I was wondering if you knew where Gary is. I haven't heard anything from him since before his trip to Australia."

Ben responds after several seconds and with a little hesitation, "Sorry Lucy, but I don't know where he is. I broke my leg on the day we were supposed to fly out of Logan. I had to cancel my trip, but I thought he was still going anyways."

"Ok thanks Ben. If you hear anything, please let me know."

There was a slight pause when Ben answered her question. Most times that hesitation, even if it is a slight one, tells a lot. Generally, it means that a person is hunting or searching for words. Lucy doesn't buy it.

She went to his hi-rise apartment in the city and could not find him. The man at the front desk knew Gary and said that he had not seen him at all for several weeks. Lucy called Gary's work number and still no one answered. Lucy started to worry. His absence and not checking in with her was very peculiar. He usually calls to let me, and others know that he's ok.

Maybe his assistant, Rose, knows where he is. Lucy met Rose several times since Gary hired her. She liked her and thought she was the perfect *anti-Gary*. She's one of those people that's incredibly meticulous and detailed. She also has no problem speaking her mind about anyone or anything. One night, Rose and her husband had gone to dinner to celebrate Gary's birthday. Rose said jokingly that the four years she had worked for him were such a chore, but she really loved it. He contradicted her claim that he hired her four years ago, Gary said it was five years ago.

Rose just looked at him like he was a little boy, like a foreigner and who didn't know how to speak English.

She raised her voice thinking that talking louder in English would translate the meaning of what she was saying.

She said "You really are a lost cause. No, you are wrong. I still have the offer letter that you gave to me, and it has been four years and three months that I have worked with you. You really are very forgetful, where would you be if you didn't have me keeping all this straight for you?"

Gary looked at Lucy and winked. Lucy knew that he was giving Rose a "win". Gary has a very uncommon type of memory. This rare gift, an eidetic memory, allows him to have a nearly perfect memory recall of anything that he hears or reads. She knew that he was letting Rose win this one.

Since Rose was always plugged in, she knew where everybody was. Lucy called Rose's cell number. She picked it up on the first ring. Lucy told her that she had not heard from Gary, and he was missing. Lucy asked Rose if she had heard from Gary or if she knew where he is currently. Rose said that she had not heard anything. In fact, she had tried to contact him and just got his voice mail. Rose said that she would look into this and if she finds out anything she will call. She also gave Lucy Roger

Tillson's contact number and said that he might have some more information about Gary's whereabouts.

The next day after talking to Rose, Lucy called Roger. When she dialed the number, the phone rang for a long time. She was just about to hang up when a woman answered.

Lucy asked, "May I speak to Roger Tillson?"

The female voice on the other end said quickly, "Wrong number." And hung up the phone. Lucy redialed but this time the line was busy.

Ironically, Roger called her a couple of days after she attempted to talk to him. He told Lucy that Gary was in a scuba diving accident. He continued by saying that he brought Gary home to Boston two weeks earlier and had him checked into the Ashwood Long-term Facility. Roger also mentioned how much money he had spent to have Gary flown home. This was Roger's classic sound bite that he likes to play. Implying, all would be lost if Roger had not been there and saved the day.

She had only interacted with him on three different occasions. The first time was at a company sponsored event to celebrate reaching a certain sales target. The event was a huge "dog and pony" show for potential venture capital investors. Lucy was a master at detecting "bullshit". Right from the start she could see through Roger's s smarmy salesman-like demeanor. It was very phony and disingenuous.

Roger asked Lucy to meet him at the Ashwood facility. She agreed to meet the next day. She met Roger at the Ashwood facility and he wanted her to sign several documents concerning Gary's care. She confronted Roger with why he had not called her almost a month ago when this happened. Roger stammered a little bit, but he told Lucy that immigration was difficult because Gary did not have his passport. Lucy half heard Roger because she knew that she would never find out the real truth about this.

Of all the documents that Roger wanted her to sign, two of the documents she would not sign. The first was a form that named Roger as the power of attorney. Gary already had a signed a document that made Lucy his power of attorney. Another document was to make Roger his Healthcare Proxy. Again, Gary already had a signed document that named Lucy and her son, Peter, as his Healthcare Proxy. The last document named the person who would be responsible for the financial charges. Lucy said that she should be the named person on the contracts. Roger looked at Lucy and made a solemn vow to her that he would take care of all the finances. He just wished for Gary to get better.

Lucy was not going to give Roger any type of power with respect to Gary's health. Once again, people thought that her good looks and pleasant personality were a sign of being ditzy or just a dumb woman who would just sign whatever was put in from of her. Nope, that will never happen.

Lucy remembered that meeting with Roger from time to time, but today she had errands to do, and Gary needed to be cared for.

Later that day....4:00 PM

When Lucy got home and unloaded all the groceries, she had time to go through her normal routine daily care for Gary. As usual, Freddie follows Lucy into the former office where Gary is staying. Several machines and IV tubes are connected to him. She starts to wash his face and arms. She puts a couple of towels under his head and does her best to wash his hair. Usually, she did this when either the kids were here to help her, or with the help of the strong hospice nurse, who stopped by twice a week. She checks that all the fluids are properly connected; and checks his blood pressure, temperature, and oxygen levels. Everything looks good.

Freddie can't stand it any longer, he wants to see his friend Gary. Freddie stands up on his hind legs and sees that Gary is sleeping. He takes two big licks of Gary's face thinking that Gary will wake up and play. He goes back down on four legs and looks at Lucy and nudges Gary's hand. Nothing happens. Freddie doesn't understand. If he does that with Lucy or her sons and if he is persistent enough, he will get a belly scratch or a treat. He likes both of those options and sometimes he gets both a treat and a belly scratch. What a life.

Lucy rewashes Gary's face and hands. And then goes to the kitchen to make dinner. Freddie usually would follow because he would always get scraps. But today he decides he's going to stay here in his dog bed until his friend wakes up. Freddie's dog bed was actually a full-size couch that Freddie had claimed as his bed. Within 15 minutes, Freddie is asleep and has dog dreams of running though fields trying to catch rabbits or something.

After Dinner

"Mom, that was great, thanks. I wish the cafeteria at school had something like this. The food there doesn't even come close to this" says Patrick McKeown as he gets up and helps his brother Peter clear the table.

"Don't worry Patrick, I made two extra pans of lasagna. One for you and one for your brother."

Patrick looked at Peter with a little grin on his face. He was hoping that she would make extra "left overs" to bring back with him to college.

After dinner was cleaned up, Lucy asked her boys if they wanted some desert.

Peter said, "I can't right now, I'm too full." Patrick nodded in agreement.

"Ok, let's sit down and catch up. Tell me what's going on with you two. How's the new job working out, Peter?" Lucy said. Peter McKeown was 22 years old and had recently graduated from Northeastern University in Boston. He had just started working at a software company in Cambridge, MA. Usually, he stayed at his girlfriend's apartment, but occasionally he would come back home, even if Lucy had to bribe him with Lasagna.

"This company is awesome. People are super friendly. They assigned another developer to shadow me and show me the ropes. We get along great. He's an older guy, like 35, and he's a wicked gamer", Peter answered.

"That's great, I'm really happy for you. My credit card is also very happy that you're working", she said and gave Patrick a wink.

Peter started to say something, but Freddie started barking and whimpering. Freddie comes rushing around the corner forgetting that he's a really big dog and that his momentum does not stop his forward motion. Freddie slams into the wall but is unfazed and keeps running at full tilt toward the couch that Lucy and Patrick were sitting on. The whole time, Freddie was barking and whimpering.

Immediately, Lucy thought Freddie had to go outside. Peter was ahead of her and opened the door to let Freddie out. Freddie didn't make a move to the door. Freddie's barking was getting more insistent. Freddie looked at Lucy and gave a big growl bark. Ok, something is up. Freddie races out of the room and down the hall to the room where Gary was staying. Lucy is now worried. Freddie never acts like this.

Patrick, Peter, and Lucy ran into Gary's room. The lights are off but most of the machines throw out a green glow and make tiny noises. Lucy turns on the lights and looks at Gary's bed. Some of the noises that the machines are making are actually alarms to signify that it was not receiving any of a dozen vital signs. Lucy looks at the bed and Gary's eyes are wide open, and he is sitting up in the bed. Lucy is too stunned to say anything. Patrick doesn't hesitate and blurts out, "Holy SHIT!" Gary looks at Patrick, Peter and Lucy and says, "Hi guys!" Freddie sticks his nose in between everyone and looks at Gary.

Gary gave a little pat on Freddie's head. "Hey buddy, WOW you have grown."

About the Author

For the last 30 years, I have been working and consulting in the software engineering field. The only rule that you have to follow in this type of career is that you will never know it all. Once you realize that you are a master at some part of technology, you can guarantee that it will change and evolve. Whether it was being an individual contributor or a managing director of teams around the globe, there was always a unique new and exciting challenge. An adventurer at heart, some of my hobbies are scuba diving, flying, and hang gliding. Debuting my first novel has been a great experience and a lot of fun.